XO
DaisyPrescott

READY TO FALL

Daisy Prescott

ISBN: 978-0-9894387-0-4

Cover Design by ©Sarah Hansen at OkayCreations.com

Interior Design by Angela McLaurin, Fictional Formats

First Print Edition December 2013

To Shawn

For showing me how sexy a man can be in flannel

ONE

A HIGH PITCHED wailing entered my dream. Slowly, I shook off the warm breeze and sunshine from the catamaran and opened my eyes to my bedroom. It took a minute or two for me to determine the sound wasn't from my dream, but coming from next door. From Maggie's house. Her smoke detector was going off.

From where he stood on the comforter facing the window overlooking the beach, Babe's barks drowned out the noise. Tossing the comforter and blankets off of me, I leapt from the bed, followed by Babe, and headed downstairs. Kelly rolled over and put the pillow over her head, grumbling about it still being dark out and what the hell was wrong with me for waking her up. Ignoring her, I grabbed my jeans and thermal from the floor, and raced from the room, not bothering to zip my jeans.

I reached the door to the deck where Babe pawed to get outside. The second I opened the door, he bounded out and barked at Maggie's cabin.

I peered through the pre-dawn gloom, but couldn't see any flames or smoke. As far as I knew, Maggie was in Portland with whatshisface. There shouldn't be any reason for her smoke detector to be going off. The battery could be dying, and if that was the cause for the ruckus, I'd give her an earful about changing her batteries with the time change next time I saw her.

The breeze shifted and I could smell the distinct scent of smoke coming from her cabin. Where there was smoke, there was fire.

I ran across the narrow yard separating our properties. Luckily, I knew she hid a key under a frog at the foot of her steps. Searching for the damn frog, I bent over, peering into the dark when the door to the deck flew open and slammed into the wall.

What the hell?

A petite brunette I'd never laid eyes on swung a throw blanket over her head while she attempted to chase the smoke pouring from the door.

Who the fuck is that? I stared at her. Now she ran around the living room, opening windows as the smoke detector continued to squawk its annoying beeping into the sleepy morning.

The smoke appeared to be coming from the wood stove. Miss Blanket Waver probably hadn't opened the flue. She must not be from around here.

Walking through the open door, I coughed and waved the smoke away from my face as I headed toward the stove.

Without introducing myself, I said, "You forgot to open the flue."

The woman stood at the kitchen sink, trying to open the window, and jumped at the sound of my voice.

"Cheesy Rice and Joseph!" she shouted and turned to face me, clutching her hand to her chest. "Who the fuck are you?"

Leaning over, I swung the lever to open the flue on the chimney stack. "I'm the neighbor. Who the fuck are you? Cause I know this isn't your house."

With the doors and windows open the room began to clear of

smoke, but the smoke alarm continued its piercing cadence. Where the hell was the damn thing? I stared at the ceiling and followed the beeping until I spied the red-lighted beast in the hallway. I reached up and knocked it from its perch, removed the batteries, and set it on the kitchen counter.

"Ah, silence," I said. Observing the woman, I noticed she had wrapped her blanket weapon around her shoulders. Sticking out below the blanket I could see a pair of flannel pajama bottoms and mismatched socks. "You going to tell me who you are and what you are doing in my friend's house? Or am I going to call the sheriff?"

She tightened the throw around her shoulders and glared at me, but not before I noticed her eyes linger at my waist and my jeans hanging off my hips.

I smiled at her to let her know I'd caught her staring before closing my jeans.

She didn't blush or glance away, but continued to glare at me. "Do you always barge into people's homes at the crack of dawn?"

"I do when the alarm wakes me up and smoke fills the air." I crossed my arms and waited.

"I'm renting the place for a few months. Arrived on the ferry last night."

She didn't tell me her name. Nope, definitely not from around here.

"Well, that explains what you are doing here, but not who you are. I'll go first. I'm John Day. I live next door. The yellow lab out on the deck is Babe. Your turn."

"Diane. Diane Watson. Well, Woodley, but Watson soon."

"Nice to meet you, Diane Woodley-but-Watson-soon. Is that hyphenated?" I stuck out my hand to shake hers, figuring it was the polite thing to do.

She laughed, but it sounded hollow, not a real laugh. Somehow the smile didn't reach her brown eyes. She shook my hand and said, "Just

Woodley. Watson is my maiden name. I'm thinking of changing it back."

"No more Mr. Woodley?" I asked.

She scowled. "No more Mr. Woodley. Or there won't be soon enough."

"If you are planning on murdering your husband, don't tell me. I don't want to be an accessory. I'm here to open the flue and prevent you from burning down my friend's house." I smiled at her. "Plus, it's way too early to hear all the gory details of your personal life."

She laughed this time and it was real. "No, no murder. Not that it hasn't crossed my mind. Sorry about the smoke detector. I thought I knew how to build a fire. The fire part I figured out, but not the flue. Obviously."

"Obviously."

"Thanks for coming over and saving the day."

"No problem. I keep an eye on the house for Maggie, it's what neighbors do around here." I surveyed the quiet beach. "In January, not many of us live down here on the beach, we have to band together."

"I appreciate it. I'd hate to have the fire department show up on my first morning here. Sorry to wake you so early. I guess I'm still on east coast time."

"Honestly, no problem. Nice to meet you," I said, backing toward the door. "Well, I'll leave you to it. You probably want to change out the batteries on all the detectors. Who knows the last time Maggie changed them."

She looked forlorn standing alone in the living room with the blanket falling off her shoulders. The Soon-to-be-not-Woodley blinked at me before remembering her manners.

"It was nice to meet you. I don't know anyone on the island, so it's nice to meet my neighbor. I hope to see you around again."

"You probably will. Island's a small place, and the beach especially. Give a holler if you need anything." I turned when I opened the door.

"And don't forget to open the flue when you start a fire."

She seemed embarrassed, but smiled. "Thanks, John."

I gave her a wave and headed back over to the house with Babe on my heels. It was weird to have someone besides Maggie living in the cabin. Diane appeared nice enough, but she was no fiery redhead like Maggie.

I crawled back into bed after shedding my jeans. Kelly rolled over and curled into my side, mumbling about barking dogs and smoke. I stayed awake for a while, thinking about the woman next door and the expression on her face as if she didn't have a friend in the world. I'd have to text Maggie later to let her know about the wood stove. And find out more about her new tenant with the sad eyes.

TWO

AN HOUR LATER I woke up alone and smelling of smoke. Wood smoke to be specific. When I stirred, Babe shook his collar, rattling his tags to indicate he wanted out. Glancing around the room, I didn't see any signs of Kelly. No note, nothing of hers left behind. Her perfume lingering on the pillows reminded me she slept here last night, but the scent of smoke overpowered the sweetness of her. Right. Maggie's new tenant almost burned down the cabin earlier. I needed to call Mags and tell her she rented her place to a potential pyro.

Stretching, I scratched down my chest. I let my fingers wander the path of hair from my pecs down over my stomach. Morning wood lay heavy against my hip, but I had no inclination to do anything with it. Kelly kept me more than satisfied last night. One thing always clicked with us. Sex. I'm sure we had other things in common, but it was too early in the day to try to remember what they were.

Coffee and a shower were needed. I rolled over to peer at the clock. 6:00. Kelly got up and out of here early. It was Wednesday. I knew she had to commute to her salon over in town. She might stay over a few nights a week, but still had her condo in Seattle. We didn't live together. Far from it.

Speaking of work, I needed to drive up to the job site after stopping in the office this morning. I would have to call Maggie from the road.

The coffee machine dripped a steady stream of dark, nearly black liquid into the pot while I shoveled a bowl of cereal into my mouth, staring out at the bay. The water reflects the same slate gray as the sky. Across the water clouds hung low, obscuring the mountains and much beyond the immediate shoreline. As I swallowed the last bite of cereal, my gaze settled on a note on the counter in Kelly's handwriting:

"Don't forget dinner with my parents tonight in Coupeville."

"Great." I rolled my eyes. Dinner with the parents. How the fuck did we get to the point of dinner with the parents in a few short months? It wasn't like I'd never met them before. The joys of growing up on the island. You knew everyone. Kelly's brother, Mark, played on the varsity soccer team with me. I'd known the Gordons since I was fourteen. Fourteen, all limbs with big hands and feet. I had an early growth spurt, but couldn't put on muscle to save my life. Gangly. That's what my mother called me. Awkward was more like it. No wonder Kelly never gave me the time of day in high school. Obsessed with soccer, I lived and breathed making All-State as a goalie. I definitely hadn't perfected my flirting ability back then. Amazing what a summer of weight training before college could do for a guy's image and confidence. I smiled at the memory of showing up for training camp at college fifteen pounds of muscle heavier.

I ran my hand over my beard and then scratched the back of my head, snapping myself back to the present. Dinner with the parents. Kelly and I hadn't had one of those "talks" where we confessed our feelings and planned for the future. What was up with this parent shit?

The coffeemaker sputtered out the last of the brew and went quiet. Grabbing one of my travel mugs, I filled it and set it next to my keys. I

7

had time for a quick shower before leaving. No time to dwell on Kelly and dinner plans.

Babe rode shotgun next to me in the truck. The roads sparkled with ice, but it would thaw. It wasn't raining, but more than a mist. According to the LED on the rearview mirror, the outside temp hovered at freezing. That meant we could finish clearing out the first site today. Not ideal work conditions for logging, but not the worst. I was glad I wasn't still a grunt out there in the woods every day. Sure I got sawdust on my boots, but being management had its perks.

After pulling into the parking lot, I dialed Maggie's cell. I figured I'd leave her a voicemail since she rarely remembered to keep it with her.

"Hi," she answered after the second ring. Startled she picked up, I forgot to speak. "Hello?"

"Hey. Hey there, Maggie. It's John."

She laughed. "Yeah, I know. That's why I said hi. What's up? Cabin okay?"

"Why do you think it's about the cabin? Can't I just call to see how you're doing?"

"Want to talk about your love life? Or mine?" she asked, laughter breaking up the last of her words.

I rolled my eyes, even though she couldn't see me. "Yeah. Sure. How's whatshisface?"

"You know his name is Gil. You've hung out. And Gil is fine. Portland's great. Writing is going well. It's nice to be amongst the living during the winter months."

"Are you calling the islanders zombies? You've only been gone a month."

"Everyone grunting greetings and shuffling around in their fleece and rain boots makes me think of zombies. I forgot how much I missed the city. Whidbey can be so quiet in the gray months. "

"Glad you're happy, Mags. Us zombies miss you."

"You do? That's sweet. How's Kelly? The two of you still fooling around in my outdoor shower?"

I blanked for a minute. There was no way she could know I used her outdoor shower. I always double and triple checked to make sure nothing was left behind.

"Aha! Your silence tells me everything," she said. "I suspected you borrowed it from time to time, but now I know there've been shenanigans. John Day, you are a Romeo."

I couldn't help but laugh. It was good to talk to her. I missed our morning coffees. I told her as much.

"I miss you, too. Biscuit misses the beach. He's not bulimic anymore now that he's not drinking seawater. And he pines for Babe. I think they had a real bromance going on there."

"Well, you won't be gone forever. Speaking of the cabin, how long will you be away?"

"Until May. Gil and I are going to move back for the summer after his semester finishes. Have you met Diane yet? I meant to tell you she'd be arriving this week."

"Yeah, met her this morning, in fact. That's why I'm calling. She almost lit the place on fire when she didn't open the flue. Set off the smoke detector and filled the downstairs with smoke."

Maggie sighed. "Ugh. Seriously? Honestly, I can't blame her too much. She's a city girl. Probably never lit a wood stove before today. So you went over and saved the damsel in distress, huh? I'm sure she swooned all over the big, hunky neighbor rushing in to save the day," she said before falling into a fit of giggles.

"Sounds about right. Although, there was no swooning. She acted pretty put out by some strange man bursting into the house. What's her deal anyway? Not the friendliest of types."

"I don't know her to be honest. Quinn and Ryan knew the cabin would be empty and asked if a friend/client/patient of theirs could rent it for the winter."

"Ah, New Yorker. Should have guessed by the attitude and stranger danger," I said. "Figures."

"From what I got out of Ryan, she's going through an ugly divorce. The ex-husband is a finance guy, lots of money and mistresses apparently. She was totally blindsided and still might be reeling."

The pieces dropped into place as Maggie spoke. The defensive posture, the hopeless expression. The mismatched socks. Emotional wreck. Danger.

"You should be nice to her. I'm sure she could use a friend on the island as she recovers. She can be the new me. Maybe less flirting, though."

"She could never replace you, Maggie."

"You're sweet. I knew there was a reason I liked you. Be friendly. Bring her fish. Chop some wood for her. Take off your shirt and give her a show while you do it. She might be anti-love, but no woman is anti-eyecandy."

I had to laugh. "Right. Bring her wood, give her a show. Got it. I'll be her dancing bear in a tutu. Anything else?"

"Do you own a tutu?" Maggie asked, sounding genuinely curious.

"What do you think?" I asked.

"I'm guessing no unless Kelly is into role playing. And my gut tells me she isn't. How are things with her?"

"We're having dinner with her parents tonight." I scratched my beard out of habit.

"Oh. Sounds serious. Is it serious?"

"It does sound serious. And it isn't. Or at least I didn't think it was. Her divorce isn't final, how serious could it be?"

"Surrounded by divorcees. Poor John. Maybe she finally knows what she has and doesn't want to let it slip through her fingers."

"We're not you and Gil."

"Aww, you said his name. I knew you'd come around." Her happiness echoed in her voice.

I glanced up when Jeff's truck pulled into the lot a few spaces from mine. "Yeah, he's not too bad as long as he makes you happy. Listen, I need to get going. I'll be nice to your tenant. I promise."

"You're the best. And thanks for keeping an eye on the place. Give Babe a scratch for me."

"Will do." I got out of the cab after saying goodbye. I did miss the woman. I wasn't going to lie, it stung a little that Gil had come back in her life, but I had Kelly. And dinner with her parents tonight.

Joy.

Dinner with the parents didn't turn out so well. Food tasted fine. The wine her father ordered was fine. Discussing playoff hopes for the Seahawks? All fine. Not until Kelly's mother brought up her not-so-ex-husband did the dinner go tits up. Turns out the not-so-ex husband was even less ex than I thought. Like lunch last week not-so-ex. Which would be fine, if Kelly had told me herself. Being blindsided by her mother wasn't. The woman clearly preferred her daughter not divorce Mr. Successful Suit and marry an "island boy". Wait. No one said anything about marriage. No one was getting married. Right. Because someone was still married and eating sandwiches with her husband.

I remained silent on the drive back to the cabin. So did Kelly. My silence was the result of anger and embarrassment. I made the assumption hers was out of guilt. Or shame. Or both.

What the hell happened?

"John, I meant—"

"Don't. I don't care if you and Rick had lunch. Lying about it is what bugs me."

"I didn't lie about it," she said.

"You lied by omission. Not mentioning having a meal with your ex to your boyfriend is lying. Or something. Something not cool."

"Boyfriend?" she asked.

I glanced at her in the light from the dash. Her eyebrow rose in a question even though she faced the road.

"Well, yeah. What else would I be?"

"We've never really talked about it. I thought we were on the same page. Having fun. I'm technically still married."

Ouch.

"Having fun. Yeah. Having tons of fun. You're the one who came on to me last summer. Didn't reveal the little detail of still being married until after we hooked up. Maybe you aren't ready to not be married."

"Wow. When you put it like that, I'm the bitch and you're the good guy. That's the way you want to see it, fine. I'm the bitch."

"I have never called you a bitch. This is a lot more complicated than I signed up for. We were having fun … for months. You invited me to have dinner with your parents, which felt like you were saying this is a relationship. You're giving me mixed signals here, Kelly."

She sighed and rolled her head from side to side like she was trying to release a knot in her neck. "You're right. I should have told you. Both about not being divorced and the lunch date. My mind's a mess. My mother is pressuring me to make up with Rick."

I asked the question I didn't want the answer for. "What do you want?" Then I waited.

She sat in silence for a while. The headlights illuminated the dark tunnel of trees flanking the road as we sped along.

"I don't know," she said. "Last summer everything was clear in my mind. Rick and I were over. Done. You were a surprise and made everything better. The sex was amazing."

I noticed she used the past tense. "Don't you mean *is* amazing?" I frowned. Sex wasn't an issue for us. We had it and it was amazing. *Is* amazing.

"I meant last summer, but yes, it's still amazing. It's all the other stuff that's complicated."

"Doesn't have to be."

"But I like you, John. A lot. I like the time we spend together. I like it all."

"Yeah, but you can't have both." The tires of my truck crunched on the gravel of my small driveway. There was no way I was inviting her back in for the night. I wasn't going to share her, and I sure as hell wasn't going to be the reason her marriage wouldn't work out. "Looks like you can catch the ten o'clock boat if you hurry. Otherwise you're going to have to wait for the eleven." My voice flat, I stared straight ahead for a moment.

She spoke softly. "Okay, I get you're mad, but can we still talk tonight? Or not talk?"

I didn't want to talk about this, but I didn't want to have sex with her either. Not tonight. I felt mad and confused. "Let's put a rain check on the talk and sex," I said. I wasn't sure I meant it, but saying no felt too harsh.

"Great." She smiled. Sounding more optimistic, she leaned over and said, "I'll call you this weekend. Maybe we can go for a hike or something." She kissed my cheek and grabbed my hand, squeezing it before scooting back to her side of the cab.

I laughed. Kelly didn't hike; she must have been desperate. "Yeah, I'll talk to you then. Tell your parents I enjoyed dinner."

We got out of the truck, and I gave her a small wave before heading to the door. Her car's headlights swung past me when she pulled out of the driveway before leaving me in darkness.

Inhaling deeply, I gazed up at the sky. I could smell woodsmoke in the air. Stars sprinkled across the clear winter sky. Moonlight gave me enough light to follow the path to the door. The beach in the winter fell into a dark silence with many of the cabins shuttered until late spring. Before I could turn on the hall light inside, I noticed a warm glow coming from Maggie's cabin. It was good to see her tenant survived her first full day on the island.

Maggie's words echoed in my head about being nice to Diane.

However, the last thing I needed was another woman in my life going through a divorce. Divorces were messy, and like marriage, avoided at all costs.

THREE

KELLY AND I never went on her hike. Not that I was surprised. Instead, she came over and stayed the weekend.

Promises of honesty and faithfulness to me followed her explanation about discussing the divorce with Rick over lunch and the two of them seeing a mediator. I wasn't sure I believed her. After the fiasco night with her parents, I decided I'd step back emotionally. We'd still have sex, but I'd guard my heart again. No reason to risk getting emotional with someone married, even if it was a technicality.

On Thursday night I found myself at the Doghouse in Langley playing pool with Tom Donnely. Or as everyone called him, Donnely. The Donnelys were one of the oldest families on the island, a place where your cred was based on how many decades your family could call this place home. Fisherman, farmers, ship builders, and loggers founded this land, and a few of their descendants still called Whidbey home. My father used to joke one branch of the Donnelys were the missing link between apes and man. It made me laugh at the time, but some days I wondered if his words were truth.

Donnely was a ladies man of the worst kind, but also a loyal and lifelong friend. Shaggy blond hair, light blue eyes and fit, everyone said he was handsome. I knew Maggie thought I slept around, but truth be told, my conquests numbered nothing compared to Tom's. He worked at the shipyard by day and on the weekends carved things with a chainsaw. He loved to brag about his signature piece being "the spread eagle" and laughed when he explained it was the bird.

Slow winter nights meant the crowd consisted of Tom, me, Olaf the bartender, and a few stragglers sitting at the bar. The woman at the far end of the bar appeared to be doing a crossword or puzzle in the paper. She'd write something, then stop, take a drink and stare at the page for a while, tapping her pen on the bar. I couldn't see her face, but she was petite, wore glasses, and had her hair in a messy ponytail/bun thing. A giant, gray sweater hung off her shoulders and she wore those tall rain boots girls always wore.

"Hey, you going to take your shot anytime soon?" I asked Tom, who distractedly stared at the brunette at the bar.

Tom turned and gave me his devilish grin. "Oh, I'm about to take my shot." He gestured over to the bar. "Haven't seen her before. Fresh bait, ya think? You know what they say about girls who wear glasses."

"What do they say?" I asked.

"The quiet types are always the most wild in the sack."

"I don't think anyone says that besides you." I couldn't clearly see the woman at the bar, but since we knew everyone who came in here during the winter, if Tom didn't know her, she must be new. "Probably a tourist," I said.

"Perfect. Tourists are the best. Just passing through and wanting some local color." After putting his cue down on the table, Tom pushed up the sleeves of his green flannel. "I'm going to ask her if she's ever gone geoduck hunting."

I rolled my eyes and walked over to our table to grab my pint. Setting the empty glass on the table, I refilled it from the last of the pitcher. Our ritual was to split a pitcher and play some pool. When we finished the pitcher, we went home. It was later than I thought.

Donnely stood at the bar, leaning over to talk into the brunette's ear. He laughed, but she leaned away from him. If body language meant anything, she wasn't interested in what he had to offer.

Great. Guess I had to be Donnely's wingman. Time to step in and either save him from embarrassing himself or save her from Donnely.

"You've never heard of a geoduck before?" Tom leered at the woman, his eyes dancing with mischief.

"I haven't. You say they're a local delicacy? And you hunt them? Are they similar to Mallards?" she asked.

Oh no. He'd asked her about geoducks. The worst pick-up line in the history of pick-up lines. Unless you weren't from around here and didn't know what the hell a geoduck was.

Donnely chuckled. "No, not so much a duck." When I headed toward the bar, he asked, "John, you wanna help me out here and tell... I'm sorry, I didn't catch your name..." He paused.

"Diane."

"Well, Diane, nice to meet you. I'm Tom Donnely, but you can call me Donnely. This here's my friend, John. He's going to explain what a geoduck is, unless you want us to show you."

I cringed at his words. I cringed even more when the woman turned on her bar stool. He was right about Diane being new around here: she was Maggie's tenant.

Maggie's tenant, who Donnely was propositioning.

Great.

"Hi, Diane. We meet again."

Donnely swung his head to examine Diane and me. "Hey, I thought you said you'd never seen her before."

"Diane's renting Maggie's cabin for the winter," I said. "We met last week. How's the wood stove working?"

Diane stared at me, but dipped her head as if she was embarrassed.

"It's great. Now. Thanks for all your help the other morning. I'll never forget to open the flue again."

Tom grumbled about me keeping secrets, but I ignored him. "Good to hear. You settling in?"

"I am. I decided to get out of the house and see a movie at the Clyde. This was the only place open after the movie let out."

"The island is pretty dead during the winter. You have to know where to look for action," Tom said. "Speaking of action, I was telling Diane here about the island tradition of the geoduck hunt. She sounded interested—"

"Hold on," Diane interrupted, "I never said I was interested in duck hunting. Just asked what type of duck a geoduck is."

I could hear Olaf chuckling over by the register, his gray beard bobbing. He shook his head when he strolled over to us. "Miss, ain't no type of duck involved. Geoducks are clams. And they look like tallywackers. These boys are being rude. Tom, you should apologize."

For an old salt, Olaf didn't take to any tomfoolery or disrespecting women in his place. He could make you feel about fourteen with a few words. We called him O for short, which he tolerated. Barely.

Diane stared at Donnely. Then gaped at me. I shrugged my shoulders. "Don't be mad at me. You didn't give me the chance to explain."

Tom wasn't deterred. "Didn't mean to be rude, O. I was trying to introduce Diane to some local traditions. Now that I know she'll be living here, there's plenty of time to get to know each other."

Diane blinked a few times, studying the three of us. The laughter that burst from her lips surprised me—loud, almost a cackle—and her face lit up with the sound. After a moment or two while we all stood there silently watching her laugh, she composed herself.

"Did you just ask me in some weird island, backwoods way to see your penis?" she asked Donnely, wiping her eyes free of the small tears collected in her lashes.

I couldn't help but laugh then. She'd completely put Donnely and his juvenile attempts at seduction in their place. I could like Diane. Somewhere under the messy hair and dumpy sweater hid a feisty woman.

Donnely shook his head. "It was more of an ice breaker. Wanted to see what kind of woman you are."

"Does that line ever work?" she asked.

Olaf interjected, "You'd be surprised how many times a woman has been lured down to the beach with talk of geoducks. Never happens to the same woman twice, nor does it happen to locals. I'm sure Tom here was sussing out if you were local. Weren't you, Tom?"

Calling Donnely "Tom" meant the equivalent of your grandfather dragging you out back by your ear. Leaning my elbow on the bar, I enjoyed watching Tom squirm.

"Sure, O. Sure. Diane seems like the kind of girl who appreciates a direct approach and a man who can make her laugh."

"I really did need the laugh, thank you, Tom."

"Call me Donnely. In fact, if you give me your phone, you can call me anytime you want."

He was relentless. Normally I'd sit back and watch Donnely dig himself into a hole deep enough to find a geoduck, but knowing Diane was somehow connected to Maggie made me feel protective of her.

"Donnely, enough," I said. "The woman just moved here. We don't want to scare her away." I smiled at her.

She stared into my eyes and gave me a small smile.

I noticed her eyes were light brown and rimmed with long dark lashes. Too late I realized I was staring, too, and glanced away.

"It's been nice meeting you, Donnely and John. Well, meeting you again, John." She acted flustered and her words jumbled together as she reached for her purse. "I'm going to head out. Maybe I'll see you here again."

"If you're living next to John, you'll see us again no matter what," Donnely said.

"Lucky girl," Olaf said, wiping down the bar. His tone clearly indicated he didn't mean it. We weren't such bad guys and he knew it; even if we did have reputations for playing the field as he called it. It wasn't easy to be an islander and be single. Most people moved off the island after high school and never came back. Or returned married with the spouse and kids in tow for the summer.

Or your high school crush moved away, got divorced, and reentered your life. Only she wasn't divorced.

Shaking away my frustration, I tuned back in to hear Diane saying her good-byes as she put on her coat. Donnely was putting on his charming smile and trying to get her to stay for another beer, but she refused.

I grabbed my jacket from our table, then put our empties on the bar, said good-bye to the guys, and followed her out.

"Since we're going the same way, I'll follow you home. Roads are kind of slick tonight," I offered, figuring I needed to show her I was a grownup and not a perpetual horny teen like Donnely.

Scanning around, I noticed Diane stood in front of Bessie.

"Maggie's letting you drive Bessie?" I asked in disbelief. Maggie didn't let anyone drive her vintage MG. Except Gil. Bastard.

Diane bit her lip. "She reluctantly offered the car when she learned I didn't have one. I promised her I'd get a car ASAP, but I haven't yet. And I swear I only drive it in good weather."

Seeing her nervousness, I covered my shock. "Maggie must trust you. I love this little car, but you can't be driving it around on icy roads. You need a real car."

She sighed and I could see her breath when she exhaled. The road sparkled with ice crystals. The little convertible wasn't road worthy this time of year.

"I know I need to buy a car, but don't laugh, I've never bought one before. Being the stereotypical woman who gets ripped off at the car dealership isn't high on my list of life goals right now. I promise I'll do it soon. Once I find the strength to face the used car salesman."

"I could help you. Go with you even. Some of those car salesmen are assholes, but I know a guy who'd give you an honest deal," I said before I thought the offer through properly.

She appeared taken aback. "Really?" she asked. "You don't know me or owe me. If anything, I owe you for saving me from your friend back there."

"Aw, Donnely's harmless. He has no bite."

"I'll take your word on it." She laughed. "Okay, you don't appear to be the type of guy to invite me to see your dick clam, so sure, I'd be stupid to not accept your offer."

I swallowed my shock at the word 'dick' coming out of her mouth. "Dick clam?" I laughed. "You're funny."

"I try." She laughed, too. "You'll help me buy a car?"

"Sure. Let me give my buddy a call and see what he has. Anything you want in particular?"

I swear her eyes flicked down to my jeans and up over my jacket before settling on my face. Did she check me out?

"Reliable. Something reliable and sturdy. No fancy bells and whistles. And I don't have a job, so I can't do a loan. Cash only."

"Okay. Cash only. Sturdy, reliable, straightforward. I think we can work with that." We were talking about cars. Pretty sure we were only talking about cars. "I'll stop by this week and give you an update. In the meantime, no driving Bessie on the ice. The top leaks, so you might want to avoid taking her out in the rain, too."

"In other words, I'm screwed."

"Pretty much." I smiled. "But if you need a ride or anything, I'm right next door."

The cold must have gotten to her because she bounced on her toes and blew warm air over her glove covered fingers.

"You're freezing. Let's head home. Unless you want to leave Bessie here and ride with me."

"No, I'm fine to drive. I had a pint of cider. I'm good."

We said goodbye and I got in my truck, blasting the heat to defrost the windows as I kept an eye on Diane in Bessie. I followed her home like I said I would, musing over the little things she revealed about herself tonight. Handling Donnely topped the things I liked about Diane so far. My new neighbor was turning out to be more interesting than I first imagined.

A few days later I called Steve, an old high school friend and one of the best mechanics ever. Steve sold cars on the side and could be counted on for all of Diane's requirements of inexpensive, sturdy, and reliable. After telling him Diane was driving Bessie in the winter, and after he finished cursing about British cars, he said he had a Jeep Cherokee that could work. If I'd help him change the oil, Diane could come see it over the weekend.

Despite Donnely's joking about calling Diane, neither of us got her number that night, so I left her a note on the door telling her I'd found her a Jeep and my cell number.

Saturday morning found me on my back under the transmission of Diane's potential car, changing the oil. I didn't mind getting dirty. Hell, I preferred dirt to a suit any day.

Steve's voice carried over the loud classic rock in his garage. The softer tones of a woman's voice responded. Diane. She refused my offer to give her a lift to Steve's, insisting she wanted to bring Bessie in for a tune up after driving her in the winter.

I could see Diane's boots standing to the side of the car while

Steve told her about it.

"You fall asleep under there, John?" Steve asked, kicking my work boot.

After securing the oil cap, I slid the creeper out from under the front bumper and gazed up, blinking under the brighter light. Diane stared, but not at my face. I tilted my head up to see the top of my boxers and happy trail exposed. My T-shirt had ridden up, exposing my stomach above my jeans, and I gave her a show.

Slowly drawing her eyes up to my face, I met her stare and raised an eyebrow in question. "Like what you see, sweetheart?"

Busted for checking me out, she quickly turned her head toward Steve and asked him about the tires. She didn't turn her face quick enough, though. Her cheeks had reddened. Lady liked what she saw.

Standing up, I grabbed a rag to wipe the grease from my hands before turning down the music.

"What do you think?" I asked.

She glanced down and her eyes swept up my body. "About what?" she asked, sounding confused.

I gestured at the car. "The Jeep? The one right next to you? Sturdy, reliable, four wheel drive, and since you are a friend of mine, and get the discount, cheap."

"It's big. Do I need something that big?"

"It's not that big. You need something with four wheel drive for the mud and ice. Not that we ever get much snow, but we could get a freak storm. Mud is a given. Want to take it for a ride?"

She nodded and Steve tossed the keys to her.

During our short drive, Diane admitted she was out of practice driving after living in New York so long. Car service and cabs had been her usual transportation. I teased her that driving was like sex. Didn't matter how much time passed in between, you still remembered where everything went.

I expected her to laugh, but she stayed quiet and turned around to head back to Steve's.

"Hey, I didn't mean to insult you," I apologized.

She nodded and then said, "You didn't. You don't know me well enough to know the intimate details of my sex life. Or lack thereof. It was a joke. I get it. No problem."

Her words lacked conviction. Obviously it was a problem. I was used to keeping things light with women. A joke here, an innuendo there, flirting a must. Clearly Diane wasn't the typical woman I met. It would be trickier to figure her out. Ogling my abs one minute, being chaste about a sex joke the next. Hot. Cold. Confusing. I backed out of friend territory and into neighborland.

"You think this will work for you? Steve's giving you a good deal, and if anything goes wrong, he should be able to fix it." I wanted to make things less awkward by focusing on the task at hand.

"It's perfect. I really appreciate it."

"No problem. It's what islanders do for each other."

"Can I return the favor? I can cook dinner for you. Or buy pizza. I'm not the best cook, so you might want to opt for the pizza."

"I eat pizza. Sure. You can buy me pizza as a thank you. Then we're even. Got it?"

She nodded. "Say when and where. I can even drive us." She smiled and patted the dash. "Same gray color as your truck. I need to name it. Any ideas?"

"Only Maggie names her cars, so I'm not going to be much help there. Let me know what you decide."

We arrived back at Steve's, and I left them to sort out the financials with a promise of pizza soon.

My phone pinged with a text message from Kelly when I got back into the truck cab.

Don't forget Valentine's Day is next weekend.

How could I forget? She'd been reminding me for what felt like forever. Chicks and Valentine's Day. I didn't get it. What's the point in putting all this pressure onto a random day in February? To sell chocolates and flowers? Sure, I'd buy her something, but I'd rather skip the whole thing. Unless I bought her lingerie. That was a gift for me. Then again, she'd probably figure it out and get mad.

What was supposed to be fun and hot sex, evolved into the opposite of fun. What was the opposite of fun? Work. Kelly had become a lot of work.

FOUR

DIANE LEFT ME a note a few days after Steve's, suggesting a night for pizza. The night we chose ended up being bitterly cold, with winds threatening to pull down trees and the power lines connecting the south end of the island to the north. Instead of going out, I offered to pick up dinner and have her over to my house. If the power did go out, I at least had a generator unlike where Diane lived. Maggie always enjoyed "disconnecting" and would live by candlelight and the wood stove. She had all sorts of romantic notions of winter on Whidbey. I wondered how Diane would fair if we did lose power for the night. Or a couple of days. Not unusual if we had high winds or ice.

After texting about our likes and "never on my pizza", I had a Hawaiian pizza with jalapeños keeping warm in the oven when Diane appeared at my door. She was dressed for the Arctic in a black parka down to her knees with fur around the hood.

Stepping aside, I let her into the house where she shook off her coat and stamped her feet on the mat. The porch light illuminated the rain pouring down sideways with the wind. If the temperatures dropped a few degrees, we could get snow. Or ice.

"Where are your sled dogs?" I couldn't help but tease her.

She blinked up at me and ran her other hand through her hair, tousling the waves before they fell around her shoulders. Shrugging off her big coat, I could see she wore that baggy gray sweater of hers and tight jeans showing off the curve of her thighs. Unfortunately, the ugly sweater covered her ass. Pity.

"Sled dogs?" she asked, leaning down to scratch Babe's ears, who sniffed around her boots.

"Yeah, with your parka I thought you might have sled dogs." My joke fell flat.

"Oh, no. No sled dogs. That's my city winter jacket. It gets much colder back east, and in the city you walk everywhere, you need the big coat," she said, explaining what didn't need explaining. Awkward silence settled between us.

"Pizza's in the oven. Hot Hawaiian like we decided," I said, filling the space.

"I brought wine." Her voice rose as if this could be the salvation we needed. She pulled a bottle of red out of the pocket of her coat from where I hung it on the hooks by the door. "I had no idea what you liked or if you even like wine. I bought a Pinot Noir. Figured everyone likes that. Do you drink wine? Should I have brought beer?"

Her nervousness was charming, but I wasn't sure what it meant.

"Pinot's fine. Three things we do well up here in the land of gray are: coffee, beer, and wine. All necessary supplies to get through a long winter."

"I like that list. What about chocolate? Man, or woman, has to eat."

"Yes, the fourth category for survival is chocolate. Maybe following fish."

I walked into the L-shaped kitchen to grab a couple of wine glasses. She pulled up a bar stool at the counter and surveyed the space.

"I like your house. It's, um …" She paused, clearly searching for the right word. "… Masculine."

I chuckled in response. Masculine was a good way to describe my cabin. I'd taken it over from my aunt and uncle who still lived on the island but built a larger home in the woods. I tried to observe the room from her point of view. Knotty pine walls, fishing photos, and a mounted king salmon above the couch my grandfather caught definitely gave the room a "masculine" feel. The furniture wasn't fancy, or as Kelly said "current," but it was sturdy and more importantly, comfortable. My aunt had sewn denim covers for the sofa facing the flat screen over the fireplace. A pair of leather chairs flanked the sofa and my collection of old soccer trophies along with old photos lined some shelves.

"Well, I'm a man and I live here alone, so masculine works for me." I watched her nod while taking in the details of the room.

"I like it. It's cozy." She gave me a genuine smile, her first of the night.

"Cozy it is. Ready to eat, or do you want to hang out a while?"

"Let's eat. I'm starved. Can I help?"

"Nope. I can manage the pizza. As you probably noted, I don't have a dining table. It's eat here at the bar or on the coffee table. Up to you."

Her eyes crinkled and she seemed delighted by the idea of sitting around the coffee table. "Coffee table. My ex wouldn't approve and it feels rebellious. Do you mind?"

"Wow, he sounds like a fun guy."

"You don't even want to know. Definitely a wolf in sheep's clothing. Or in his case, a suit."

I grabbed the pizza box and plates, and asked her to bring over the wine and glasses. She settled in on the sofa and I took one of the leather chairs. I had a fire going in the small fireplace and it gave the room a warm glow. Diane was right about the cozy.

"I can't believe I found another person who loves jalapeño and pineapple together. Lauren, my best friend, hated it."

"This Lauren clearly doesn't know what she's missing. New York friend?"

"Best friend from college. She's a teacher. Our lifestyles were so different when I was married, but after the divorce she was the one person I could count on. I miss her."

"Sounds like a great friend, other than the whole bad taste in food part. How did you and the wolf meet? If you don't mind me asking." Curious about her past, and since we were neighbors, getting to know her felt like the thing to do.

"Do you really want to know the whole sorry tale?"

"Sure."

"If I tell you mine, will you tell me yours?"

"My what?" I asked. "Sorry tale? I have a long list of them. You'd be bored or go running for the hills with all my woes."

"I doubt that. You seem like a nice guy." She meant it. What she didn't know was I was a wolf in flannel.

"I can be a nice guy. Very nice. But I can also be an asshole," I admitted.

Her eyes wandered my face, searching for something. "Okay, so the brief history is I married right out of college. Whirlwind romance. Wealthy, ambitious, good looking—the whole family was like the Kennedys. Only they summered in the Hamptons and not Hyannis."

She said these places as if I knew what they meant.

"It was a fairy tale. After the perfect wedding, life fell into place. I quit my entry level PR job and became 'the wife'." She frowned and picked a pepper off of her slice of pizza. "Being 'the wife' was a full time job of making sure everything about us and our homes were perfectly presentable to the outside world."

"I'm going out on a limb here and guessing things weren't so perfect with Mr. Perfect."

"At first, yes. Then his career took over."

"What does Mr. Perfect do?"

"Hedge fund. Big money. Taking money from the wealthy and making more money for the wealthy. Our lives became about money. How much we had, if we had more than so-and-so. We weren't keeping up with the Joneses, we were the Joneses. And what was once perfect began to feel like a brilliant trap."

My mouthful of pizza, I gestured for her to continue.

"Turned out money and things weren't his only acquisitions. My husband also had the reputation for collecting girlfriends."

"Ouch," I mumbled with my mouth full. Swallowing some wine, I found my voice. "He sounds like a tool." I wanted to call him an asshole, but refrained.

"Tool is too nice. Long story short, I caught him in flagrante delicto and the fidelity clause in our pre-nup kicked in. The affairs and even the divorce were kept hush-hush because of his family's reputation. His parents strongly suggested I take an extended vacation while the final proceedings and settlement are ironed out."

"What year is this? I swear you are talking about some 1950s bullshit, pardon my language, about controlling parents and making the problem literally disappear." The part about controlling parents reminded me of Kelly's mother and her own meddling in my life.

"At least they didn't ship me off to Reno for a quickie divorce like the fifties." Laughing, she hid her mouth behind her napkin. "Sorry, I'm talking with my mouth full."

"No problem. As long as you don't choke. No fancy rules in this house. That's it? You've been banned to an island? For how long?"

"I wasn't banned. Honestly. I could have spent the winter out in the Hamptons. Instead, I told the whole fiasco to Quinn over lunch and he offered Maggie's cabin. Isolated on a beach in a place where no one knew me as Mrs. Woodley sounded like heaven. In reality, it's a cold, dark, wet heaven."

"I've never been to the Hamptons, so I can't give you an honest comparison, but Whidbey is heaven on earth. You chose to move here during the challenging months. Wait until summer."

"I'd love to see the summer here, but I only have the cabin until May. Then who knows where I'll go. Maybe back to New York, start over. Or someplace new."

"Did you grow up in New York?" I asked.

"Not the city. I'm from Upstate, which basically means the rest of the state except Long Island. Small town. Dad was an accountant, Mom ran the PTA, and my two older brothers were track stars."

"Sounds idyllic. Your folks still alive?"

"They are. Happily retired in Florida—my second option for a hideout."

"You had the option to be in Florida where it's warm and sunny, but you chose here? Are you crazy?" The incredulousness obvious in my voice.

Sipping her wine, she stared at the fire crackling and hissing. "Moving in with my parents would feel like utter failure. They invited me, but I'm not sure it was heartfelt. Having their thirty-year-old divorced daughter sleeping in the guest room would be difficult on all of us. I believe the saying 'You can never go home' and so do they."

"I can't imagine living with my parents." I shook my head at being trapped in Arizona, driving a golf cart around a neighborhood in a planned golf community.

"We agree about that. We have our first thing in common." She raised her glass in a toast.

"Actually, that's about the third thing we have in common. First, jalapeños on pizza. Second, we both like Pinot."

"Are you keeping a list?" A soft smile formed on her lips.

"I wasn't, but I am now." I raised my own glass to clink with hers. "To things in common."

"To things in common," she echoed.

31

"Are you looking for a job? Not to pry into your financials, but do you need a job?"

"I'm okay financially. I'd love to get a job, but have no idea what's out there. Working again would be another nail in the coffin of my old life."

"What do you want to do? Or what can you do?"

"Ah, therein lies the rub. I don't know. It's been so long since I've worked, I'm out of practice. I can join a committee, plan a fundraiser, host a party, but not sure if any of those things will get me a job on the island."

"Think about it and let me know. I know a lot of people. Figure out what you want to do and I'll get the word out."

"Thank you. Now, I've told you the horrible story of the demise of my perfect marriage, your turn." She turned the tables on me.

What could I share with her? I wasn't going to spew my life disappointments at her. We might have a few things in common, but I wasn't ready to go deep tonight.

"I've never married, so no ex-wives lurking around."

"I've seen a brunette around here. Who's she?"

Ah, who was Kelly? The easy and partially true answer would be my girlfriend. Or would have been a few weeks ago, pre-dinner revelations. *How do I define her?*

"The brunette is Kelly. Someone I've been dating."

"Girlfriend?" she asked, apparently unashamed she might be prying.

"Not really. Things are complicated."

"Complicated how?"

"Like you, she's getting a divorce. Or was. Maybe still is. Pretty sure she still is." My words tumbled out in a mess of uncertainty. Fuck, I sounded like a pussy.

"You don't know if she is or isn't getting a divorce?"

I took a deep breath and stretched my neck, rolling it from side to side before running my hand over the scruff of my beard.

"That about sums it up. We ran into each other again last summer. At that point, she was legally separated and it was only a matter of time. Then a few weeks ago I hear from her mother of all people she and the husband are still talking. Like I said, complicated."

"Sounds messed up. Are you in love with her?"

Am I in love with Kelly?

"Look, I don't mean to pry, but since I already am, I might as well give you some unsolicited advice."

I couldn't help but snort at her offer of advice, but waited for her to continue.

"Yeah, I'm the last person who should be giving anyone relationship advice. If you don't know if you're in love, then you probably aren't. Marriages and divorces are complicated, and not something you want to be the third leg to."

I listened to her words, knowing she said them from a place of kindness. "Tell me about it. Right now I'm in a holding pattern."

"She's a fool if she tosses you aside, but love makes fools of the best of us." She reached out and gently touched my forearm. "I've sworn off the L word for now."

"L word?"

"Love. For the time being I want uncomplicated, straightforward interactions. Nothing romantic. Nothing serious. No promises of fairy tales or happily-ever-afters."

"Sounds like a smart choice. I don't normally do the whole relationship thing. Kelly was the first for me in a while. Probably because of my stupid high school crush on her."

"Ah, I wondered when you said you ran into her again. So she's the one who got away?"

"Hardly. She was the one who never paid me any attention in school. I played soccer with her brother and I don't think she ever looked in my direction twice."

"Like I said before, she's a fool. Who wouldn't look at you twice?" Her words had a flirty edge to them I didn't miss.

"I was a long, lanky guy who was more obsessed with soccer than girls. I didn't fill out until college."

"You definitely filled out." Her eyes widened and her hand covered her mouth. "Did I say that out loud?"

"You did." I watched as her cheeks turned crimson.

"No more wine for me. I've lost my filter. First, I'm giving you love advice when I don't even know you. Now I'm ogling you out loud. Clearly I'm not fit for human company these days. Maybe I should get myself a dog."

Her squirming and clear embarrassment made me want to laugh or hug her. I did neither.

"I should head home before I completely embarrass myself."

"You're cute when you're embarrassed. Your cheeks turn bright red."

"Please, can we blame that on the wine?" Her blush deepened.

"Honestly, I've enjoyed spending time with you tonight. We should hang out more often. You've probably figured out it's pretty quiet down here on the beach in the winter. It's nice to have the company."

"You're too nice. I'm going to hide now." She wrapped her cardigan around herself like armor.

"I'm not that nice."

"You are. You saved me from the closed flue, you helped me buy a car, and presently you're overlooking my foot-in-mouth syndrome. All nice things."

"If you say so. Give yourself time to get to know me before you make that decision. Bachelor for a reason."

"I have no problem with that. I've sworn off relationships and you're in a "it's complicated" situation. Only thing for us to do is be friends. I could use a friend on the island."

Friends sounded good. Diane fit the mold of one of the summer wives who arrived every Memorial Day, but there was something else about her. Something deeper and maybe wounded tugged at me to be her friend.

"Friends it is."

"Let's shake on it." She stuck out her hand and I shook it.

"We don't have to spit swear or anything like that, do we?" I asked.

"I thought maybe a blood pact. I'm sure you have a knife around here somewhere in this manly house."

"You aren't serious?" She couldn't be serious.

"The expression on your face right now. No, no sharing of bodily fluids as friends. Spit, blood, or other fluids." With a resolution to her voice, she nodded and shook my hand again since I still held hers.

"Good on the no knives. I don't like human blood."

"Are you telling me you aren't a vampire so I'll invite you into my house, and then you'll actually be a vampire and kill me?"

This time I didn't hold back my laughter. "Your mind works in wild ways," I said after the laughter died down.

"You didn't answer the question. Are you a vampire?"

I started to answer no when two things happened simultaneously: the power went out and Diane screamed.

FIVE

DIANE NOT ONLY screamed, but practically jumped into my lap. Her hand clutched my shirt and her nails dug into my chest through the flannel. The whole scenario couldn't have been timed better. Talk turned to vampires and then the lights go out. A warm glow from the last of the fire lit the room, so we weren't in complete darkness. My laughter broke the silence that descended with the dark.

"Are you laughing at me?"

"I am. I'm sorry, but you have to admit, it's pretty damn funny."

"My being scared out of my skin is funny?" She attempted to sound offended, but I could hear amusement in her voice. "Vampires are scary."

"If they're so scary, and you believed I am one, why jump toward me when the lights went out? Have you no sense of self-preservation?"

Full giggles erupted from her. Leaning back, she released my shirt, tilted her head back, and let her laughter out. After a moment, she composed herself. "Oh my god, I'm the idiot girl who goes back inside the cabin or upstairs in the horror movie! I'm the one everyone yells at for not running for help when I had the opportunity."

"Pretty much. You're toast." I leaned forward toward her exposed neck and spoke in a Transylvanian accent. "Don't worry, I bite, but it will be painless after the fangs sink into your flesh."

When I stopped about an inch from her neck, she froze in place. Her laughter stopped, and I wasn't sure if she was breathing. Pulling back, I stared into her eyes, which were wide in the low light of the fire.

"Breathe. I wasn't going to bite you," I said.

She shuffled and sat more upright, breaking whatever tension was rising between us. "I know. I never believed you were a vampire. That accent gave you away. What was it? Jersey?"

I chuckled and rubbed my nails over my scruff. "Transylvania, of course. Jersey? Really?"

"Maybe Philly. Not Eastern Europe. You might want to work on that a little more." Her words teased, but her posture had slipped into something more formal. I'd clearly crossed a line, but I had no idea what that line was.

The wind howled outside, lashing rain against the windows. Babe raised his head, gazed outside, and sighed before dropping back down on his bed.

"Do you think the power will be out for a long time?" Worry crept into her voice.

"Hard to say. Might be an hour or a few days."

"Crap."

"You have enough wood. There should be flashlights, candles, and extra blankets a plenty over there, but you're welcome to sleep here tonight." My offer was genuine and without ulterior motives.

"How would Kelly feel about that?"

How would she feel about me having Diane here? Good question. "She wouldn't like it. Let's say she gets a little possessive of me."

"Can't blame her. I'd hate to create any trouble for you. If I could borrow a flashlight, I'll be fine once I get inside. I can sleep by the wood stove if it gets colder. Maggie has several down comforters; I should be warm tonight. I'll be fine."

Her words were brave, but an undertone of concern and uncertainty lay beneath them.

"You sure? I've got the generator, which should kick on pretty soon. You'd be more comfortable over here."

"I'm sure. Now that I have confirmation my fears about a paranormal monster living next door are unfounded, I'll be able to sleep at night."

"Glad we cleared the air. If you're worried about Dave down the road, you know the guy with all the hair, I can assure you he's not a werewolf or shape-shifter."

"Good to know. I have no idea who you are talking about, but I appreciate you letting me know. I really do." She grinned at me.

"Good, everything's settled. Let me find a flashlight and get you home."

"It's miserable out there. You don't have to walk me home."

"I insist. I want to make sure you have everything you need. A little rain won't hurt me."

I turned on a few LED candles and found a flashlight in the drawer by the door. After bundling up in our coats, we sprinted for Maggie's door. Despite the short distance, we were both soaked by the time we got inside. I shook the water from my hair with my hands and pushed it out of my face. Diane laid her dripping coat on a chair and searched for candles or a flashlight. Finally locating both in the basket on top of the fridge, she thanked me again. For what, I wasn't certain.

"Listen, if the power is out tomorrow morning, come over and shower at my place. I'll be up early and off to work, but there'll be coffee and food. Best not to open the fridge or freezer here unless you have to. Food should be okay for a few hours without power. There's still the landline if your cell battery dies."

"You're very resourceful," she complimented me, and my chest puffed out at the praise.

"Years of living on the island. You'll find we're hearty people who can handle whatever is thrown at us."

"I'm beginning to see that." She smiled at me in the darkness save the light of the flashlight where it laid on the island.

"Well, I'll let you settle in. I had fun tonight. We'll have to do it again."

"I'd love that. You're the only person I know here. I think we're going to be great friends."

Normally when a woman put me into the 'friend box,' I bristled, but I liked Diane. She was cool. Definitely not without baggage, but as far as a friend went, yeah, I could definitely hang out with her again.

I headed back out into the rain. When I reached my door, I turned back to wave at Diane. She waved her flashlight in response. Smiling, I walked inside. It was good to have a neighbor again.

The power came back on the next morning around five. I know because Babe woke me up barking at the silence after the generator turned off. Good guard dog.

Part of me felt disappointed Diane wouldn't be coming over for coffee. I missed my morning coffees with Maggie, and Diane might be a good substitute. I wondered if she was a morning person like me, or a cranky witch without her caffeine like Mags. Hopefully I'd find out.

I'd left my phone downstairs last night, so I hadn't seen that Kelly had texted me a few times. She acted perturbed and asked more than once why I didn't respond to her texts. I failed to mention having pizza with Diane. It wasn't a date, far from it, but somehow I knew Kelly would be annoyed. Diane was right. There was no way in hell Kelly would be okay with another woman showering here. Funny, given she was okay with seeing her ex/not-ex. Yeah. Double-standards.

I sent her a short reply telling her we'd lost power.

She responded with a snarky comment about rural living.

Not in the mood for her jabs, I ignored my phone while getting ready, and headed to work. If trees were downed, our equipment could be needed by the county. I'd have to check if power was still out around the island. People might need more wood, and I made it a habit to drop off split wood to those who needed it—the elderly or struggling families. Something I started doing a few years ago, but didn't brag about. For one thing, I didn't want word getting out we were a source for free wood, cause firewood isn't our business. Second, people tend to take advantage of generosity. Messed up, but true.

The storm let up in the afternoon, but I still dropped off a few loads of firewood at the end of the day. Left them on the porches or filled empty wood holders on my usual route. No thanks needed or expected.

Arriving home, I could see the power was back on at Diane's. The early evening darkness highlighted the glow from lamps in her living room flowing out onto the lawn. I debated for about a minute before deciding to check on her.

The chords of classic rock sounded through the front door when I knocked.

Diane clearly hadn't expected company. The baggy gray sweater had been replaced by a tight long sleeve T-shirt and what Maggie always called yoga pants. The curves I suspected where hidden under the oversize sweater were on display. And what curves they were.

A cough brought my eyes up to hers. "Um, hi."

I knew I'd been busted. Meeting her eyes, I could see the delight in them.

"Hey."

"Um, hey. Just checking to make sure you're okay. Power came back on about five this morning."

"Hey, thanks. Come on in. Unless you're a vampire." She raised an eyebrow and waited, her lips twitching to fight back a smile.

"Nope, not a vampire." I smiled and her own smile broke free.

"Good, come on in. I'm making dinner."

"Doesn't smell like anything's burning." I walked down the hall into the airy living room, sniffing the air. Some kind of stew simmered on the stove in the open kitchen, and I could smell something baking in the oven.

She padded over to stir the stew. "That's a relief. I was afraid it would smell of smoke in here forever. Lesson learned, though," she said, pointing at the fire in the wood stove.

"Fire going, dinner cooking, and whatever smells amazing in the oven, looks like you've settled in to living here."

"I have. I can't believe it's only been a few weeks, but this place feels more like home than my co-op ever did. Want to stay and eat? I made stew and there are biscuits in the oven."

"Stew and biscuits sound amazing. Are you sure you're a snooty city girl? This is simple fare."

She laughed at my teasing. "I'm a simple girl at heart. Guess I forgot along the way."

"I need to let Babe out. He's been cooped up all day."

"Bring him over. I'm sure he knows the run of the house over here."

After letting Babe out, we walked back to the house. Diane had set the dining table. I guess old patterns died hard.

"I brought a bottle of Pinot." I set the bottle down on the counter.

"Thanks, but I love beer with stew. You can have either."

I liked this stew and beer Diane and smiled. "Beer's fine."

Steam rose from the stew as we ate dinner. Conversation didn't lag between us, but no great personal revelations either. We talked about storms and our dependence on modern conveniences. I teased her about winning me over through my stomach when she brought over an apple crisp from the counter.

"I wasn't expecting company. I'm embarrassed to admit all this would have been for me. There would've been leftovers all week. I don't know how to cook for one," she said.

"I'm happy to help out any time. I was spoiled by your predecessor, who's a food blogger. She was always trying out new recipes on me. I'll never forget the tea brined chicken. It tasted, um, interesting."

"You don't seem the fancy food type of guy."

"What was your first clue?" I asked.

"Well, you appear pretty straightforward all around. Sturdy work clothes because you need them. A truck which functions more than impresses. Loyal dog. It's all without pretense."

I glanced at my Carhartt jacket thrown on the stool and down at my jean covered legs. Flannel shirt, thermal underneath. "I'd never considered my clothes as a personal statement. They serve their purpose. Never been one of those guys who wears fancy socks or designer jeans."

"It's refreshing. Something about being on the island lets me shake off all the pretension of the city." She tugged at her messy bun. "I never would have had company for dinner dressed in work-out clothes or without a shower first. I got a job today."

"Does the job explain the smell?"

"It might. You know the Pilates studio in Langley?"

My blank stare told her I didn't.

"Well, I've been taking classes there and they needed a new teacher. I'm filling in and it might be permanent."

"They'll let anyone teach classes?"

"Oh, no. You have to be trained. I've taken Pilates since college. In New York, I took so many classes, my instructor suggested I complete the training because there were no other advanced levels beyond what I took. I had plenty of time on my hands. I've never officially taught before, though. The job of Pilates instructor wasn't posh enough for the Woodleys."

"Well, good for you. Work related stink I can support. I intended to comment on the stench, but didn't want to be rude." I grinned at her.

"Oh, no. I do smell, don't I?" A look of horror passed over her face.

"Not that I noticed. All I smell is your fabulous cooking. I was teasing."

"You do that a lot," she said.

"Do what?"

"Tease. Is it me, or is that one of your standard forms of communicating?"

Her question took me off guard. I'd never thought about it. "I didn't realize I was a tease, although I have a reputation for being a flirt." I held her gaze, testing her to see if she'd look away quickly. She didn't.

"Flirting and teasing can be the same thing. Since you have a girlfriend, I guess you're teasing."

"Does it bother you? I can try and stop." The offer felt hollow. I liked teasing her and getting her to laugh.

"I doubt you could stop." She clearly didn't buy my bullshit offer. "And I don't mind. At all. It's been a long time since a boy pulled my ponytail."

"That's what I'm doing? Ponytail pulling?" I reached over and tugged on her bun.

Swatting my hand away, she said, "Didn't say it's a bad thing. I can't tell you the last time a guy flirted with me. I was starting to think I'd lost all my appeal." Her words were light, but between the lines I could see her hurt. Mr. Perfect had done a number on her.

"If you're fishing for compliments, let me tell you, you have nothing to worry about." I touched her arm before pulling my hand back and rubbing my beard. "Don't forget Donnely at the Doghouse. He was all about hitting on you."

"Ah, Donnely. Does his line ever work? The whole gooey duck thing?"

"You'd be surprised. He's very popular with the ladies. Not that he ever sticks with anyone long enough. If people don't call him Donnely, they call him Tom Cat for good reason."

"Oh, really?" Interest sparked in her eyes. "I figured he was teasing the new girl, kind of like you do."

"Seeing who you were and if you were up for fun was part of it for sure. If you were willing, you could have gone home with him that night. Probably still could. He isn't easily discouraged." My words sounded harsher than I meant.

"Thanks for the warning. Like I said last night, I'm not up for a relationship and am going to avoid the "L" word for as long as possible, but it doesn't mean I want to live like a nun."

"Well, Donnely would be more than willing to flirt with you. Give him an inch and he'll take a foot." Was I warning her against Donnely or approving of this? "Just know what you're getting in to with him."

"His bed, probably, from what you're saying."

I nodded. "Yep. Pretty much sums it up."

She eyed me and tapped her index finger against her lip in thought. "Before Kelly, were you and Tom pick-up partners?"

Chuckling, I glanced away from her face. "Yeah, I guess you could say that. I hadn't dated anyone seriously for a long time before Kelly. I was young, single, and healthy. Let's leave it at that." For some reason I wasn't comfortable discussing my single days with Diane. Not embarrassed or ashamed, hell no, but something about her made me want to protect her from the ways of men on the prowl.

"I figured as much. You're handsome and nice. Not as sleazy as Donnely. I can see why you were popular."

Nodding in agreement, I pushed back from the table. "Those days seem to be behind me for now. I honestly can't imagine being Donnely's wingman for the rest of my life."

"You're the settling down type? Is that why you're with Kelly? When you fall, you fall hard?"

"Not sure about the hard part, but I'm loyal. If I make a commitment, I'm in. One hundred percent. That's what has my head all messed up about the Kelly thing."

"I'm sure you'll sort it out soon. She can't stay 'almost divorced' forever. Then you two can move on."

"Right."

"Okay, then. Looks like we've talked ourselves into the awkward corner. Change of subject?"

"Actually, I need to get going. Early morning tomorrow." I took my plate and empty pint glass over to the sink.

"John?" she asked from the table.

"Yeah?" I turned to face her, keeping the island between us.

"Sorry I keep prying into your life. I haven't been alone in a long time, or had real conversations with new people. I'm out of practice. I'm sorry if I made you uncomfortable."

"No problem. Let's make a pact next time to talk about work, or dogs, or football. Something neutral."

"Well, I don't think you want to talk about Pilates. And I never watch football. Or have a dog. But I get your point. We can do that."

Smiling, I nodded. After whistling for Babe, I thanked Diane for dinner and she thanked me for eating her food in return. Odd, but endearing.

SIX

AFTER LITTLE DELIBERATION, I bought Kelly chocolates for Valentine's. The idea of shopping for lingerie and running into someone I knew decided it for me. The island was too small, and somehow I knew my luck would follow me over to town where I would've run into Sally or one of her gossiping cluster of women. Plus, a bearded guy in Carhartt's and boots standing amongst a bunch of nighties and bras came too close to Monty Python's lumberjack. Even I laughed at the image.

Chocolates, dinner, and sex—we had a classic Valentine's Day celebration. Kelly acted into it and into me. I couldn't complain about that or the hot sex with her.

The complaining happened the next morning when she got in the shower. I asked to join her, but she said she didn't want to miss the ferry, so I headed downstairs to make us some coffee.

Her phone rang.

Normally, I never picked up her phone, but it was ringing and vibrating on the kitchen counter. I reached over to turn it off. Rick's name flashed on the screen.

What the hell?

Curiosity got the best of me and I answered it.

"Hello." I tried to sound disinterested.

"Hello? Who's this? Is this Kelly's phone?" His voice revealed his confusion mixed with a touch of anger. He was calling my girlfriend, or whatever she was, how dare he be angry.

"This is John," I said. "Kelly's in the shower. You want to leave a message?"

"John who?"

Are you fucking kidding me?

"John Day, the man whose shower she's using right now."

"Well, John Day, this is Rick, her husband."

Like I didn't know who the fuck Rick was. He either didn't have the same knowledge of me or he was being a dick and pretending he didn't. Asshole.

"Don't you mean ex-husband? I know who you are."

He had the nerve to laugh. Yeah, he was an asshole.

"Ask her about the ex part when she gets out of the shower, buddy. Have her call me."

He hung up.

No good-bye. Nothing.

Asshole.

I slammed the phone down on the counter.

Kelly strolled downstairs a few minutes later and wrapped her arms around my waist before standing on her toes to kiss me.

I turned my head.

"Hey, what's up?" she asked, kissing my neck.

"Rick called."

I could feel her stiffen against me before sliding down and stepping away from me.

"Were you snooping on my phone?"

Knowing there was no point in denying it, I told her I saw his name and answered it. "Why is he calling you first thing in the morning? What's going on with you two?"

She strode over to one of the bar stools, spun to face the beach, and then back toward me. Even though her body turned in my direction, her eyes landed anywhere but mine.

"I don't know what's going on. We've been talking. More. A lot."

Gut punch.

"I thought we talked about this. You were going to keep me in the loop. What gives?"

"I don't know. I really don't. He's different. He wants to try. He says he wants kids, the dog, the picket fence. Everything."

A growl rumbled in my chest. "He only wants you because you've moved on. You believe him?" My anger simmered.

"I might. My mom does." She paused. "I knew you were upset at dinner last month when she brought him up and I didn't want to fuel any fires."

"Fuel the fire? Give me a fucking break, Kelly." My voice lowered. The simmering turned into a slow boil. "If you want to get back together with him, then do it. Don't play both teams. Are you fucking him?"

"He's my husband."

"So that's a yes?"

"No, we're not having sex. He wants to, but I told him I've been seeing you."

I knew he was being an asshole on the phone. Asshole.

"He acted like he didn't know anything about me during our chat. But he has every right to be pissed some guy is answering his wife's phone first thing in the morning."

"I was separated and getting divorced when we met. *And* I'm not cheating on you with my husband."

"Sure feels that way. Everything is different now."

She blinked at me, finally meeting my eyes.

"Are you breaking up with me?"

"You're married. Still. Despite my reputation, I don't fuck around with married women." I'm not my father. Her marriage status changed everything for me.

"Seriously? I'm still separated. We don't even live in the same house anymore."

"Fuck the details. I'm not going to entertain you while you figure out if you want to stay married. No way. I'm not that guy." I tossed my coffee cup into the sink, where it clattered around but didn't shatter.

"Wow. Kind of harsh, John." I could see her eyes getting wet with tears.

"Tell me about it. Last summer you were all about moving forward, falling for me. How you couldn't believe you overlooked me in high school. What a catch I am. You used me."

"I didn't. I swear. I meant all of that, I do. You're a catch. I'm the one who's confused. I don't want to lose you." Her voice wavered and cracked.

"You never had me. You never did." I crossed my arms.

It was her turn to say ouch. Wiping her tears, she pushed back from the counter and stood, her body swaying in my direction, but she didn't move toward me.

"What do you want me to say to make it right between us?"

"'I divorced my husband' is a good place to start. Until that point, maybe we need to keep our distance. I'm not getting involved in your divorce. Make up your mind and let me know." I stuffed my fists into the front pockets of my jeans and leaned against the fridge.

"That's it? You're done?"

"Done."

My anger had returned to its simmer, beneath it hid a bruised ego and a scratched heart. This moment was the reason I didn't get involved in relationships. Drama. I didn't need the drama.

Buried even further beneath the anger, ego, and scratched heart lingered fear. I pushed it down and covered everything with my practiced nonchalance.

"You're going to miss your ferry." I nodded toward the clock on the oven.

"I might be the one with the messy life, but you're a jerk." She grabbed her bag and slammed the door on her way out.

Happy Fucking Valentine's Day. At least I didn't spend the money on lingerie she'd probably wear for Rick. Asshole.

I took my frustration out on the woodpile. I chopped, split, and stacked a cord of wood the week following Valentine's Day. Diane had enough wood stacked next to the house to last all winter. So did the three neighbors' houses on either side. That might be exaggerated a little, but I had a lot of pent up anger and frustration.

According to Donnely, those weren't the only pent up things about me. That's how he convinced me to tag along with him to Everett to see some band. He promised we wouldn't run into anyone from high school or any exes. Or for him, "Repeats." Donnely was all class.

The band played mostly classic rock covers. I may have been born in the 80s, but my music taste definitely leaned a decade or two earlier. Listening to the band crank out *Mustang Sally*, I got lost in my head. I missed Kelly. Missing her made me angry. Angry about her stupid non-divorce-divorce and marriage. Angry at myself for letting myself start to fall. Yeah, she was a lot of work, but she was Kelly Gordon. The girl who held my teen heart in her hands for four years. She thought I kidded when I told her about my crush. I should've known better than to think things would have worked out for us. Second chances in love were bullshit.

Maggie's face popped into my head. She'd found her second chance with Gil. I blamed her for my current situation. I believed in her fairy tale. Confused it with my own life. What did I have to show for it? A lot of chopped wood and an empty bed.

After draining the rest of my beer, I scanned the room. Fuck second chances. I was going to take a page from the old me and listen to Donnely.

Where was Donnely? I scanned the room. He sat at the bar next to a blonde. At least he had a consistent type. I remembered his attempts to pick up Diane at the Doghouse. Crashed and burned. Yet he continued to put himself out there, thinking eventually he'd hit gold.

I ambled over to him. It turned out the blonde had a friend— a bored looking brunette. She eyed me and then smiled, pleased with what she saw. Worked for me.

Her name was Stacey, with an 'e'. She worked as a bookkeeper, was twenty-six, and had two cats. That's all I can remember. She didn't make me laugh, but she made me miss the last ferry that night.

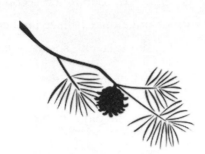

SEVEN

SUNDAY NIGHTS FAMILY gathered for dinner at my uncle's house. Every Sunday. Some people attend church on Sundays, I went to my aunt and uncle's. Honestly, I didn't mind it. Home-cooked meal, family, and sometimes laundry. My aunt doted on me. My uncle told fishing tales and complained about ferry lines. They were family, and on the island, traditions were important. Opening day of hunting season, opening day of fishing, and opening day of crabbing—time on the island could be measured by what was being hunted, caught, trapped, or the length of the ferry line.

Usually a cousin or two would be there. Maybe a grandkid. The dryer would be clunking in the laundry room next to the small kitchen while my aunt, and whichever female cousin or girlfriend or wife showed up, would make dinner.

Tonight was only the three of us. Quiet. Lasagna baking in the oven and the scent of garlic bread filled the house. Uncle Peter sat in his recliner, his round belly protruding, and told me about the time he had a halibut the size of a VW on the line in Alaska and lost it. Classic

Peter. Always about the one who got away. Sometimes I pretended he spoke metaphorically, but more often than not it was about a big fish.

Helen called us to the long, pine dining table and coughed until Peter said grace. Once we were all seated, the grilling of John began.

"Why don't you bring that girlfriend of yours to dinner sometime? What was her name? Kalie?" Helen passed me the basket of warm bread, keeping her eyes on my face. She could read me better than anyone.

"Kelly. And she's not my girlfriend. We're not seeing each other anymore. Turns out she's more married than divorced."

With a soft expression of pity I hated, she gave me an extra piece of eggplant. Feed the feelings was the motto in this family. "Well, she doesn't know what she's missing if she can't see what a good man you are."

My uncle broke into the conversation and spouted on about fish in the sea and baiting your hook with the right lure. This time I was pretty certain he wasn't talking about fishing, but with him you could never tell.

"What about your neighbor? She's a nice lady." She didn't let the subject of my bachelorhood drop easily.

"Maggie? She's living in Portland with her new guy … well, old guy. He showed up last summer and they picked back up again after all that time. Meant to be I guess." I stuffed a piece of bread in my mouth to shut myself up.

"Anyone living in her cabin?" Peter asked.

"Yep. She's rented it out to some woman from back east. Seems like a real city girl. Didn't know to open the flue for the wood stove."

"Oh, dear. She could have burnt the place down. Can you imagine?" My aunt held her hand over her pink sweater covered heart at the horror.

"Good thing I was home to help her. She appears to have gotten the hang of things. Steve hooked her up with a car."

"Sounds like you're keeping an eye on her. Is she single?"

"Helen, enough," my uncle chastised her. "Leave the poor man alone."

"The 'poor man' being alone is exactly my concern. His folks are down in Arizona. He has us and that's it. A person needs a family of their own. I worry. I'm allowed to worry."

"Thanks for your concern, but I'm okay. I work, I have friends, stuff to do, and in case you're worried, my health." I patted my toned stomach, despite her best efforts to fatten me up. I might have been single, but I wasn't letting myself go. "I like being single. Women are too much work."

"Hard work is what life's about, John," Peter said. He had been a logger same as me, but spent his years in the woods working the saws and loading trucks. From him I knew what it meant to work hard and break your back doing it.

"I work hard. I've known hard work all my life. Nothing was ever handed to me. Taken away, yes. Handed to me on a silver platter, no."

He nodded. "You're one of the best workers I know. And you don't have to tell me about loss. I've got the eight and half fingers to show for it." He wiggled the remaining fingers on his left hand. Scars, missing fingers, a missing leg, and even death were hazards of working in timber.

"My wedding ring saved the rest of my finger. That says something about things being worth the hard work."

Pretty sure that was a metaphor.

My aunt gave him a sweet smile. "We want you to be happy, honey. You deserve to be loved and happy. Have a family. Have someone to come home to every night. If it didn't work out with Kelly, there's someone else out there."

I found myself deep in dangerous territory. I missed the chattering, gossiping, giggling girlfriends, wives, and cousins. This almost felt like an ambush.

Sweeping the last piece of bread through the pool of sauce on my plate bought me some time. "I think I've heard this speech before. I get it. You know, there are lots of men out there who arc lifelong bachelors or settle down later in life. Thirty-two is not so old that you need to worry."

"Some of those bachelors are homosexuals."

My uncle's words startled me and I laughed. "I'm not gay. Trust me on that one. I love tits as much as the next guy."

"Never said you were. I'm just saying some of those bachelors are homosexuals. They keep to themselves and they don't bother me."

My aunt joined in the laughter. "For a man in your sixties, you're very open-minded, Peter."

"What? Nowadays you can't be too sure, so it's good to know these things. Know where you stand when you shake a man's hand."

Images of my uncle at a gay bar dropped into my mind. I tried to shake them away before I saw things that couldn't be unseen.

"Are we all good here? I'm not gay, I'm not lonely. I'm single. No complaints from me. New subject?"

She patted my arm. "Sure, sweetheart. You talk to your dad lately? I spoke to Joyce last week. Said they've been playing a lot of golf. I swear she likes to rub it in a bit."

When I wished for a new subject, I meant anything but this one. Joyce was my stepmother. As my real mother's sister, Helen never took to her, but put in the effort because they were family. I felt lukewarm at best about both Joyce and my father.

"Haven't talked to either of them in a while. Jim said he planned on going down to visit."

"Your brother always manages to squeeze in a trip down there. Don't know how he does it given he has his job, a wife, and kids."

Here came the guilt.

"Guess it's important to him." I shrugged and moved to stand. I'd had enough of the interrogation and guilt for the evening. "I hate to miss dessert, but I told Tom I'd meet him for an early game of pool."

Her frown showed her disappointment. I felt bad being rude, but I couldn't take it anymore. Still feeling raw from the whole Kelly situation, I didn't need my inadequacies laid out and discussed ... well anymore than they already had been.

"I'll wrap you up some things to take with you. I baked a chocolate cake. You can take a slice for Tom, too." She smiled and stood up to fix me a plate.

My uncle drummed his fingers on the table next to his glass of water. "John, she means well. You've always been special to her. Especially since we lost your mom. You're her connection to her sister. Be patient with her if she mothers you too much."

I blinked a few times after my uncle spoke. It was rare for him to talk about feelings. Even more rare for him to bring up my mom.

"Yeah, I'm sorry," I told him.

"Don't apologize to me. Tell her." He nodded in the direction of the kitchen. "Helen, I'm going to have my dessert in the family room," he called out as he stood from the table.

"I'll see you next Sunday," I said.

"You betcha. I bought some new fly fishing rods I want to show you. Planning a trip to Montana."

"Sounds good." I gave him an awkward one armed, patting the back hug men in my family perfected.

Strolling into the kitchen, I observed Helen while she put together a container of leftovers for me and sliced two enormous pieces of chocolate cake.

"Mom's recipe?" I asked, swiping my finger through the icing on one of the slices. Her hand caught air when I dodged her swat. Instead she pinched my side and turned back to the leftovers.

"I'm sorry I'm a jerk." I rubbed my side. When she turned around, I hugged her. She hugged me back, still holding the cake knife.

"About the cake? Nah, you always steal the frosting."

"No, I meant in general."

"You're not a jerk. Life hasn't turned out the easiest for you, John. I only want you to be happy. Your dad and Joyce feel the same. Your mom would want that, too. She always did."

"Thanks for saying so. Not sure I believe it, but thanks." Changing the subject, I added, "You think that's enough cake for me and Tom?"

"It might be too much, but heaven knows we don't need it." She patted her plump middle under her apron. "Better you young men eat it and work it off. No worries about diabetes for you."

"How's he doing?" I lowered my voice and tilted my head toward the family room and the blast of the television.

"He's good. His doctors still want him to eat better and exercise. He tells them he fishes, but they don't count sitting in a boat all day drinking beer as exercise."

"You'd tell me if anything serious was going on, right? You know how much I hate being kept out of things." I gave her a pointed look which said everything I didn't want to discuss.

"I will. I promise. Don't worry about us. Now you take your food and go. Invite your new friend to dinner sometime. Might be nice for her to meet some more people. Although heaven knows we aren't very entertaining. Maybe bring her when your cousins will be here."

It took me a minute to realize she meant Diane. Bring Diane to meet my family?

"I can see your mind trying to figure out a way to say no. What's her name?"

"Diane."

"Is she pretty?"

Was Diane pretty? I hadn't considered it. She was attractive, but so busy hiding it under thick gray wool and messy hair I hadn't given it much thought.

"Yeah, I guess she is. Dark hair, petite, but not a stick. She's going through a divorce, too. Guy sounds like a royal asshole."

"John."

"Sorry about my language, but he is. Unlike Kelly, this divorce is almost done. He's being an ass—jerk about alimony."

"Such a shame. Definitely bring her to dinner. She probably could use some family too." She stretched to kiss me on my cheek. I had to bend for her to reach it. I gave her arm a squeeze before saying goodbye.

Diane was perched on a stool at the end of the bar when I walked through the double doors at the Doghouse. Donnelly stood next to her, chatting her up and leaning a little too close. He didn't give up. Her laughter assured me he wasn't harassing her, but I still didn't like it.

I shed my coat and hung it on a peg in the hall leading toward the back room. My eyes stayed trained on Diane as I walked toward them while my aunt's question echoed in my head.

Was she pretty?

I took in her dark hair, which she wore down tonight. It hung past her shoulders, not super straight, but not curly either. Pretty. She had a nice profile and her face lit up when she laughed, revealing straight, white teeth framed by plump lips. Lips made for kissing.

I stopped myself. No one was kissing anyone. I wasn't kissing Diane.

Neither was Donnely.

I couldn't make out her body under the fleece jacket and jeans, but I remembered what she wore the night I ate dinner at her house. Nice tits, round ass, curvy hips and thighs. No bony girls for me. I liked somewhere to put my hands and something to hold onto that wouldn't break.

Yeah, I guess she was pretty. Very pretty, if I was being honest.

Focusing my eyes, I caught Diane staring at me, which meant she caught me staring at her. I coughed and gave her a little wave. Like a kid waves, but less enthusiastically and more embarrassed.

What was wrong with me?

Tom turned and greeted me, "Hey, I wondered when you'd drag your sorry ass here. Not that I mind you being late and giving me the chance to catch up with Diane here. We were chatting about her yoga and pilots. Both of which are great for flexibility." He winked at her.

Rolling her eyes, she corrected him, "Pilates, not pilots."

"You didn't deny the flexibility." Tom grinned at her, draping his arm around her shoulders. "I like bendy."

Seeing him touching her caused me to grumble and it came out more as a growl. Diane faced me and quirked her eyebrow.

I had growled. Like an animal. Next I would be beating my chest with my fists. I wasn't the jealous type, not ever, but Donnely hanging all over Diane annoyed me. He didn't know her backstory. He didn't know her dislike of players.

"Give the woman some room to breathe, Donnely," I said.

"Oh, he's no problem. I can handle him," Diane said, but subtly shifted away from his arm. "You two going to play pool tonight?"

"That was the plan. Unless you want some company, sweetheart." Donnely gave her what he called his "panty-dropper" grin.

She didn't fall for it and rolled her eyes at me. "Is he always this bad?"

"Didn't we establish this the last time we were here? Yes, he's that bad."

"Standing right here, you two. Standing. Right. Here." Donnely's voice bordered on petulant.

"Right, you want to rack 'em up?" I asked.

"Racks are my thing." Donnely stared down at Diane's chest and then gave her shoulder a final squeeze before he covered the short distance to the pool table.

I smiled at Diane. "If he gets too bad, give me a sign. He doesn't know any better."

"Thanks, John. Really, he doesn't bother me much. He was telling me about his wood sculptures when you arrived. I would like to see them. You don't meet many chainsaw sculptors in Manhattan."

"Many?" I had to tease. "You mean you've met a few men who wield chainsaws to create eagle and bear lawn art?"

"Okay, none. You don't meet any such artists in New York. I bet Quinn would love to see Donnely's work."

"You know Quinn?"

"I do. My husband … I mean ex-husband, and I own a couple of his works. How do you know him?"

"I met him at Maggie's mom's funeral and again last summer. He's a character, for sure. I can't imagine what his stuff is like."

Her answering laugh brightened her face. She was even prettier when she laughed. Beautiful even. Her brown eyes sparkled. "Oh, it's hysterical. I'll have to show you sometime. Everything's in storage. My ex admitted he hated Quinn's art, confirming not only is he an asshole, but he has no sense of humor."

"You're beautiful when you laugh." The words flew out of my mouth before my brain caught up.

Diane stopped her chuckling and stared at me. Her smile was soft and she appeared unsure of the compliment. "Thank you. You're more of a flirt than Donnely is."

Her words reminded me of my buddy a few feet away. "That's a lie. We know Donnely considers himself the king of the flirts."

"I'm king of what?" he asked, handing me a pool cue.

"King of the flirts, but I think John might be the dark prince." Diane placed her hand on my arm. I flexed my bicep under her fingers and she tightened her grip.

"Hey man, don't be moving in on my lady. You might be the

neighbor, but I'm the one with the mad skills with my axe."

Diane and I both groaned at his double-entendre.

"Right, let's play pool before you get too full of yourself. I'm going to kick your ass." I nodded at her before returning to the table. "I'll break."

The crack of the cue ball sounded over the music and I tried to focus on sinking my balls into the pockets. Whenever it was Donnely's turn, my eyes tended to wander over to Diane at the bar. She leaned over the paper most of the time, but occasionally I'd catch her watching us play, a wistful expression on her face.

"Hey, you want to play the winner?" I asked, knowing I had one ball left and the eight ball while Donnely had four solid balls on the table.

"I haven't played since college. You'll wipe the floor with me," she replied.

"Nah, I'll take it easy on you. I'm sure it will all come back. Like sex." With a wink, I reminded her of one of our first conversations.

Her blush told me she remembered, too.

With two more plays I won the game. Donnely grumbled his way over to his pint glass on the bar. Diane hopped off her stool and grabbed a pool cue from the rack on the wall opposite the bar.

I handed her the chalk and she rubbed it on the tip of her cue. "All right, so who breaks?" she asked, all business.

"I won the last game. I'll break."

Balls scattered across the table and two solids dropped into pockets. I reminded her of the basic rules and we began the game.

Every time she bent over to make her shot, I caught Donnely staring at her ass. Twice he winked at me and made a rude gesture. Diane's words about Tom and I being alike echoed in my head. I hoped I was never that bad. Thinking back, I probably was.

Paying too much attention to Donnely's antics, I lost track of how many balls she'd sunk and was surprised to find she was beating me.

With one more shot, she won the game.

"What was that about you haven't played since college?"

She gave me a sly grin. "Nope, not since college. Back in the day I was pretty good."

"You may have forgotten to say you're a shark. Maybe you've forgotten to mention other things too."

"Oh, John." She lightly patted my cheek. "There's so much about me you don't know."

The woman flirted with me. The gray sweater was gone and so was her shy sadness.

If she wanted to flirt, we'd flirt.

I lightly swatted her ass and leaned down so I wouldn't be heard by anyone but her. "I'd like to know all about you."

Her soft intake of breath told me she didn't see that coming and I may have turned it on too strong. She didn't know Kelly and I had ended things. She probably thought I was a cheater. Great.

I peered into her eyes where I saw not only surprise but something else. Something that surprised me. Fire.

Was she mad? Turned on? Both?

EIGHT

"SHE LOOKED LIKE she didn't know whether to slap you or fuck you. What did you say to Diane at the end of the pool game?" Donnely asked when we walked out to our trucks.

Diane had left a few minutes ago. She didn't say anything before she left; just grabbed her coat and said good-bye.

"I flirted with her. No big deal."

"You must have lost your touch, dude."

"She doesn't know I broke up with Kelly. Now she thinks I'm a cheating two-timer."

"Oh, man. Sucks for you."

"Thanks for your sympathy."

"What? I have a clear shot at her. Before she was too busy staring at you. You're the asshole and I'm the good guy. Win for me."

"Donnely," I said with a threat to my voice. "Neither of us had a shot with her. She's ruled out relationships. Nasty divorce, asshole ex."

"How do you know?"

"We've had dinner."

"Oh, like a date?" He wiggled his eyebrows. "What's the deal then? You've already hung out."

"Dinner happened before Kelly was gone."

"Ah. Yeah, you're screwed. What's with you and the divorcees lately? Aren't there any single women left for you to fuck?"

"Ha ha." My voice lacked all emotion. "If I'm not willing to take your sloppy seconds, it rules out the majority of single women under forty left on this island."

"True that." Donnely puffed up his chest in pride. "Nothing sloppy about my women. Cream of the crop."

"Sure. What's the name of the woman you went home with in Everett?" I knew I had him after a moment of silence.

"Kim? Karen? Kami? I know it started with a K. Keri?" He shook his head. "Okay, maybe I need to pay more attention. But you know me, I'm a good guy. I give them a good time. I never lie or lead them on. Not once."

"Don't you ever worry you'll get tired of not remembering names?"

Tom scrunched up his face. "Yeah, sure. I mean, some days I want the lazy comfort of the same woman in my life, but it's too much work, man."

"Maybe it feels like too much work because it isn't the right woman."

"You feel this way because of things with Kelly, but maybe it's that way with every relationship."

Taking in a deep breath, I exhaled a cloud of air in the night's damp cold. "I hope not. Things with her were great at the beginning."

"That's my whole point. Stick to the beginning of fun and you'll never get to the point of the work and the pain in the ass shit which comes with relationships."

There was no way I would take advice from Donnely. The more he said, the stronger I felt living the life of Donnely wasn't the right path. Somewhere between trying to remember last night's name and feeling trapped had to be the good stuff. The question was how to find it.

"You are a wonder with words. It's no wonder you're so popular, D."

"I have a gift. Well, I'm heading home. Gotta rest up for the weekend. You up for a trip to town?"

"Maybe. Supposed to go to the movies with Diane."

"Sounds like a date. Dinner, too?" Donnely teased.

"Not a date. We're friends."

"Friends can screw too, dude. Try the whole friends with benefits thing. Maybe that's what you're missing out on."

"Right. Cause that works out."

"Did with me and whatsherface."

"Yeah, you and whatsherface were something to be envied." I laughed at him. He was a piece of work, but as far as guys in my life, he was a loyal friend. No bullshit when it came to Tom Donnely.

"Maybe not the best example. Let me know if Diane's off the market. I'll cut you some slack and tone down the charm to give you a chance."

"Thanks, man. You're the best."

"That's what she said."

I grumbled and waved good-bye. On the drive back down to the beach and my empty house, thoughts floated through my head about friends, love and hard work. The funny thing was I never shirked hard work, physical work.

Later in the week I found myself back at the Doghouse again with Diane after a movie at the Clyde. Light snow fell but didn't stick to the ground, giving everything a slight shimmer and softness.

"Maybe if you lose the big sweater you'd have more attention than you'd know what to do with. Island's a lonely place in the winter." I teased Diane about her gray sweater, which had made another appearance tonight. We were sitting at the bar having a pint of beer before heading home.

"You hate this sweater, don't you?" she asked, picking a ball of fuzz off the shoulder.

"It looks like it's swallowing you whole. You have a nice body. Don't hide it because you married an asshole."

"Ouch. My sweater's comfortable and warm!"

"And ugly." My smile showed her I teased.

"Your opinion is duly noted. I won't wear it around you again."

"Maybe we should ceremoniously burn it?" I asked, half kidding, but mostly serious. The sweater was an abomination. Or her security blanket. "I'm going to start calling you Linus."

"Why Linus?"

"Instead of a blue blanket, you have a sweater. I think I've only seen you without it once."

"That's not true. I wore my fleece when we played pool. And I didn't wear it the night you came over for stew."

"Okay, that's twice. Still, I think we should burn it come spring. We'll do it on the beach. First bonfire of the year."

"Bonfires on the beach sound wonderful, but you're not burning my sweater." She petted her wool covered arm as if protecting the damn thing from my loathing.

"Fine," I huffed, crossing my arms.

"Maybe I'm using it as my superhero power to ward off the men. Maybe I don't want any attention."

The mention of super powers hinted she was joking, but her eyes

66

showed she meant the part about not wanting attention.

"You'd use your one super power to ward off men? Seriously? No ability to fly? Read minds?"

Her shrug told me she was serious about hiding herself. Unacceptable. That asshole did a number on her ego. Somebody needed to remedy all the shit her ex left her with. I told her as much.

"It's your superhero power to do with what you want. Invisibility it is."

"What would be your power?"

"Strength, of course." I put my elbow on the bar and flexed my bicep, wiggling my eyebrows and nodding my head to get her to touch it.

"Nice. You must work out." Her humor returned as she clamped her hand around my arm.

"Chopping wood is hard work."

"I saw you outside splitting wood. You were going at it pretty hard. Working out some frustrations?"

Here was the chance to come clean about Kelly. I took a deep breath and exhaled. "You might say that. Kelly's out of the picture."

Her face showed genuine concern. "Oh, John. I'm sorry. What happened? The ex?"

"Pretty much. The not-so-ex is less ex than I thought. I told her I'm out until she knows what she's doing. I might be catnip for the ladies, but I've never gotten mixed up in a marriage."

"Catnip?" Her lip quirked and she fought a smile.

"You'd be surprised. I'm the whole fantasy. Beard. Brawn. Wholesome."

Her eyebrow raised at the last word.

"Yes, wholesome. Dinner every Sunday night with the family kind of guy."

"Really?" Her voice filled with surprise.

"Honest. In fact, you've been invited to join us some time. Being friendly islanders, they want to show you some hospitality. My aunt is worried you don't know anyone."

"Wait, your family knows about me?"

I realized too late I had admitted to telling my family about her.

"Sure. Small island. They asked about Maggie and I told them you'd moved in." The truth, not the whole truth, but still honest.

"That's nice of them. Everyone here's been pretty welcoming on the surface. I get the feeling people don't get attached to the new arrivals."

"A lot of people have the romantic idea about living on an island. Most don't last. Isolation and rural quiet aren't for everyone."

"I can definitely see that. I could use a change of scenery and I've only lived here a few weeks."

"The rest of the world is only a ferry ride away. You could take the boat over to Everett and go to the mall."

"Thanks!" She swatted my arm.

"What? Girls like shopping and malls. We don't have that much here unless you drive up to Oak Harbor."

"I'm good, thanks. Not like I have a life and need clothes. I have my sweater, I'm good."

I chuckled watching her pet her arms. "Okay, you're atypical. No malls for you. Still, might be good to go blow the stink off once and a while."

"You think I smell?" She huffed and turned to take a sip of her beer.

"It's an expression my uncle uses. Means get out of your routine. Maybe we should head over to Port Townsend sometime. You'd like it."

"I could use a change of view. Stink or no stink."

"Then we'll go. We take the ferry over from Ft. Casey."

"I have no idea where that is. I'm realizing I haven't explored the island. I come to Langley, I buy groceries, I get coffee from the

Fellowship of the Bean … sometimes I even go out to eat by myself. Pretty boring."

"Totally boring. You need a life, Diane."

"Geez, it's a wonder why the women swarm. You're so flattering on a girl's ego."

"They don't like me for the ego stroking." I winked and we both cracked up. "Seriously, I'm an honest guy. I never lie. I compliment what I like and don't think telling a woman she's pretty should ever be held back."

Her eyes met mine and we stared at each other for a beat or two. I noticed her eyes had flecks of green and gold in the middle. What had at first appeared to be average brown, was in fact beautiful.

"You have beautiful eyes," I said, emphasizing my words about not holding back compliments.

She broke our eye contact and mumbled a thank you.

"See? Never miss the opportunity to compliment."

She scanned my face. Resolving herself, she straightened on her stool, and she set down her pint glass. "I think we should make a pact."

"What kind of pact?"

"Neither of us wants to swim in the relationship pool again anytime soon, right?"

I nodded.

"And we've already agreed we're friends," she said.

"Sure." Where was she going with this?

"Friends hang out and do things, fun things, all the time. Look at tonight, for example. This was fun. A movie and a drink. Some might think of it as a date. But it isn't a date because we're friends."

The idea tonight could be conceived as a date never crossed my mind. Sure I liked Diane, but I'd never even considered this being that kind of night out. Dates ended in good night kisses or sex.

"Okay. Where are you going with this?"

"We do all the fun things, blow the stink off together, but avoid the romance."

"Date without dating?"

"Yep. Unless you'd rather hang out with Donnely around here."

Hanging out with Donnely had its time and place, but did get boring after a while. "I do stuff other than hang out with D." For some reason, I felt the need to defend my life.

"I know you do, but I don't know anyone and you already offered to show me around. We'll make a pact it's not romantic."

I gave her a half-smile. "If you need a pact to fall back on in order to keep your hands off of me, then so be it. I'm well aware of how tempting I am."

She chuckled and held out her hand. "I think I can resist. It's you I'm worried about. You'll eventually be unable to resist the power of the sweater."

"We're shaking on the pact to date without dating?" I held out my hand, but didn't shake hers.

"That's the point."

"What about sex? You didn't say anything about sex."

"Implied in the "not dating" part of the pact." Our hands still hovered over the bar, not touching.

"Who says you have to date to have sex? I think Donnely is living, breathing proof of that fact."

"Sex is off the table."

"Forever? Or just between us?"

"Between us," she whispered and the words lacked certainty.

"Okay. No sex. No dating. Tour guide and eye candy at your service." I reached my hand out and shook hers. Her grip was firm and she didn't release my hand right away. Neither did I. Her smile reached her eyes when she glanced back at me.

"Done and done." Her hand slipped from mine and reached once again for her beer.

The thing I'd learned about pacts in my life so far was they were made to be broken. I was curious to see how long this one would last and who'd break it first.

"One more point of clarification."

"Yes?" she asked.

"Just because we aren't having sex together, doesn't mean we've agreed to a vow of celibacy, right?"

"You should have asked before shaking on it. No take-backs after." Her laughter was throaty and she shook her head, letting her long waves shake down around her shoulders.

"Not taking it back, only clarifying. No sex in this not dating dating thing, but we're free to get laid should the desire or need arise."

She remained silent for a minute, her eyes sweeping over my face. "Should the need arise? Nice wording there."

"Thanks. I'm proud of that one, too. Now, answer my question."

"This doesn't apply to me, since I only know you, Donnely, and the women at the studio. And I'm not having sex with Donnely. So sure."

"You know Olaf here." I gestured behind the bar to Olaf, who so studiously ignored us I knew he had to be eavesdropping.

"Sorry, but Olaf's off the table, too."

"Sorry, O." He lifted his head and gave me a blank look. Maybe he wasn't eavesdropping.

"For what?" he asked.

I was about to explain Diane wouldn't have sex with him when I felt the sharp sting of her fingers pinching the hair on my forearm. Swatting away her hand, I said, "Ouch!"

"Zip it, Day," she whispered in my ear.

"Nothing," I told Olaf. "Another round?" I asked her.

"No, I'm good."

"What do we owe you, O?"

I paid for both of our beers despite Diane muttering about not being a date and me not having to pay.

"Shut it, Watson. Friends still pay for shit."

"Fine." She sounded resigned. "Thank you. I'll get it next time."

"There's the spirit. To next time." I raised my glass and clinked it with hers.

"To friends," she said.

I may have said it didn't feel like a date, but I admitted I had more fun hanging out with her than I had on any real dates I could recall.

NINE

DIANE BLEW ON her cup of hot chocolate as we stood on the deck of the ferry to Port Townsend. A warm Chinook wind blew away the cold temperatures, giving us an early taste of spring. The sun shone for the first time in a week, brightening not only the sky but everyone's mood. The crossing lasted longer than the trip to Mukilteo, but what awaited on the other side was less of a culture shock.

I had left my truck parked along the road near the ferry. We'd be exploring town on foot, so the good weather was a relief.

Sipping my black coffee, I stared out at the water, absorbed in my own thoughts.

"It's a gorgeous view," Diane said, gesturing at the far coast. From this vantage point the mountains loomed to the southwest. Their sharp peaks whitened with winter snow above deep evergreen forests.

"That it is. If you look back, you can see the Admiralty Lighthouse." I turned her shoulders to face Whidbey and Ebey's Landing.

"What are all those buildings and bunker things?"

"Fort Casey. Those bunker things are gun batteries."

"Gun batteries?"

"First line of defense against a sea attack."

She squinted at the retreating shore, trying to make out the details. "It all looks so *Officer and a Gentleman*."

I had to laugh. "You have a thing for young Richard Gere?"

"Who doesn't? Bad boy turned good guy with a heart of gold. Plus, the buzzed haircut and uniform? It's one of my mom's favorite movies. I grew up loving him." Her sigh and swoon let me know she was serious.

"Girls and their bad boys."

"You're kind of a bad boy, so don't knock it."

"You think? How many bad boys take pity on their lonely neighbors and offer to show them the local sites?"

"Hmmm." She scrunched up her face. "This's true, but you're still trouble."

"If you say so." I tugged the ball on the top of her hat. "*Officer and a Gentleman* was filmed around here. We could do a tour if you want."

"Can we recreate the wet pushups scene?"

I searched my brain for what she was talking about.

"You know. Richard Gere in a wet T-shirt doing pushups. All kinds of hot."

"You're weird."

"That isn't a no." She winked. "We can wait for warmer weather so you don't catch cold."

"Thanks. Ogling your friend should be an amendment to the pact."

"Unspoken rule, my friend."

"Then it goes both ways, friend." I let my eyes wander down her body, unfortunately hidden by her coat.

"Nothing to ogle here," she said, patting her puffy covered torso.

"Spring will come soon enough." I gave her my sexy grin.

"Thank goodness. I don't think my feet have been warm since I got here."

"Welcome to the Pacific Northwest."

"No kidding. Tell me more about today's adventure."

While the ferry made its way across the water, I told her about the town and nearby fort which mirrored Fort Casey.

Wandering around the streets lined with Victorian era storefronts was more amusing than I imagined. My ulterior motive for going to Port Townsend was pizza, but Diane's delight over the used bookstore trumped even that. She dragged me through the musty stacks despite my protests I didn't read. Ignoring my grumbling, she bought me a vintage copy of *The Story of Paul Bunyan*. Something told me it was to get me back for all my teasing, but she insisted it was an act of kindness.

"You, the beard, the axe, the dog named Babe. Come on, it all fits!"

"Babe is a dog," I grumbled. "Not a blue ox."

"Okay, besides that detail. You work in timber. You're tall. How tall are you anyway?" She stood on her tiptoes and reached up to touch the top of my beanie covered head.

"Six-four," I said, straightening up to my full height.

"That's tall." She continued with her inventory and comparisons. "You have broad shoulders, wear plaid and boots all the time. And you smell of wet pine and something earthy."

"Are you saying I smell like a tree?" I cocked my head and stared down at her.

Again she stood up on her toes and leaned closer, but this time she sniffed my neck.

"Did you sniff me?" My voice broke into laughter.

"I did. Hold still while I decide what you smell like." Placing a palm on my jacket, she leaned closer. Her own fragrance filled my nose. The scent of something citrus and floral mixed with warm wool when I leaned down to inhale more of her.

Her hand clenched at my jacket and our faces were inches apart. The sounds of the shop faded away and electricity crackled between us. A small turn of my head would bring my lips to hers. I froze in place, waiting for her to move. Another moment passed and she released her grip, never turning her head the minuscule, yet monumental inch.

Her breath trembled when she exhaled and stepped away from me.

"Yep, wet pine needles and earth. You do smell like a tree." She chuckled nervously and a new pink colored her cheeks as she avoided my eyes. Grabbing her bag with my gift, she turned to leave the store. I trailed behind, my head cloudy with thoughts of what happened.

Outside, we strolled in silence along the sidewalk toward the dock. I could smell pizza on the breeze and suggested we grab lunch before heading back home.

We entered the little pizzeria, more of a hole-in-the-wall, and ordered their signature sourdough crust.

The awkward silence continued after we sat at a small table in the back.

"Pizza is kind of our thing," I said, breaking the silence.

She smiled and her shoulders relaxed. "It is our thing. We have a thing."

"We do. It's nice."

"John …"

I waited for her to continue while she fiddled with her silverware and napkin.

"I have to ask you something."

"Shoot."

"Okay, you have to promise to be honest."

"Sure. Although, now you're making me nervous."

"Sorry, but back in the store… were you thinking about kissing me?" She peered up at me, but her eyes settled below my eyes, barely meeting my gaze.

I debated whether or not to tell her the truth. Honesty won out once I decided we were friends and friends don't lie.

"It crossed my mind. I'm not going to lie. From the electricity between us, I'm guessing it crossed your mind too." I tilted my head down to meet her eyes. "Yes?"

She nodded and aligned her knife with her fork.

"What would you have done if I kissed you?" she asked, not meeting my eyes this time.

"Kissed you back." There's no doubt in my voice.

Her eyes snapped to mine. I know she saw complete honesty in them. Hell yeah I would kiss her back.

Her full lips turned up in a smile and her eyes narrowed as she sought deception or mischief in my eyes.

"I'm not lying. I know we have the whole friend pact and we're both members of the 'Please Lord, no more shitty relationships club', but I'm still a man. A beautiful woman is a beautiful woman and I'm going to want to kiss her, especially if she's an inch away from my face."

"You think I'm beautiful?"

"You are. There's no thinking about it. It's a fact."

"You're just being nice."

"I'm not and I'll prove it." I flagged over our dreadlocked and Patchouli bathed waiter. "Hey, what's your name?"

"Gabriel."

"Nice to meet you, Gabriel. I'm John and this is Diane."

Gabriel gaped at me like I was crazy, but said hi.

"Do you think Diane is beautiful?" I asked, ignoring Diane's embarrassed groans.

Gabriel scrutinized, his eyes lingering on her face before sliding down her curvy frame highlighted by her sweater.

"Yeah, sure," he said, not sounding exactly enthused.

"See? A neutral and unbiased opinion. Thanks, Gabriel."

"Sure, man," he said before wandering back toward the kitchen.

I smiled at Diane, who looked as if she wished the floor would open up and swallow her.

"Do you really think he was going to say no to my face? That completely doesn't count!"

"Fine. We can do a wider survey and ask everyone on the ferry too."

"Please don't. I get it." Her crossed arms and defensive posture disagreed with her words of agreement.

"Somewhere in there is a confident woman. I know it. I've seen glimpses of her. She's sexy and she knows it."

"Ugh, I feel like a loser who needs self-improvement lectures. Can we drop it?" Her tone was light, but she'd closed up again same as she had in the bookstore.

"There's only one way to prove it to you."

She crossed her arms and stared at me. "Prove what exactly?"

"You are desirable, sexy and beautiful."

"More surveys?"

"No."

I leaned over the table and took her chin in my hand. Her mouth opened slightly with her surprise. I studied her eyes before leaning closer, as close as we were before. "By doing what I should have done in the bookstore."

I kissed her. It wasn't hard or deep. More of a soft whisper with only enough pressure I could feel her begin to return the kiss before I pulled away and slid back in my chair.

Slowly, she opened her eyes, but remained speechless.

"You're beautiful and deserve to be kissed."

She blinked a few times before finally closing her mouth. Opening it to say something, she was interrupted by the return of Patchouli Gabe with our pizza.

Ignoring her fish-gaping, I pulled out a slice and slid it onto her plate, then put one on mine. I grinned at her stunned silence. "Now that we have that settled, eat your pizza."

Without a word, she ate her slice, giving me sidelong glances. Eventually the pink in her cheeks faded and she spoke, "Thank you."

"For what?" I asked.

"For not letting me wallow in self-pity."

"No problem."

"You're a great kisser," she said, another blush deepening on her cheeks.

"I know." I winked at her. I had no doubt about myself in that area. My heart may have been off limits, but I was comfortable in my skin.

"You're cocky," she teased me, her smile returning.

"I am."

A wadded ball of a napkin sailed across the table and landed in the middle of my plate.

"Now, now, there's no reason to start throwing things. I'm honest. You like that about me."

She narrowed her eyes at me, but nodded. "I do like your honesty. Sometimes. Let's agree not to involve Gabriel in any future debates. I think he's stoned."

When the waiter returned, neither of us could stop ourselves from laughing when the telltale scent of pot hung around him in a cloud.

Grabbing the pizza box, I pulled Diane up with my other hand.

"Are you going to kiss me again?" she asked when we stood close together.

"Do you need to be kissed again?" I smiled at her.

"No, I'm good."

"Okay, you let me know. Always happy to help a woman in need." I helped her with her coat and hat before saying, "Let's catch the ferry. There's someplace I want to show you before it gets dark."

My truck stood alone on the shoulder of the road when the ferry docked. Instead of heading toward it, I led Diane a short distance down the road and through a gravel parking area.

"Where are we going?"

"You'll see. Have faith in me."

We walked through the empty lot and into the narrow strip of sea grass, rocks, and sand before hitting the first row of driftwood. I stepped up on a large log, then turned to give her a hand up. Her glove covered hand stayed in mine as we traversed the piles of logs between the grass and the water.

"What is this place?" she asked.

"I like to call it the driftwood graveyard, but its real name is the Keystone Spit."

"Your name is better." She let go of my hand when we reached the rocky beach.

"It's a great place to come and think. Or beach comb, if that's your thing."

Turning to peer down the beach and then back, she took in the curved strip of land. It wasn't late in the day, but given the time of year the sun sat low on the horizon, casting a golden glow on everything.

"It's beautiful." Her words echoed my own thoughts.

"Thought you might like it. Let's hike up the beach." I opened my arm and gestured for her to follow me.

"Is this where you're from? You said you grew up in Coupeville."

"Yeah. Not down here at the beach, but up the road toward the highway is where I grew up. Beachfront property was too rich for my parents. They built a simple A-frame, but had a few acres."

"Do they still live there? You mentioned Sunday dinners with family, but didn't say what family."

I bristled at her innocent question. Steeling myself, I resolved to be honest, despite wanting to change the topic more than anything.

"Nah, I have dinner with my aunt and uncle only. A few cousins show up now and then. They're the only family left on the island."

"What happened to your parents?"

It was the logical next question. The nice thing about living on the island all your life is most people already knew the answer.

"My father remarried and lives in Arizona with Joyce, his wife." I never referred to her as my stepmother.

"And your mother?" she asked.

I didn't answer right away. Diane touched my arm and said, "I'm prying, aren't I? It's evident you don't want to talk about it."

"My mom isn't around anymore. Just my brother, me, my dad, and Joyce." I knew I wasn't being completely honest, but she didn't need to know everything about my past.

"Ah. I'm sorry." I didn't meet her eyes, not wanting to see any signs of pity there. I had enough of that the last decade. The sympathetic looks from the various benevolent women from church, hospital, or grocery store were something I couldn't stand then. Or now.

"No problem. Let's change the subject."

"Sure." She let her hand fall from my arm, but kept pace with me.

I bent down to pick up a feather and handed it to her. "It's an eagle feather. Won't find one of those in New York."

She accepted it from me and twirled it. "Can I keep it?"

I stared at her for a beat. "No way. Only Native Americans and eagles can be in possession of eagle feathers."

She frowned and gently propped it up between two rocks near a driftwood log.

Whatever flirty tension or mood existed between us in Port

Townsend had disappeared. A cloud passed in front of the sun, casting a shadow on the whole beach. Without the sun's warmth, the chill of winter returned. Diane shivered and stuffed her hands in her pockets.

Time to call it a day.

TEN

I DIDN'T SEE Diane for more than a week after the kiss, which led to the awkward talk about the parents on the beach. Not that I avoided her—I hadn't. A stretch of good weather meant work picked up again. It had been so busy I had donned my orange safety gear and hit the woods to help clear. Despite my helmet and face protector, my hair and beard itched with sawdust. If I ever smelled like a tree before, I most certainly did today. Laughing at the memory of Diane's description, I stared at her house from my position behind my truck in the driveway. I wasn't hiding, but I involuntarily crouched behind the bumper when her garage door opened. Realizing how strange it looked, I straightened up and squared my shoulders.

Diane appeared, carrying a box of recycling to the back of her SUV. I trotted over to her and reached to take the box, so she could lift the tailgate.

She jumped away from me and dropped the box. "For the love of— " She cut her words off and glared at me holding a hand to her chest. "What are you doing?"

"Sorry. I was trying to give you a hand. I didn't mean to scare you." I gave her a sheepish grin, then picked up the spilled recycling, placing it back in the box.

"Next time warn a girl when you're going to be chivalrous."

"Sorry. Hi," I said, grinning at her. "You jumped about a foot, for the record. Impressive."

"I'm a city girl. Someone coming up and grabbing something out of your hands usually means you're being robbed. Old instincts die slowly."

"I didn't even think of that. Looked like you needed a hand and I was giving you one. You headed to Island Recycling?"

"I was. Time to stop hoarding the empty wine and beer bottles in the garage."

"Want some company?"

She cocked an eyebrow at me. "To the recycling center?"

"Sure. Have you been?"

"Not yet. Hence the hoarding comment." Her words sounded more clipped than they had been a few weeks ago.

"Well, you're in for a real island treat. Let me grab my stuff." I turned back toward my garage, but didn't get far before changing my mind. "Let's take my truck." We needed to clear the air and I'd rather do it on my turf.

"Okay." I could hear the doubt in her voice.

"Trust me. This will be fun."

"Okay, whatever you say. Want to grab that?" She pointed at the box sitting at her feet. "I have more back in the garage."

"Great. The more the merrier. Grab it and I'll meet you back here in a minute."

She gave me a sidelong glance before shaking her head and tromping back inside. Being excited about a recycling center probably sounded strange, but Island Recycling was no ordinary place.

Everything loaded, we drove up the hill from the beach and

headed up island.

"What's the helmet for?" she asked, patting the orange plastic creating a barrier between us on the bench seat.

"Safety. What else are helmets used for?" I slipped back into my easiest way of communicating.

She responded with a roll of her eyes and a deep sigh. "I know that. Is this going to be similar to the last time we hung out where I ask a question and you deflect or ignore?"

My eyes wandered away from the road again to her face. "That wasn't the extent of the last time we hung out. I remember something else more."

Her lips twitched into an almost smile before clamping down into a straight line.

"Okay, no teasing. Sorry I didn't answer your questions. You hit a nerve without realizing it. Wasn't your fault," I apologized.

"Yeah, I got that feeling. Why not say as much then, instead of clamming up and stewing?"

"Who's stewing?" I asked even though I knew the answer.

She turned her body and tucked her left knee up on the seat to watch me while I drove. "Okay, I was prying, but I'm curious. We know some things about each other, but not the back story, not the history that makes us tick."

"You want to know what makes me tick? I'm pretty straightforward."

Her mouth gaped open. Maybe I hadn't been so straightforward.

"You play things close, John Day. Other than your relationship with Kelly and you wear an orange helmet to work, I don't know much about you. Same goes for me."

"The orange helmet is so you can be seen in the woods and to protect your head from falling branches."

"See? That's a start. You are a real lumberjack?"

"Lumberjacks sing songs and eat flapjacks. I work in timber. Or if you want to be fancy, say Silviculture. If you must, you can call me a logger. Although I don't work with saws and chokers on a daily basis."

"Okay, logger it is. I suspected as much. That's why the Paul Bunyan book is perfect."

"And probably why I smell like a tree, according to you." Talk of how I smelled took my mind back to the bookstore and what happened after at the pizza place. From her silence, I'd guess her mind went to the same place.

"It all makes sense now. See? This sharing stuff isn't awful. Let's start with the simple stuff."

I turned to glare at her, narrowing my eyes at her motives. "Simple stuff?"

She nodded. "Like favorite food, favorite movie, favorite Turtle … basic get-to-know-each-other stuff. No sticky emotional questions or skeletons."

"But how will we know when we hit something sticky or run into a skeleton?" I asked.

"We need a code word. Something which changes the subject without either of us feeling put out for being defensive or shut down."

"Code word?"

"A code word. And you can pick it. A word that won't come up in normal conversation or is the answer to a question."

I took a moment to think over her offer of a code word as I turned off the main road to the dirt drive which led into the center. I spied my answer stacked into a pyramid.

"Bowling ball."

"Bowling ball?" she asked.

"Yes, bowling ball." I pointed toward the stack.

"Oh cool. Look, over there's a bird sculpture!" She leaned forward toward the window, eyes wide taking in all the magic of the found objects.

"I thought you might like this place." Pulling the truck up to the bottle bins, I turned off the engine. "Let's dump this stuff, and then I'll show you around."

"This place is so cool," she said, turning her head to rubberneck behind us at the stacks of old rusted cogs, scrap metal and the brightly painted lavender school bus. "Weird, but cool."

I led her over to the bus after we dumped our stuff. Inside housed a small collection of used books.

"It's a book bus. At a dump."

"It is. Since you like old books, I figured you'd love this."

She climbed up the narrow steps and entered the bus. I followed her into the tight space crammed with shelves and the smell of old paper. There wasn't much room to maneuver or turn around, and we found ourselves standing shoulder to shoulder while she scanned the shelves.

"Thank you," she whispered.

"For what?" I whispered back, unsure why we were whispering. We weren't in a library.

"For bringing me to the dump because you thought I'd like it. I can honestly say no guy, or woman, has ever taken me some place like this."

"I'm nothing if not a classy guy."

"Do you bring all the girls here?"

"No, only the ones who'd get excited by some rusty metal and a slightly musty smelling copy of a bird book." I pointed at the book she clutched to her chest.

"How many women do you know who fit that description?"

"Only one." I smiled down at her. "Ready?"

"Sure."

I stepped down and turned to help her off the last step. She gave my hand a squeeze before letting go.

"I love this place. It's full of amazing things others have thrown away because they thought they were trash."

"The saying is true. One man's trash …" I didn't need to finish the statement.

Bent over to examine a large triple-domed birdcage resting on its side in the mud, she turned and smiled up at me. "Don't take this the wrong way, but we're kind of like this stuff."

"Garbage? Gee, you think so highly of us." I frowned.

"No, the treasure. Only they didn't see it."

Not getting her meaning, I asked, "Who?"

"Mr. Not-so-Perfect and Kelly. They tossed us aside, not realizing what they were giving up."

I nodded, but I still wasn't getting it. "Which one of us is the birdcage?"

"We're everything. Misfit toys, broken window frame, old Encyclopedia Britannica volumes."

"Useless and outdated crap?" My eyebrows pulled together as I tried to figure out how this flattered either of us.

"If you want to see it that way. I prefer to think it takes the right person to see the treasure inside someone else. You're not useless or worthless to me. Or to anyone else who matters in your life. That's my point."

She was either incredibly wise or crazy. Or both.

"I think I get it. I'm the cool stack of bowling balls, not expired meat."

"Are you saying the code word?"

I licked my bottom lip and chewed on the scruff right below it before smiling at her. "Nope. I'm embracing my bowling ball status."

"Good. I'm the birdcage."

"And what a lovely birdcage you are." Our tension lifted and we settled back into right. The even keel comfort between us returned.

"You have enough fun at the dump?"

"Best time at the dump ever." She grinned up at me, her eyes alight with happiness.

"Glad to hear it. I still don't know what your favorite ice cream is, but I know you identify yourself as an old birdcage. I think it says more about you than the simple stuff."

"I agree, bowling balls." She reached out and grabbed my hand and swung it between us.

"We need a new code word."

"How about pyramid? I don't see us managing to bring that into conversation."

"We might if we have a heated discussion about Egypt."

"Or Mexico."

"Or Mexico," I said at the same time, swinging her hand when we walked over to the truck. "Pyramid it is."

"Hopefully we won't have to use it."

I liked her optimism.

Winter's iciness thawed into rain and the sun broke through the gray more often when February turned to March. Diane and I hung out, often playing what she dubbed "Truth or Pyramids"—a nod to our code word. The need for an out faded as we learned about each other.

"Favorite Star Wars?" she asked.

"Star Wars."

"Favorite city?" I asked.

"London."

"Favorite tree?" she asked

"Cedar."

"Favorite body of water?" I asked.

"A lake."

"Favorite fish?" she asked

"Salmon."

And so it continued for weeks. Neither of us ever said pyramid.

We talked about other stuff: weather, island gossip, zombie apocalypse preparedness, and the probability of a zombie apocalypse. And if zombies existed, then other supernatural creatures must exist, too, which led to reminiscing about our vampire story. Normal stuff. Sometimes we went to the movies. Once we drove to Oak Harbor when she swore she craved fast food only to figure out she had lost her taste for it after going so long without it.

Occasionally, I'd have a guys' night out with Donnely. On some of those nights we headed over to town and flirted with women we hadn't known our whole lives. But I never missed the last ferry. The appeal wasn't there. Donnely commented, but didn't make a big deal of it, which surprised me at the time. He also toned down hitting on Diane. Guess he figured she was sticking around and wasn't giving in to his charms any time soon. Could have been that or she beat him at pool every time they played. Losing damaged a man's ego.

After much reminding from my aunt, we found ourselves in her Jeep driving to have Sunday dinner with my family. I kept warning her they might be overbearing or my uncle would probably say something homophobic, but they were good people. She'd never asked about my family again and I'd been nervous she'd find out all the ugly truth. I could have told her upfront, but the topic hadn't come up. And I was a chicken shit.

While we bumped along the unpaved driveway through the woods to the house, I filled her in on the list of cousins who might show up. I felt relief when only two cars sat in the driveway. We'd lucked out and my explanations were for naught. No big family inquisition.

Helen and Peter were as nice as could be to Diane, offering her wine and inviting her to help herself to the homemade cheese-ball or smoked salmon. She politely tried both, asking if Peter had smoked the salmon.

"John and I did it together. I'm surprised he hasn't shared some with you already."

"I've heard legend of his fish sharing, but he's never brought me any fish."

I wondered where she'd heard that … ah, Maggie. They must have talked. Of course they talked. Maggie was her landlord. Made me wonder what else they spoke about. Specifically, what did they say about me?

Dinner tasted delicious. After we finished eating, Peter invited Diane to sit with him while I helped my aunt with the cleanup. He insisted, even after she offered. Damn him. I hated doing the dishes.

Helen waved me away from the sink. "Stand here and keep me company while I clean up. You'll only get in the way."

"I knew there was a reason I loved you," I said, leaning down and kissing the top of her head.

"I talked to your dad last week. They're thinking of bringing the RV up this summer. We figured they could park it here on the property for a visit."

My spine stiffened at the idea of my father visiting.

"I can see how happy you are about the idea. He's your dad, John. The only parent you have. You only get one set to start out with and there isn't a return policy."

"I know," I grumbled and picked at a spot on her counter with my thumbnail. "I'll play nice when they come. I promise." Even to my own ears I sounded like an insincere child.

"You have a couple of months to practice." She sighed and patted my arm.

A change of subject was needed and she chose the exact one I'd rather not discuss with her. If only my code word worked with everyone.

"Diane seems like a nice girl."

Pyramid.

I leaned back and peered around the corner to see Peter and Diane in the living room. Her soft laughter carried into the kitchen. Nothing appeared out of sorts, nor did she sound uncomfortable.

"Yeah, Diane's nice. We've been hanging out."

"Is that code for dating?"

"No, in this case it means spending time together, but not dating."

"Is that the same thing as hooking up?"

Pyramid.

"No, not hooking up. Hooking up is the benefits of dating without the dates if you know what I mean."

"Oh." She paused. "Well."

"Yeah. Not that."

"Good. A nice girl should be respected and treated like a lady. I think your generation would benefit from courting."

"Seriously? Courting? My generation? You're not that old. Dad got Mom pregnant before they got married. Sounds like your generation could have benefitted from it too." I bumped her hip with mine to emphasize my teasing.

"Oh, those things have always happened."

'Those things' were my brother James, born fourteen months before me.

"Speaking of the bastard child, how is Jim?"

"Don't call your brother a bastard. Haven't spoken with him, so I guess he's fine. You should call him."

Pyramid.

"Sure. I'm going to check on Diane. We should probably get going."

Peeking into the living room, I spied Peter showing her a framed photo. The familiar frame and the picture in it would open a whole big box of pyramids.

Why did I think bringing her to dinner was a good idea?

# ELEVEN

DIANE WAITED UNTIL we climbed in her car and hit the main road to ask the question. It would have to be asked sooner rather than later. Either way I knew she'd give me the out if I needed it.

"What happened to your mother?" she asked, her voice soft, concerned. Full of pity.

Fuck.

I sat in silence while I debated which answer I'd give her. "Pyramid?" I said, the question evident in my voice.

"If you want. I won't pry, but I'm curious. Your uncle didn't tell me, if you were wondering. He showed me a couple of family pictures and in the later ones she's missing."

"She's dead."

"I'm sorry."

"Me too."

Her hand found mine on my thigh and she gave it a squeeze before saying, "Pyramid."

The word conveyed more empathy than any frown or words of

pity. Diane got it. She wouldn't push and accepted death for the answer. The how's and why's didn't matter.

"Favorite sport?" Diane asked.

"Soccer."

"Do you still play?" Her question was innocent.

"Not anymore."

"But you did?"

"I did."

"But now you don't?"

"Nope."

We'd run out questions of ice cream flavors and childhood memories. Lately our conversations wandered more into first kisses, weird scar stories, and beloved, but dead pets.

"I blasted out my knee in college. Tore both the ACL and MCL."

"Playing soccer?"

"Yeah. I played goalie. If YouTube had been around then, the video probably would have gone viral. Legs aren't supposed to bend in that direction."

I watched Diane cringe and curl up further into a ball in one of my leather chairs. Rain beat the windows and we had blown off a hike for sitting around, watching movies, and waiting for the storm to pass.

"Ouch," she said, rubbing her own knee. "Were you good? Before the injury?"

Chuckling, I absentmindedly rubbed the faint scar on my left knee. "Was I good? Yeah, I was good. Full scholarship and being scouted for the Olympics when it happened."

"The Olympics? Really?" I could hear both the surprise and respect in her voice.

"It would have been a long shot, a very, very long shot, but yeah. I spent the summer training. Stupid asshole slipped on the wet grass when he missed the kick. I dove for the ball and he used my knee to stop himself."

"Shit." Diane rarely swore.

"Shit is right. I think I blacked out on the field. I've never felt pain like that."

"What happened after?"

Pyramid. "I learned what it was to lose everything."

"No more Olympics?"

"No more Olympics, no more soccer, no more scholarship."

"How old were you?"

"Nineteen."

"Wow."

If she only knew how fucked up that summer was. Sucking in a deep breath, I decided to spill the whole horrible tale.

"It was the beginning of a shit storm in my life."

"What happened next?"

"My mom died."

"Oh shit, shit. Shit. The same summer?"

"A week later." No turning back now. "You sure you want to hear the story?"

"Only if you want to tell it."

"My mom had driven over to be with me when I had the surgery and set me up in my apartment after."

"She sounds like a good mom."

"She was."

We fell into silence while scenes from that summer flowed through my mind.

"I didn't know it was the last time I'd see her, that any of us would

95

see her. She hit a summer snowstorm up at the top of Snoqualmie Pass. White out."

Diane stood up from her chair and joined me on the sofa. Tears already crested her lower lids, but she didn't say anything. If I was going to finish the story, I couldn't watch her crying. Turning my head toward the windows, I continued.

"The news said the pass closed because of an accident involving a jack-knifed semi. No one knew if she got trapped on the other side because there isn't great cell phone service up there. We didn't know for hours. Everyone kept calling her cell phone. She was dead and her phone kept ringing. And we kept leaving messages thinking she'd forgotten to charge her phone or stopped for something stupid like going to the mall. She never heard any of our messages."

"Oh, God." Her voice nothing more than a whisper, a quiet prayer.

"She never would've been on the pass if not for me and my knee. If I hadn't pushed to stay for soccer camp that summer, I would've been working in the woods with my uncle. It's my fault she was there."

She reached over and took my hand. I contemplated our fingers and then peeked up at her face. She shook her head no. I chose not to argue with her over the facts. It was my fault. All my fault.

"I guess the state bulls got in touch with the sheriff here on the island so they could let my dad know." I rubbed my eyes, anger replaced the sadness. "They couldn't find my dad at home. Or at his usual bar."

"Where was he?" Trepidation clouded her words.

"At Joyce's house. He was closing his pants when he opened the door for the officer."

"No," she gasped.

"Yep. Island's a small place. Didn't take long for the story to get around."

"Oh, John."

"Don't. Don't give me your pity."

"I'm not. I'm just… that's really…" Her words faded away.

"Fucked up. It was fucked up."

"Beyond fucked up." She rubbed her nose on the sleeve of that damn gray sweater. "Joyce even showed up at the funeral."

"Wow. Wait … Joyce? As in your stepmother?"

"My father's wife. Yep. Same woman. He married her less than a year later."

"Wow. That's so wrong."

"Yep."

The silence wrapped itself around us, cocooning us in our thoughts while we sat on the couch. Diane crept closer and half hugged me, resting her head on my shoulder. I extended my arm behind her, embracing her against my side. Outside the rain fell, making ripples in the puddles on the deck. The house felt like an ark with the two of us alone in the world, alone in the silence of my fucked up past.

TWELVE

TALKING ABOUT MY mom put an end to "Truth and Pyramids" for a while. Diane tried to stop frowning when she regarded me, but she often failed. Our visits became further apart. I told myself I wasn't pulling away, but I knew I was lying to myself. There was something uncomfortable having my story voiced aloud that changed everything. I expected the pity and found it. And who wants to see that in someone's eyes? Not me.

Storms passed and the skies would clear up for a day or two before another wall of gray clouds descended. Trees and earth began the long thaw into spring while each day grew a little less dark in the morning.

One Saturday toward the end of March, I stood at the window facing my deck, drinking my coffee while deciding what I'd do for the day. The clouds floated high over the Olympics and the weather guy said they'd clear by the afternoon. Could mean rain all day, but my guess was it would mist rather than pour.

A knock at the door and Diane waving at me through the glass broke me out of my thoughts. She wore jeans and the ugly cardigan. My eyes wandered to her face and I saw distress in her eyes.

After motioning her inside, I offered her coffee as a way of greeting.

"You want cream in it?"

"Milk's fine. Sorry for barging over. I know we didn't have plans, but I needed someone to talk to about this." I noticed she held an envelope in her hand, crumpled from her grip.

"Whatcha got there?" I asked, handing her a cup.

"Letter from Kip."

"Who's Kip?" My brain wandered through the names of her friends and family I'd learned over the past few months. No Kip came to mind.

She stared at me with her mouth agape. Guess I should have known who Kip was. I shrugged.

"Kip! Kip Woodley? My ex-husband?" Her voice raised with each word until it reached a high-pitched level of incredulity.

Racking my memory for some story of her telling me her husband's name, I still came up blank. "You know, I don't think you ever told me his first name. We called him Mr. Not-so-Perfect or Woodley. You married a man named Kip?"

"Kenneth Pennington Woodley Junior, thank you. And I divorced a man named Kip."

"Seriously? Could his name be more pretentious?"

"You're not listening!" She took out her frustration by throwing the envelope on the counter.

"Okay, okay. Sorry, I was distracted by Kip. What's up?" I backed away from her with my hands held up in case she turned completely feral, and attacked.

"I divorced him. Done. Finito. He's agreed to the settlement." She gestured to the crumpled paper.

"That's a good thing, right? Being finished with it?"

"It should be. It is. Only Kip had to add a personal letter to me. Asshole."

"And? What did it say?"

"I only read the first paragraph and headed over here."

"Okay. Want me to read it?"

"No. Yes. No. Gah! He can't have this hold on me anymore. He lost that right." She turned and paced to the window and back. Babe watched her from his perch on the couch. Back and forth. Back and forth. On her third lap, I made the decision this wasn't an event for coffee. We needed whiskey.

I poured some into her coffee. Maybe a finger or two's worth. Maybe a little more.

"Thanks." Sipping her coffee, Diane flopped on the couch next to Babe and petted his head.

"Right. Now we're prepared, do you want to read his letter?"

"Not really. But I should. I think."

"Up to you. You're legally done with him. There are no 'have-to's' in this situation. Should you? Maybe. Must? No."

"Okay, I'll read it. But not out loud. Is that okay?"

She was ridiculous, but who was I to push on emotional issues?

I handed her the envelope and she pulled out the letter— a single typed sheet. What asshole types a personal letter? Right. Her ex-husband. Asshole.

Her eyes scanned the letter quickly, then settled on the top of the page and moved slowly over the paper. I waited, sitting on the arm of one of the chairs next to the couch.

Finally, she scrunched up the paper and threw it across the room. Her aim indicated the fireplace, but she missed wide right. She drained the contents of her mug and held it out to me for a refill.

"Want me to bother with the coffee this time?" I asked, eyeing her before taking the cup.

"No. Don't bother."

Oh boy. Emotional women were not my thing. I added more coffee to my cup along with some whiskey before facing the potential emotional bomb on my couch.

Diane drained her cup in two big swallows and cringed. After wiping her mouth on the back of her hand with her eyes closed, she shook her head a few times when the whiskey burned down her throat.

I kept silent and waited.

A few minutes passed while she glowered at the crumbled paper sitting on the floor.

"He's engaged."

"He's engaged." I confirmed more than asked.

"To one of the girlfriends. Who was married when they 'dated'. Dated. As if they were both single at the time. You can't date when you're married."

"What an asshole."

"That's not the worst part."

I braced myself when her eyelids turned pink with the coming tears. Fuck, there was going to be crying. Last time we hung out on this sofa there was crying. Clearly it was cursed and probably should be replaced. Or burned.

"What's the worst part?" Getting up, I refilled her cup before returning with the bottle and setting it on the coffee table.

"They're pregnant. He wanted me to hear it from him before someone else told me when she starts showing."

"Wow." I wasn't sure what else to say.

"Pregnant! She's pregnant! He always said he wanted to wait. Wait until we were thirty. Wait until we had the house in Greenwich in the best school district." The tears broke the dam and spilled down her cheeks. She pulled down the sleeves of her cardigan and wiped at her eyes and nose. We could burn the sweater with the couch.

"I see you giving my sweater the stink eye, mister."

I had to laugh. Falling apart on my couch, well on her way to drunk, and she was mad about my sweater hate. "Let me get you something so you don't have to use your sleeves."

I pulled out a bandana from the clean laundry basket down the hall.

"Here." I handed it to her. "I wouldn't want you to damage your security blanket, Linus."

"You hate this sweater." She sniffled and blew her nose into the bandana.

"I do hate it. I hate everything it stands for."

"Comfort and warmth? Harsh." Her tears still tracked down her cheeks, but talk of the sweater distracted her from Kip. Kip the asshole.

"Yes, I'm against comfort and warmth. Both are overrated. No. I hate it because you use it to hide. It's a sign of sadness."

She responded by wrapping it more tightly around herself the same way she did on her first visit here. Damn this cursed couch. Definitely going into a bonfire.

"I'm sorry. Here I am, once again sitting on your couch being an emotional girl."

"Well, the girl part you can't change. If I got a letter from an ex like that, I'd be upset, too. I'd probably punch something or split wood, but I get it. Did I tell you yet your ex is an asshole?"

She smiled, barely lifting the corners of her mouth. It didn't light up her face, but was better than a frown. Or more tears. "You may have said it once. Or twice."

"Good. I'll keep saying it. He didn't deserve you, but sounds like he deserves her. Marriage vows are sacred. You don't walk out on them and fuck other people."

"Like your dad." She clamped her hand over her mouth. "Sorry," she said into her palm.

Fuck.

She knew about my parents, of course she'd make the connection. I nodded. "My dad was an asshole, too."

"I'm sorry."

"Don't."

"Sorry."

"Stop saying sorry. I'm in the minority about my dad still being an asshole. My aunt thinks it's wonderful he found someone to spend his life with rather than be alone. My brother even calls Joyce 'Mom'." I scowled. "But we're talking about your asshole, not mine."

Her laughter sounded genuine and loud. "I didn't realize the conversation had turned to our anatomy."

"We weren't—" My own laughter joined hers.

"I think I'm feeling the whiskey." She giggled.

"Listen, I'm sorry your ex is an asshole. But you're done with him. He's out of your life completely. You're an entire continent away from him here."

"You're right. Fuck him and the entire eastern seaboard!" She raised her cup and gave a salute.

"There's the spirit." I leaned forward from my chair and clinked cups with her.

"We should do something to honor this day."

"What did you have in mind?"

"I don't know." She flopped back into the cushions of the sofa. "Drink whiskey and then nap?"

"You're on your way with the whiskey, but we need something more than napping."

"Naps are the best." To emphasize her point, she snuggled into the couch, curling around Babe who shifted to expose his belly to her.

"Not dissing naps, but you need something to blow the stink off from Kip." I couldn't say his name without frowning or laughing.

She pinched up her face and squinted at me through one eye. After she gazed out at the brightening sky, she nodded and said, "Okay. Stink blowing off first. Naps later. Let's go see something I've never seen before."

"What haven't you seen before?"

"Lots of stuff." Tapping her chin with the lip of her mug before continuing, she said, "I've never seen a banana slug. Or one of those gooey ducks."

"I don't think phallic creatures should be our focus today. You might want to kill one in a symbolic gesture."

"True. Keep yours in your pants, just in case."

My eyes widened. Was she talking about my cock?

"Let's forget I said anything. Let's never speak of it again. Ever." She attempted to hide behind her mug.

"Okay, change of subject. How about we get in my truck and drive. We'll figure out where we're going when we get there."

"Sounds like a plan." With a final pat to Babe's belly, she attempted to get off the couch and stumbled. I held out my hand and pulled her up to standing.

"I'm going to hug you, John, but wanted to warn you first. You don't seem like the hugging type." She wrapped her arms around me and buried her face in my shirt. I pulled her closer and crossed my arms behind her back.

"You're going to be okay," I whispered to the top of her head.

She nodded, then peered up at me. "We both are."

We drove north up the island until we hit Oak Harbor. And then kept going.

"What about Deception Pass?" I asked after we figured out we'd explored most of the island already.

"Deception Past?" she asked, her brows furrowing. "What a weird name for a place, but all sorts of appropriate for today."

"Pass, not past." I laughed at her switching of words and how she was right about it being the perfect place.

"Deception Pass? Haven't gone there."

"Then that's where we're going." We drove past the air base and up ahead I spied a small shingled building on the side of the road. After pulling over and stopping, I told her to wait in the truck.

Inside, I bought a selection of smoked fish and snacks. Because of the whiskey this morning, I figured Diane needed something in her stomach. The sky had cleared, and while it wasn't balmy, it was warm enough for a picnic and a short hike.

I carried the sack of food back to the truck. Babe wagged his tail in Diane's face when he greeted me from his spot in the middle.

"Ack! Dog butt!" she screeched, swatting at his tail.

"Babe, sit," I said and he did.

"What did you get in there?"

"Food for a picnic."

"You're the best. Next stop, Deceptions Past!"

Her deliberate word play and arms waving caused me to chuckle again. If her humor returned, there was hope her sadness would pass and we could resume normalcy.

During the rest of the drive, I explained how the narrow body of water earned the name when early explorers mistook it for an inlet rather than the tip of the island. The single span bridge we drove over was breathtaking for the view and the long drop down to the churning water below.

Once on Fidalgo Island, I took a left leading down to a parking lot and narrow beach. We were close, but hadn't arrived at our final destination. I parked and loaded up my backpack with everything we needed.

"What's wrong with the picnic tables?" Diane asked, pointing to the flat lawn with park regulation grills and picnic tables beyond the smooth sand and calm water of the bay.

"We're going someplace better."

"Will we be sitting on the ground?" She gazed longingly at the tables and benches.

"We will. On a blanket." I patted my backpack, then swung it over my shoulder. "Like a proper picnic. Come on," I said, before wandering toward the pier and the trailhead off to the left.

Babe ran ahead down the beach and into the trees. Following behind, we left the beach for the shadows of the woods and the smell of old growth Douglas firs. Behind me, I could hear Diane inhale and exhale, then sigh.

"Smell good?" I asked.

"Smells like you. This is you."

I inhaled the scent of sea, pine, and earth. Not a bad smell to be compared to, but internally I still rolled my eyes at her.

"Come on, sniffy. Quit huffing the woods."

"It's either the woods or you."

Her words caused me to turn. Was she flirting or only being silly? Her face confirmed nothing.

"You only have to ask. Happy to share my pheromones with you."

"Good to know, Day. Good to know. Where are you taking me?"

"You'll see. Tide's out so we should have no problem getting there." The path led us along a salt marsh, the grasses still golden and dry with winter. A bend brought the trail back into the woods before we found ourselves in the sunlight again.

I pointed to a short trail splitting off to the left, across a narrow spit of sand, and up a rocky incline. "We're headed up there."

Diane raised an eyebrow. "Short hike is one thing, straight up rock climbing is another."

"Come on, it's worth it. I can either give you a push from behind or pull you up. You decide."

Her face scrunched up while she weighed her options. "Pull."

I scrambled up the rocks and turned to offer her my hand. Her hand felt warm and I didn't let go once she found her footing at the top. Instead, I led her up and over the top of the small island, which revealed itself to be more of an outcropping of meadow covered rock crested with a small stand of trees. Below the rocky cliff, dark, slate blue water swirled in eddies, creating circles on the surface demonstrating the ruthless current.

She smiled and stared at the view of the arched bridge span and water.

"Worth it?"

"Definitely worth it. It's our own private island."

"I'm glad you like it. Let's eat."

Babe trotted down the hill and joined us. His fur dripping water and dirty from his explorations. Rather than plopping down, he shook and sprayed us with bits of sand and droplets of water.

"Ugh!" Diane turned her body to escape.

"Sorry about that. Sometimes I swear he does it on purpose." I attempted to shield her from the spray with my body.

Babe gave a self-satisfied 'humph' and flopped down in the dead grass.

From my backpack I pulled out the bag of food and a blanket.

Once we settled on the blanket, I opened the various spreads and smoked fish along with some crackers and two containers of chowder.

"Good thing I like fish," she said, smelling the steam from her cup of soup.

My mouth dropped. It had never crossed my mind she wouldn't like fish.

"How could you not like fish?"

"A lot of people don't like seafood. Or clams. Some people have allergies."

I stared at her in horror. "Bite your tongue."

"It's true. Or don't eat shellfish for religious reasons."

"Fishing *is* my religion."

107

"Is it?"

I nodded. "Think about it. Jesus was a fisherman. What more honest hobby or profession is there?"

She blew on her spoonful of chowder. After swallowing a bite, she said, "I'm converting to your religion. This is amazing."

"To convert, you have to go fishing with me."

"What does that entail?"

"Sitting around in a boat mostly. And getting up early. Being cold. Sometimes being wet. It's not glamorous."

"Is it gross?"

"Gross?" I asked.

"Smelly. Fishy. Baity."

"Baity? That isn't even a word. Guess it depends on the bait. But not gross. I'd even bait your hook for you 'cause I'm a nice guy that way."

"Chivalry isn't dead!" She held her cup and spoon over her heart and blinked her eyes at me.

"If hook baiting is your idea of chivalry, you need to meet some better men." From the slump of her shoulders, I immediately knew I'd said the wrong thing and brought her mind back to the letter. Fuck. "Hey, sorry. I didn't mean—"

She cut me off before I could continue. "No, please don't apologize. I do need better men in my life."

"Well, I'm here. And I'll bait your hooks, so that's a good sign."

"And you buy me fishy foods for lunch. Delicious, fishy foods."

Something about her caused me to feel like a good guy because I bought her something as simple as smoked salmon pâté. Silly, but after feeling like I continually disappointed Kelly with my "island guy" lifestyle, it felt nice to be appreciated.

"We'll go fishing."

"We will. Jesus, you, and me. Fisherman all." She nodded.

"Not sure my boat is big enough for the three of us."

"It's not the size of the boat, it's the motion of the ocean." Her giggles showed she was still loose from the earlier whiskey.

"Wait, you did not just say that. Right after talking about Jesus?"

"What?" She played innocent. "I was talking about boats. You said you had a small boat."

"My boat is just the right size and gets the job done."

Her eyes wandered up and down my frame before settling back on my face. "I've no doubt. When will I get to see this boat?"

"We're still talking about fishing, right?"

"Of course."

I didn't believe her.

She set down her food and stretched out on the blanket. I played with a piece of grass as I rested my elbows on my knees and looked down at her. With her eyes closed and her hair loose from her ponytail, her typical guarded sadness disappeared. Left was her natural beauty, the softness of her cheeks, dark lashes against light skin, rose-colored lips parted and welcoming. She should be kissed. Kissed thoroughly.

Our brief kiss from Port Townsend flashed through my memory. I hadn't given her an opportunity to respond. As strong as the urge was to give her another opportunity, I hesitated. Today wasn't the day.

Dark eyes met mine. I'd been caught staring.

"What are you thinking about?" she asked, shielding her eyes from the sun to look at me.

"Nothing."

"Are you sure?"

"Yeah. I'm sure."

A cloud passed between us and the sun, dropping the temperature. More clouds gathered on the horizon and the breeze strengthened, bringing with it the smell of coming rain.

"We'd better head back. Rain's coming in." I stood up and pointed to the gray clouds west over the water.

"At least we had a little time in the sun. Thank you."

"For the picnic? Sure."

"For everything. For letting me be a girl and cry, for giving me the whiskey like a man, and for bringing me someplace new and perfect. There couldn't have been a better place to be today than Deception Past. Or better company. So thank you." After she stood up less than a foot separated us before she hugged me.

"You're welcome," I said into her hair.

"Two hugs in one day, you're turning into a hugger, Day."

"Don't tell anyone. I have a big, mean gruff guy reputation to protect," I grumbled, but hid my smile by ducking my face beside her head.

"I won't. It'll be our secret."

The windshield wipers beat a soothing rhythm while we drove back down the island that afternoon. Something shifted between us that day at the bridge. Our worst secrets and the ugliest of our pasts laid exposed, but those truths didn't make me want to run or shut down. Instead, they drew us closer. Wrapped in a comfortable silence in the cab of the truck, warm and dry, it felt like the three of us were a team.

THIRTEEN

THE IDEA CAME to me when we were in Port Townsend. Diane needed cheering up, and if we were ever going to kiss again, she needed to forget about Mr. Asshole. The woman needed to be reminded other men were out there, real men, who didn't hide behind their bank accounts and snooty families. Real men. With beards and trucks and real names, not like Kip.

I found myself leaning on the wall across from the studio where Diane worked Saturday afternoon. I still wasn't sure what she did, but she was clearly happy to say she had a job. Through the glass doors I could see her standing next to something that appeared to be torture equipment while a woman twisted and turned, opening and closing her legs, and then bent over on all fours, thrusting her chest out.

My mind went blank.

Did Diane do this? The bending and the opening? My mind descended to the gutter and I had to adjust myself. Seeing myself through someone else's eyes, I looked like a creeper loitering around watching women work out. Not the best impression for what I had planned.

Leaning over, I picked up one of the helmets and held it in front of my jeans. Movement through the door caught my eye. Diane and the other woman stood by the counter, talking. When the woman exited, Diane smiled and waved.

"What are you doing here?"

"I'm here to whisk you away from your tedious job."

"My job isn't tedious."

"That's the first clue to why I'm here."

She peeked over her shoulder at me while gathering her stuff. "Go on."

"I'm surprising you with an afternoon adventure."

"Is that the same thing as afternoon delight?" She wiggled her eyebrows.

"No idea what you're talking about, but it should be a good time." I held up the two helmets. Her blush told me whatever an afternoon delight was, it was dirty. I liked where her mind went.

"Are those motorcycle helmets?"

"They are indeed. That's your second clue."

Her face scrunched up into her puzzled expression I found adorable.

"I'm all gross and not dressed appropriately for a bike ride." She gestured to her black stretchy pants and tank under a light fleece hoodie.

Shit. I hadn't planned this out. "No jacket?"

"No jacket. Only my hoodie."

"Well, drive home and I'll follow you. We can start our adventure from the beach."

"Deal."

We strolled out to the parking lot behind the studio. She froze when she saw the motorcycle parked there.

"Since when do you own a motorcycle?" she asked, stroking the seat of the bike.

"I don't. It's Donnely's. '74 Triumph Bonneville."

"It's beautiful." Her eyes sparkled with excitement. "I can't wait!" She sprinted to her car a few spots away. "What are you waiting for? Last one to the beach is a rotten egg."

I fired up the bike and stashed the extra helmet before straddling the seat.

I beat her back to the house by four minutes. As an island boy, I knew all the short cuts she didn't.

Her pout broke into a smile when she saw me leaning against the bike in her driveway.

"Damn you!" After jumping down from the Jeep, she swatted at my arm. "You cheated."

"I didn't cheat. I'm faster.

Narrowing her eyes at me, she took in my body from my boots up over my jeans to the beat up leather jacket. "You look good on a bike. Is that a clue, too?"

"Nah, I'm hot. Can't help it." I grinned at her. "Go change. Wear something warm."

Diane's arms wrapped around my waist in a vise-grip. I kept telling her to loosen her grip, but every time I gunned the motor or took a curve fast, her arms tightened. Not that I complained. She felt amazing. The Triumph wasn't a big bike and her thighs pressed tight against mine. Might have been one of the reasons I'd borrowed it.

"You warm enough?" I asked when we stopped at a light.

Her words were lost to the noise, but she gave me a thumbs up. I revved the engine and pushed off. We headed toward the Keystone ferry and the peninsula. I wondered when she'd figure out my plan and our destination.

She hadn't clued in after we boarded the ferry. Sitting in the sun on the deck while we crossed over to Port Townsend, we warmed ourselves with paper cups of coffee.

"Still not telling me where you're kidnapping me to?"

"Where's the fun in that?" I asked, nudging her leg with mine.

Her huff said she wasn't nearly as amused as I felt.

"Don't you like surprises?" I asked.

"Not really. The last big surprise I had was finding out about Kip."

I growled at his name. "First rule of this adventure is no bringing up the asshole. Got it? Today's supposed to be fun."

"Sorry," she said, tucking her arm under mine and giving me a sheepish smile. "No assholes."

"Good."

"Do I get another clue?"

"Sure. You're on it."

"I'm on the clue?" She shifted her body weight into me while she attempted to peek underneath her ass.

"Not literally. The ferry and where we're headed are the clue."

Her lips twisted up into a sideways pout while she thought it over. "Okay, let's review what we know so far. You picked me up from work. On a motorcycle. Now we're on a boat to Port Townsend."

"Vintage motorcycle."

"Vintage motorcycle is important?"

"It is."

"Okay." She dragged out the word while her mind attempted to add things up.

"No idea?"

"None."

"You'll figure it out soon enough."

"I kind of hate you at the moment."

"Why?" I was stricken with her words and sure it showed on my face.

"Not real hate. Stop worrying. I'm having fun, like always, but I hate you know something and I don't."

"I know lots of things you don't. How to bait a hook or where the short cuts are between Langley and Sunlight Beach." I grinned at her glowering.

"Fine, but I'll figure this out soon enough."

"Don't ruin the fun. Enjoy the ride."

We disembarked first and headed away from downtown, up the hill. Passing through residential neighborhoods, I had a few doubts this would work out the way I'd hoped.

When the sign for Fort Worden came into view, Diane gave my waist an extra squeeze, then let go to pat my shoulders in excitement. I pulled to a stop and her squealing rose above the quieting engine.

"Oh my God! Oh my God! You didn't!" She jumped off the back of the bike and took off her helmet before bouncing up and down.

"You figured it out?" I grinned.

"Vintage motorcycle, Port Townsend! You remembered!"

I set the kickstand and leaned against the bike, smiling at her while I removed my helmet.

"I can't believe you remembered." She gave me a full-fledged hug, nearly tipping the bike over when she leaned into me. "You're giving me the *Officer and a Gentleman* tour! This is the best afternoon adventure ever!"

I'd seen Diane smile the past few months—not nearly as often as I thought she should—but I'd yet to see her gleefully happy. The woman was gleeful. Downright about to lose her mind.

"Want the tour?"

"Will there be push-ups?"

"Probably not."

"What if I beg?"

"Maybe."

I settled the helmets and the bike before we headed off to see the gun batteries and buildings.

"I think this is the first date in the history of dates that involves gun batteries."

"Who said this is a date?" I asked, my brain shutting off from surprise at her words.

"No one." Her smile faltered for a second before returning. "Date, afternoon adventure … who needs a label. I'm just saying what guy takes a girl to a place like this? No guys I know."

My brain worked again. "You know me. Date or not."

Did I want this to be a date? If I had, I suppressed what that meant. Good thing The Tides Inn wasn't still part of the tour. What first date ended up at a dingy motel?

This wasn't a date I reminded myself.

Diane's hand found mine after she took off her gloves. Our fingers intertwined and she swung our arms back and forth.

There wasn't much to see around the fort, but the view out over the water was spectacular.

After we climbed to the top of one of the gunneries, Diane brought up the push-ups again.

"Is it because you can't do push-ups that you don't want to?" She baited me.

I didn't bite. "I can do them."

"There isn't a physical reason you won't indulge me? Just you being mean?"

"I'm not being mean. I don't want to do push-ups."

"What if I bribe you?"

"With what?" I was definitely curious to hear her bribe.

"Hmm … let me think of something good."

I stared at her while she stood there, tapping her finger on her lips and her left foot on the ground.

"Stop staring at me. I can't think," she said.

"Well? Did you come up with something?"

"You are a difficult man to bribe. That's what I've come up with."

"Why's that?"

"For one thing, money isn't going to work with you. Neither are material things. Food might.." She paused, and her face lit up with an idea. "Fishing!"

"Fishing?"

"If you do push-ups and recreate my hot, young officer fantasies, I'll go fishing with you."

"A few push-ups and you'll go fishing with me?"

"Yep. But I have conditions."

"What are these conditions?"

"First, the fishing can't be out in the open ocean. I need to be able to see land."

"Okay." I nodded. Easy.

"Second, you need to do the push-ups in your T shirt. No flannel, no leather jacket." She crossed her arms in confidence.

"That's it?" Her demands were simple enough, but a gleam appeared in her eyes which wasn't there before.

"That's it."

"Okay. Push-ups for fishing. Deal." I unzipped the jacket and tossed it on the ground. Next I unbuttoned my shirt and shrugged it off. "Good thing I wore a T-shirt today. Otherwise I would have had to do this bare-chested." I figured out the gleam in her eye. It was lust.

Her eyes snapped to my face from where they'd lingered over my biceps.

"Damn it," she cursed, making her hands into fists and shaking them.

"Should have insisted on shirtless as one of your conditions. Just sayin'."

"Sometimes I hate you."

"You said that already today. You didn't mean it before, and you don't mean it now. How many push-ups are we talking about?"

"How many can you do?"

"We could be here all day."

She groaned low in her chest and mumbled something under her breath. "How about twenty?"

"Twenty it is."

On the final few push-ups, I lifted my arm and did a few with one hand.

"You're trying to kill me," Diane said when I bounced back up to standing.

"You made the request. Don't ask for what you can't handle."

She handed me my flannel. "That was one of the hottest things I've seen in a while. Thank you."

"Me doing push-ups? We need to get you out more."

"Maybe, but I'm standing by it. Maybe it's the location or the motorcycle, but yeah, hot. Not taking it back."

"Don't take it back," I said, stepping closer to her. She didn't back away.

"What's next on the tour?"

"Well, there's the paper mill. Scenic as it is. Sadly the motel isn't the same."

She blinked a few times. "Were you going to take me to a motel?"

Shit. That didn't come out the way it sounded. "No, not like that. I mean the motel from the movie."

"Oh." Disappointment tinged her voice.

"I was thinking more along the lines of food, drinks, maybe some pool, jukebox …" I felt awkward and scratched my beard near my ear.

She took a beat or two before answering me. "Sure, yeah, no motel. Food, jukebox."

A short drive back into town and we walked into one of my favorite local places. It wasn't a dive, but it wasn't touristy either. Okay, so maybe it was a dive.

"What's good?" Diane asked, studying the menu.

"Burgers. Fish and chips. Don't get anything fancy."

"Got it. Burger for me."

"Beer?"

"Sure. I could use something to warm up."

"Sorry about that. April isn't the warmest around here."

"At least it isn't raining."

"Bite your tongue." I turned to survey the bar. "If you acknowledge the good weather, you're asking for rain."

"Me talking about it won't make it rain."

"You've done it now." I grinned at her. "Hope you don't mind it raining on the ride home."

She laughed at me, clearly not understanding the power of the jinx.

"You're kind of a superstitious guy," she said.

"How so?"

"Controlling the weather for one."

"Not only me. Ask anyone around here."

"Do you have other superstitions?"

I considered her question for a minute. "Some. Mostly to do with fishing, but you can blame my father and uncle for those. Handed down generation to generation. What about you?"

"Superstitious? Maybe. I believe there are no coincidences. Everything kind of works out."

"In what way?"

"Well, like today. I only had one class, so the whole afternoon was free and I ended up here with you."

"Okay. Not really seeing it."

"I'll give you another one. I rented Maggie's cabin and met you. If I hadn't told Quinn and Dr. Gooding about my woes, I wouldn't be sitting here with you with thoughts of push-ups dancing through my head."

"Everything's connected?"

She nodded. "It is. There's a whole long list of things that had to happen for me to be sitting in this dive bar with you today."

"I'm glad you're sitting here."

"Me too. More than you know."

"Why's that?"

"I was very sad when I first got here."

"And now?"

"I'm less sad. Getting the letter last weekend then finding a place called Deception Pass, it made all my sadness feel like the past."

"Good." What else could I say? I was glad she wasn't as blue as she had been.

"Yeah, good. I have a job and a place to live. A car. And it's all stuff I did on my own. Well, with the help of friends, but you get my point."

"You get by with the help of your friends."

"I try," she said and smiled. "Hey, speaking of butchering lyrics, I see they have karaoke here in a couple of hours. We should stay. They have prizes."

"You sing?"

"Terribly, but I do. You?"

"What do you think?" I pretended to glare at her.

"Doesn't matter. It's karaoke."

Something about her happiness and joy made me want to do things that gave her more of both.

"You're going first," I said.

A few hours later, people much drunker than us sang pop songs and country songs. I stopped after two beers, knowing we'd be on the bike later. Diane appeared pleasantly buzzed, but nowhere near drunk or even tipsy.

As one of her weird ideas, we swore not to tell each other our songs. I flipped through the list and ruled out most of the songs until I found one I knew I could do justice.

Her turn for karaoke arrived before mine.

Diane walked up to the stage while I clapped and whistled for her. Blushing, she waved at me while her music cued up.

When I recognized the opening notes, I cracked up. Never did I imagine Diane would pick "Hit Me with Your Best Shot" by Pat Benatar for her song. Not only did she know all the lyrics without reading the screen, but she had choreography to go with it, involving some punches and even a few kicks. It was the most hysterical and awesome thing I'd seen in a long time. The crowd, especially the guys, ate it up. This annoyed me, until I remembered she came with me and would be leaving with me.

She bowed to the clapping and the cheers before making her way back to me. I stood up and hugged her. More to congratulate her than to mark my territory, but both worked.

"That was sexy, Linus." I smiled down at her, pushing a stray lock of hair behind her ear.

"Glad you thought so." She met my eyes and smiled back. "You better bring it if you want to beat me."

"Oh, I'm bringing it."

The two drunk girls finished their sloppy version of "Summer Nights" and my name was called.

"Hold onto your heart," I said with a wink.

Diane clasped her hands over her heart before I turned to walk up on stage. Once there, I stood still and tucked my head down to study the monitor.

When I began to sing, I kept my eyes cast down and my voice low during the first lyrics.

Her laughter carried over the crowd when she figured out what song I was singing.

Yeah. I rocked some Taylor Swift.

At the chorus, I lifted my head and found Diane in the crowd. She stood next to our table, with a huge grin on her face. I smiled back, nodding my head before continuing with my version of "You Belong to Me".

Throwing on the charm, I flirted with a few of the women near the stage, but I sang only for Diane. When the ladies clapped along, I went for it, singing the final chorus in falsetto.

No one expected a big guy with a beard, wearing jeans and flannel, to rock the teen pop. That was my ace.

I had to fight my way back to Diane through the groups of women with wandering hands, offering me congratulations. She was still standing there grinning when I reached her.

"How was it?"

She answered me by throwing her arms around my neck and jumping her legs around my hips.

Did not see that coming.

I wrapped my arms under her thighs so I could find my balance.

"Does this mean you liked it?"

She met my eyes and smiled. It wasn't the grin she wore all through my performance. This was soft and intimate. "You have no idea," she whispered.

"Glad to hear it. Wanna get out of here?"

"Yes," she said, loosening her legs and sliding down. I would've carried her out, and frowned when her body warmth left me. "Now."

FOURTEEN

THE RIDE HOME was dark and much colder. I felt Diane shiver behind me and bury herself closer into my back. At least it wasn't raining. Maybe she hadn't jinxed us with her earlier words.

A single raindrop hit my visor when we turned onto the main road from the ferry. Unfortunately, all of its friends followed it. By the time we approached the darkened Greenbank Store, there was no denying it was more than a mist. Jinxed.

I pulled the bike off the road and we ran for the overhang of the store. Standing in the shadows next to the bagged ice freezer on the side of the building, I took off my helmet and brushed the rain from the back of my neck. Diane was dry on her front, but the back of her jacket appeared nearly soaked.

After she took off her helmet and set it on the ground, I gave her a stern look. "See what I mean about not talking about the weather? Around here it can rain when the sun's out."

Brushing the water off her jacket, she peered up at me with a sheepish smile. "Sorry. How long do you think we'll have to wait it out?"

I left the dry safety of the overhang to stare up at the fast moving clouds swirling above us. "Hard to say. Might turn back to being a mist. Might not."

"Can we ride home in the rain?" she asked, leaning against the wall. Her wet jeans clung to her legs and I found myself staring while she lifted one leg to brace it on the wall.

"Sure. Do we want to? Not really."

"What should we do?"

I lifted my eyes to her face. Her eyes sparkled same as they did back in the bar. I swept my thumb across my lower lip and then ran it across my chin.

Since our hike at Deception Pass, I couldn't stop thinking about kissing her. The day she received the letter from the asshole wasn't the right time. Normally, I didn't give this much thought to making a move. If I wanted to kiss a woman, I did. As long as she gave me the right signals. Maybe that was part of the problem with Diane. I didn't know her signals. We flirted, we teased. I caught her staring, but it never moved from thoughts to action. My hand was getting tired of all the time I spent thinking.

There was a time and place for action.

That time and place was now.

"Store's closed. Nothing to do but stand here and watch the rain fall." I moved closer to her along the wall, my shoulder brushing hers when I mirrored her posture. My hand dropped between us and brushed against her leg, but I faced the line of water dripping from the roof gutter.

"Nothing?" she asked, her voice more of a whisper.

"Can't think of anything," I whispered back while I turned to gaze down at her. "You?"

I could see everything in her eyes. I wasn't the only one thinking about kissing. When I entwined our fingers, her breath hitched. I broke eye contact and stared down at her mouth. Her lips parted and her tongue peeked out to wet the bottom one.

"John …" Her words faded away when I leaned down. My gaze flicked up to her eyes. Her nod answered my silent question.

Our lips met, soft and slow. So slow. The sound of the rain dripping from the roof and our heavy breaths broke the silence. She moaned and reached her hand behind my head, threading her fingers into my hair. I rolled my body until I pressed her into the wall. Even on her tiptoes, she was short. Too short. I cupped her thighs and tugged her to me.

Breaking the kiss I whispered next to her ear, "Lift your legs."

She lifted and wrapped her legs around my hips. I easily held her weight with my arms.

"Much better."

"Mmmm," she murmured, rubbing her cheek and chin along my jaw. "Much."

I didn't answer because her lips crashed into mine again. Nothing slow or gentle this time. She leaned away from me and rested her shoulders against the wall, giving me access to her neck and chest. My hand dragged along her neck and collarbone before wandering down to the zipper of her jacket. Again I stared into her eyes to make sure she wanted to cross this line.

Without opening her eyes, she moved her hand down to cover mine and pressed. Message received.

Her skin beneath her jacket felt warm and dry, an oasis in the cold rain. I traced her breast through her shirt and watched as the skin below her collarbone broke into goose bumps.

"Cold?" I asked, stroking the back of my index finger along the curve at the top of her bra.

"Yes, but that's not why I shivered. Keep going."

Enough talking. My tongue found hers. All words and thoughts beyond her mouth and her body left my mind. Whatever blood rational thought required thickened in my cock. I thrust into her, grinding my erection along the denim covering her warmth.

Moans came from both our mouths when we tried to catch our breath.

Fuck.

Diane felt amazing. So amazing I was practically fucking her up against the Greenbank Store while the occasional car splashed down the road, the headlights throwing our shadows along the siding.

Realization hit me like cold rain water down my back. We were making out, dry-fucking against the wall of a store, only half-hidden by the freezer. Slowing down my kisses, I pulled away from her. My hand stayed over her heart and felt the racing beat matched my own. Blood thrummed in my dick to the point of pain. We needed to stop.

"Don't," she said when I moved my hands to her waist to shift her down.

"I could kiss you all night standing here, but we are in public. The road is right there and anyone driving by can see us."

"I don't care."

I raised my eyebrow at her. In the dim glow of a beer sign in the window I could see her flushed face and her eyes wild.

"You want me to fuck you here?"

She blinked up at me as she slid down my body. I waited for her to find her footing before releasing my grip on her waist.

"You want to fuck me?" she asked, needing confirmation of what I'd said.

"Pretty obvious I do. Only not here."

"Okay." She tugged my hand while reaching down to pick up her helmet. "Let's go."

"You sure? It's still raining."

"I'm sure. And I'm also pretty certain if we don't leave right this moment, you'll switch back into nice guy John and change your mind."

"Nice guy? No nice guys here." I strapped on my helmet and

zipped up her jacket, intentionally brushing across her nipple. "Let's go."

Despite the wet roads and the rain, or maybe because of them, we arrived back to my house in record time. The moment we got inside our mouths found each other again while hands grappled to remove jackets and feet tangled. Babe wove in between us, barking and jumping. I lost my balance first and pulled Diane down on top of me when I hit the ground.

"Umph," I said when the wind was knocked out of me and my head bounced against the floor. My body had cushioned her fall and luckily she managed to avoid kneeing me in the groin on her way down.

"You okay?" she asked.

"Great. Just great. My plans to get you horizontal worked out exactly as I imagined." I tugged her up my body so her torso lay across mine. "See? Perfect." My lips trailed along her jaw and she squirmed.

"Your beard tickles."

"Sorry about that. Want me to stop and go shave?"

"Never. Every time it brushes against my skin I think of how it would feel other places."

"Other places?" I nipped at the skin behind her ear, which caused her legs to contract around mine.

"Everywhere. I want to feel it everywhere."

With those words I rolled us over and pinned her arms above her head.

"I love it when you tell me what you want." I stared into her eyes before I lowered my face to the top button of her shirt. My nose ran up to the place where her shoulder met her neck and I inhaled her scent. A musk mixed with her usual citrus scent drove me wild.

Babe whined and scratched at the door.

"You need to take care of him?" She gazed up at me and smiled.

"Damn dog. First, he's the best wingman ever and puts us in the exact position I've been thinking about the whole drive home. Now he's cockblocking me."

"No cockblocking here. Only a small delay. Point me in the direction of your room and I'll meet you up there."

My eyes snapped to hers. There was no doubt or hesitation in hers, and there sure as hell wasn't in mine.

"Door at the end of the hall, bathroom on the left." I reluctantly lifted myself off of her. She took my offered hand and pulled herself up to standing.

Her hands found the buttons of her shirt and she slowly undid the first few, never breaking eye contact with me. "You going to stand there and stare, or take care of Babe so we can get back to what we were doing?"

She didn't need to ask me twice. I raced across the room and opened the door before her shirt hit the ground and her feet pounded up the stairs.

Damn.

A few minutes later, I bounded up the stairs, stripping off both of my shirts and leaving a trail behind me in the hall. The door to my room stood open, but the lights were off. When I entered, my eyes focused on the bed. Diane laid across the comforter, on her stomach, her knees bent with her feet in the air. She'd stripped down to her pale purple underwear.

"Took you long enough," she said, crooking her finger and motioning for me to come closer. She didn't have to ask twice.

"Sorry to keep you waiting." My eyes adjusted to the dim light enough to follow the curve of her legs over the swell of her ass and around to her full breasts spilling out of her bra. Meeting her stare, I undid the button of my jeans and lowered them down my thighs. My boxers couldn't contain my hard-on, which tented out toward her. Her lips quirked into the same lustful smirk from earlier in the day.

"Come here," she said, shifting her body closer to me. When my knees hit the edge of the bed, she reached for me, grasping my cock firmly in her hand.

I moaned like a teenage boy about to get a hand job. Not knocking hand jobs, but tonight I wanted more.

"Everything about you is big," she said more to my cock than me.

"I'm in proportion."

"Yes, yes you are." She licked her lips when she released me from my boxers. "Yes you are."

With a quick flick of her eyes to mine, her warm mouth engulfed me. Fuck. I would never get tired of this feeling of warm, wet suction. To stabilize myself, I placed my hand on her head but didn't direct. As much as I wanted to thrust, I held back.

I wove my fingers into her tangled, windswept brown waves and gently guided her into a rhythm. She was a quick learner. Her teeth only pushed me closer to the edge. I tightened my grip in her hair, but didn't pull. The nerves at the base of my spine fired as heat moved down my body. Everything tensed and tightened while I fought the pull between pleasure and release.

Sensing my struggle, she slowly dragged her mouth to the tip and waited.

"Your mouth is fucking unbelievable." I met her eyes. "But you better stop because I have other things in mind for you tonight."

A final swirl of her tongue and her mouth left my tip. Her hand still kept a steady hold at the base, giving me the occasional squeeze.

"Oh do you?" Her smile was anything but innocent.

"You don't even know." I stepped back and her hand slipped away. "More than standing here with my jeans around my thighs and my boots still on."

She laughed. "I guess you need to take care of that."

Boots, socks, jeans, and boxers fell into a pile at the foot of the bed. The only clothing left between us were a few scraps of lace.

In a swift motion, I lifted her up and flipped her on to her back, her head resting in the pillows. She gasped and smiled. She didn't expect that, but she liked it.

I trailed my hand down from her round breasts to the top of the purple lace at the juncture of her thighs. Her legs spread open for me.

"Patience," I said, my tone stern.

She closed her eyes, a smile toying at the edge of her lips.

My eyes shadowed my hands when they moved around her body, watching for her reactions. When she sighed, I took note. When she moaned, I memorized the place. When her skin pebbled, I wanted more. Kneeling over her, I slipped my hand under the lace and pushed down the bra to play with the soft flesh of her tits. I needed to put my mouth on her.

My arm snaked underneath her back to undo the clasp, and the bra joined the pile of my clothes on the floor.

I kissed her again and my hand continued to explore her body while I took her hands in my other hand and pushed them above her head.

"Hold on to the headboard," I told her. She didn't even open her eyes to question me, but grabbed the wood in silent compliance. "Good."

Shifting again, I laid down alongside her body. My beard brushed against her neck when I kissed, licked, and nibbled my way south. She squirmed when the rough texture hit a sensitive place. Rough, wet, soft—each texture produced a reaction on her skin. Cool, pale flesh heated and turned rosy with each pass of my lips and scruff.

Not remaining idle, my hands pinched and tugged her nipples.

"More," she said, nothing more than a whispered moan.

"Mmm … not yet," I answered, nipping at her pink bud.

Following the path burned by my hand, my mouth lowered down her body until it reached the last of the lace. Her legs opened further when I nudged her with my nose. I inhaled deeply before skipping over her heat. Down her left thigh and back up, I moved over to her right leg, dragging my beard lightly across her skin.

"Gah," she said. "You're torturing me."

"Am I?" I smiled into the lace. I wouldn't admit it, but torture was exactly what I was doing. To both of us.

"John Day, if you don't stop …"

I cut off her words with a small bite to her hip.

"I'll …"

Another nip to the other hip caused her to pause. When I exhaled over her heat and met her eyes, she clamped her mouth shut and her eyes rolled back in her head.

"Aha. That's how I get you to stop talking," I said while tugging on the sides of her underwear. Her ass lifted off the bed, and with a final pull, she was naked. And fucking gorgeous. I stopped my actions to take in her body. My stillness caused Diane to open her eyes.

"What?" she asked, her brows pulling together in concern. She lifted up on her elbows. "What's wrong?"

"Absofuckinglutely nothing." I grinned at her and leaned over to kiss her. "Nothing. You're beautiful."

We kissed and slid our bodies together while we tumbled around on the bed. Lifting her leg, I flipped her over and she straddled me, never losing contact with her mouth.

"I want to taste you," I said, sharing our breaths. I lifted our entwined fingers over my head and put her hands on the headboard behind me. My hands wrapped around her thighs and I showed her where I wanted her. Once she situated herself above me, I was in heaven.

Each pulse, twitch, and contraction I felt with my tongue when she moved over me. All of my senses were consumed by her, only her.

Her body told me when she started to climb. I let it lead me, teaching me what to do and when to extend her pleasure until she stilled and moaned. Easing back, I kept contact until she quivered and collapsed next to me.

I wiped a hand across my beard, feeling the well earned wetness. Damn. I could do that all day. Maybe she'd let me.

When I rolled onto my side facing her, she opened one eye to peek at me before leaning up to kiss me.

"You're soaked," she said, embarrassment tingeing her words. When she pulled back, I wrapped my arm around her.

"You're not going anywhere. Nothing to be embarrassed or ashamed about. You don't know how much that turns me on. The sounds you made, the way your body responded to me. Nothing is more sexy."

"Really?"

"Honest truth. I don't think we're done here." I rolled us over toward my nightstand to grab a condom before settling over her.

When I pushed, she opened. When I retreated, she tightened. We found our rhythm and increased the tempo. Each movement brought us closer.

My mouth couldn't get enough of her lips, her neck, or her tits. I hitched her leg higher, going deeper, wanting more until the warmth returned and the tightness warned me I was at the point of no return.

"I'm close," I warned. She kissed me harder, her hands on my ass, guiding me.

A few erratic thrusts and I came, pulsing inside her.

My vision narrowed from the overwhelming sensation and I closed my eyes, drawing out every second.

When I opened my eyes again, her eyes were the first things to come into focus.

"Hi," she said.

"Hi." I kissed the tip of her nose. "You okay?"

"Better than okay. Best."

"Best what?"

"Best as in beyond better than okay."

I chuckled and shifted, separating my body from hers.

Her head lolled on the pillow but her heavy, hooded eyes followed me when I stood up.

"You've ruined me forever for clean-shaven men, John Day."

"Damn straight." I leaned over and kissed her forehead.

Her eyes closed completely. "Damn bearded lumberjack," she said, fading into a mumble of words as she fell asleep.

I stood there and gazed down at her body. When I woke up that day, I hadn't planned on having sex with Diane. Now that I had, I didn't plan to stop.

FIFTEEN

BECAUSE DIANE FELL asleep immediately it never occurred to me to think about her leaving. Diane in my bed wasn't awkward or uncomfortable, unless I considered she slept like a starfish and stole the comforter. Nothing about this was normal to me. Sure Kelly and I spent the night together, but we worked up to it. First time Diane and I had sex, she stayed the whole night and I cooked breakfast the next morning.

"Thanks for not kicking me out into the cold, wet night last night," she said, as if knowing my past behavior.

"Do you honestly think I would do that? Make you take the long hike home in the rain? I figured the very least I could do was to let you do the walk of shame in the morning."

"You're teasing," she said.

"I am. Pancakes?" I held out a plate stacked with three golden circles flanked by fat slices of bacon.

"Yes, please. I'm starved. Can't imagine why."

"No idea. Syrup?"

Syrup formed a moat around the island of pancakes on her plate. The woman liked it sweet. I made a note for future reference.

We ate in silence … silence broken by her random moans, which I felt in my cock. Morning wood was no excuse. Not after waking up to her mouth blazing a trail down my chest and her hand bringing me to full alert.

Speaking with her mouth full, she mumbled, "Meese are smoo goob."

"Meese? Goob?" I repeated while attempting to translate in my head.

She held up a finger and finished chewing. My eyes focused on her mouth while she licked the syrup off her fingers. "I said these are so good. I never figured you for a man who could cook."

"Pancakes aren't cooking. I use the box stuff." I shrugged. "My cooking abilities are limited. Trust me."

"No need to get defensive. Not calling your masculinity into question. Certainly not after last night."

I smirked at her. "Don't forget this morning."

She lowered her eyes to her plate and swirled her finger through the pool of syrup. "Oh, I haven't forgotten." Her tongue licked the tip of her finger before she sucked the tip into her mouth.

"Fuck." My cock twitched.

"What?" she asked innocently, but her motives were splashed across her face.

"You know exactly what."

"What are you going to do about it?" A giggle burst from her mouth in a whoosh when I picked her up off the stool and lifted her onto the counter. "Oh, well then, carry on…"

I lowered my mouth to hers. She tasted of syrup and bacon and her—the perfect combination. Her chin was sticky with sweetness, so I licked it.

"You smell of syrup. I think it's my new favorite scent." I moved down her neck to kiss the skin peeking out from my shirt she wore. "Mmm … it's my new favorite taste, too." I kissed her again. And again.

At some point her plate crashed to the floor and my shirt ended up in a puddle of syrup. Not that I cared with Diane splayed out in front of me. Nothing in the world mattered when she exhaled a moan when our hips met again. Everything disappeared as we found the rhythm we discovered last night. Nothing and everything met when my orgasm raced through me.

Coming back to our senses, we examined the mess. Somehow she had a bit of bacon in her hair and my beard was sticky with syrup.

"Shower?" I asked, settling her on her feet safely away from the mess of syrup and plate on the floor.

"Join me?" she asked.

At that point, I would have followed her anywhere.

The rain from the night before never let up. Sunday meant a day for being lazy or fishing. Despite her sworn promise of going fishing with me, I knew today wasn't the day to call in that promise. Plus, we'd spent the morning fooling around and wasted the best fishing hours. Not that I complained.

Instead, we found ourselves showered and lazing around the living room debating what to watch on TV. Easy.

Except she had the worst taste in movies. I didn't expect her to like action movies, but not only did she love them, the more ridiculous and terrible the better. And she had all sorts of rules.

"Let me get this straight, you hate horror movies because of the gore and scary, but you can watch two guys kick the ever-living shit out of each other?"

She shrugged and smiled. "Don't try to analyze it. And for the record, I'll watch kickass women kicking the shit out of men, too."

"You're scary. Remind me to never get on your bad side. You'd probably be able to take me out with some kind of ninja move, despite your size."

Her eyes narrowed and I knew I was in trouble.

"Listen, lumberjack, I don't need the ninja moves to take you out. It's all about strength and speed."

She'd straddled me before I knew what was happening, and tugged my head back by pulling on the hair at my neck. My throat lay exposed, my legs pinned by hers. Her mistake was leaving my arms free. Despite her best effort to keep me pinned to the couch, I lifted her up and tossed her back on the cushions, trapping her with my body. I didn't make the same mistake she did, and pinned her arms above her head. Her thrashing and squirming only brought our bodies closer together.

"What were you saying?" I smiled down at her, knowing I had the gleam of victory in my eyes.

She leaned up and found my lips with hers. My thoughts forgot all about … well, everything.

First rule of wrestling, don't become overconfident.

The pressure I felt at my groin snapped me back. It wasn't painful, but it wasn't pleasurable. Should she have wanted to, she could have inflicted real pain with her knee, precariously positioned against my testicles. I arched my hips back and away from her pointy knee.

My eyes found her and my triumphant gleam from earlier shone in her eyes.

"Never leave your most vulnerable assets unprotected."

"You don't play fair, ninja girl," I said, resigned, releasing her arms and sitting back on my heels.

"You know what they say about love and war."

"Didn't know we were in either." I laughed.

But she didn't.

"No one said we were." Her tone of voice lost the lighthearted teasing of earlier. She scrambled up on the sofa and straightened her clothes.

I sensed I had done something to change the mood, but while I watched her and tried to figure out what it was, her smile returned. Softer and less bright, she smiled at me, then tucked herself into the corner of the sofa.

"All this talk of ninjas and badass women has me wanting to watch *Kill Bill.* Let's watch that."

Not a huge Tarantino fan, but if it made her happy, who was I to deny her?

Later when it got dark, she returned home and I drove to family dinner. Simple. No drama. She even agreed next weekend we'd go fishing.

"How do you feel about camping?" I asked Diane.

"Like sleeping out in the woods? With bears and serial killers lurking, waiting to kill me?

"Are the bears and serial killers working together to kill you?"

"Don't mock me. There are many stories about people being mauled to death because they aren't smart enough to sleep in a bed behind a locked door."

"Not sure about the bears, but I'm pretty sure a locked door isn't going to stop a serial killer."

We'd been talking about new experiences for the past hour. Sitting out on a boat in the early morning while waiting for Blackmouth Salmon to bite required interesting conversation topics to keep Diane awake. Most men fished for the quiet and to get away from the chatter of their girlfriends, or wives and families. Two men could sit in a boat for hours and not say a word. We liked it that way.

Bringing Diane out on the boat wasn't a huge mistake. Only a little one. For some reason, being out on the water made her chattier. Maybe it was nerves. Or excitement. After an hour out here without even a bite, nerves were the obvious answer.

"Muffin?" she offered. Muffins. On a fishing boat. What nonsense was this?

"Sure. You didn't have to bring food."

"I know, but it seemed a polite thing to do. Plus, I didn't know how long we'd be out here. We could get lost at sea or something, and later think if not for a few cranberry orange muffins, we'd be dead."

She definitely wasn't an island girl. "For one thing, we're not 'at sea'. We're in a sound, which means land on two sides." I pointed over my shoulder at the coast, and then turned to point behind her at the island. "Second, we'd be in more trouble with dehydration than starvation."

"See? These are good things for a girl to know. I feel prepared with this lovely vest." She patted her life vest over her windbreaker. I'd insisted she dress in layers and wear my beanie. The morning was warm for mid-April, but that didn't say much.

I tugged at her braid sticking out beneath the knit cap. "You look adorable."

"Thanks."

"Back to camping. I think we should go."

"Go where?"

"Camping."

"In a tent? With bugs and peeing in the woods? Not to mention the mauling bears and lurking serial killers?" Her eyes widened with each question into something that was a mix of fright and disgust.

"Yeah. We'll camp someplace with toilets and hot showers.

There's something magical about sleeping outside." I absorbed her frozen expression. "By outside, I mean in a tent. Cooking over a fire. Telling tall tales."

"No ghost stories though. That's how every scary movie starts. Overconfidence in the face of the limitless terror of nature."

"Limitless terror of nature? Honestly? I was going to make you my famous campfire roasted bananas." I wasn't certain when the idea of going camping with Diane first entered my mind, but I knew it had to happen. "Don't say we can make those at a beach fire. It's different."

"You want me to go camping with you?" She tilted her head and smiled at me.

"I do. It'll be fun. We'll stay on the island ... for the first time."

"First time?" She caught my hint there'd be more than one time.

"Trust me. Once you do it with me, you'll want to keep going."

She raised her eyebrow. "Is this conversation going the same way the fishing one went? By the way, your boat is bigger than I thought it would be."

I choked on the coffee I'd attempted to swallow. She leaned over to pat my back. "Thanks. I'm glad you like my ... boat."

"It doesn't look new like so many I see around the island."

"That's because it isn't. It was my grandfather's. I inherited it when he passed away. Donnely helped me restore it."

"She's very yar."

"Yar?"

"Don't you say yar about boats?"

"Not fishing boats. I think that's a sailing term."

"I only know it from *The Philadelphia Story*."

"Is that where you got the muffin idea? From the movies?"

"Maybe. I read something somewhere about dried out bread or biscuits eaten on those long crossings. Figured muffins would work for us."

"You're weird." I couldn't help myself. She was weird.

"You're weird." Giving me a gentle shove, she let go of her pole. The tip bent toward the water. She had a bite.

"Grab your pole!" I shouted at her and simultaneously reached out for it before the whole thing fell over the side.

It wasn't pretty and it wasn't fast, but that morning Diane caught her first fish. And that night we ate fresh salmon inside, in my house, no bears or lurking serial killers around to test the locks.

"This is the best salmon I've ever eaten in my entire life." She moaned.

I stared.

She licked her lips and met my eyes. Raising her glass, she toasted to the chef. "To a man who can not only catch dinner, but cook it, too."

"You caught it, I only grilled it."

"We make a good team," she said. "I bet you'll be a hot commodity come the apocalypse."

"But not until then? Gee, thanks." I attempted to glower at her, but failed. I couldn't keep a straight face when she grinned at me.

Her hair undone from her braids, I wrapped a long strand around my finger and tugged her closer. "I'm sure I don't need to remind you how hot I am right now."

I watched her throat when she swallowed before speaking. "So hot," she whispered, leaning forward to brush her lips against mine.

"Don't forget it."

"Never."

"Do you believe in the coming apocalypse?" I asked.

"Zombie apocalypse? Or rising seas and economic crisis apocalypses?"

"Either?" I asked.

"Both are terrifying in their own ways. I'd hate to think of a world where this beach didn't exist, but the looming threat of flesh eating humans is terrifying."

"This keep you up at night?"

"Not really. I have an active imagination, so maybe that's why I can't watch scary movies. At least action movies might somehow give me fight skills through osmosis."

"Or you could take some karate or self-defense classes."

"I have. Well, the self-defense class. I think everyone in my dorm in college had to do it. College campuses are dangerous places for girls. Where do you think I learned that trick with my knee the other day?"

My hand instinctively protected my balls. "I wondered about that. Good to know you can defend yourself against monsters of the human kind."

"I wonder if kneeing a zombie man would have the same benefit."

"I don't think you want to ever get that close. Better to aim for the head. You ever fired a gun before?"

She shook her head. "Even though I grew up in a small town, my parents were always anti-gun. My dad didn't hunt. Didn't have to since patients brought him venison and duck, sometimes as payment."

"Everyone should know how to fire a gun."

"Do you hunt?" Her eyes widened and I could sense part of her was appalled at the idea.

"Is hunting any different than fishing? Still catching food. Providing for your family."

"It feels different. I mean, consider Bambi." She pouted her lips and gave me a wide-eyed look of horror.

"I don't hunt Bambi. Have I? Sure. But I prefer fishing."

"Good. For some reason that makes me feel better."

I laughed at her. "At least we'll still have those skills when the zombies come."

"Right! Excellent point. All is right in the world. You and me against the zombies."

"What do you bring to this equation?" I asked.

"Hmmm …" She furrowed her brow and pouted her lips. It

wasn't attractive, but the more I saw it, the more I found it adorable.

"You don't cook, you can't bake … you have questionable ninja skills."

"Hey now, Lumberjack. Let me think." Her fingers tapped on the edge of her plate.

I crossed my arms and waited.

"I've got it. My womb."

"Your womb?" Where was she going with this?

"Yes, my fertile womb will nurture the hope for humanity. I'm also good at staying up late. I can take the night watches against the undead."

"Well then, you can stay." Talk of wombs and fertility. This conversation had veered off into strange territory.

"Do you want kids?" she asked.

I raised my eyebrows in surprise. Very strange territory.

"I'm not talking with me and my womb of hope for humanity. In the grand scheme of life way."

I exhaled. "Um …" I was at a loss for words.

"Does this freak you out?" Her hand rested on my arm.

"I'm, um …" Why did this freak me out? "Um, sure. I mean I like kids. You?"

"I do. I did."

"Did past tense?" Turning the conversation back to her helped me breathe easier.

"I'm single at thirty. Doesn't bode too well for my chances."

"Thirty's not old."

"Oh, I know. I'm saying the whole life plan I had with Kip got blown to pieces. Who can say what the future will bring? Best not to have a plan."

I growled at the name of the asshole. Good thing he lived on the other side of the country.

"Well, I totally put a damper on this conversation. Ugh. Sorry for the kid and baby talk."

"No problem." I meant it.

"I know I freaked you out. Please don't be freaked out."

"I'm not," I lied. "You and your hope for humanity womb will be good assets during the zombie siege."

"Your face says otherwise, but thank you for lying."

"That obvious, huh?"

She nodded. "I'm learning your ticks. You stroke your beard or tug your earlobe when you're uncomfortable or embarrassed."

I didn't remember doing either.

"If I've learned anything over the last year or so it's to read people's body language better. You'd be surprised what people give away if you pay attention."

"Oh really? What does this tell you?" I stared at her lips. Enough with weird conversations about zombies and wombs.

"I'm not sure about that one. Better to tell me. Or show me." She smiled, knowing exactly what I was thinking.

I kissed her and her tongue found mine. A few minutes later all talk of zombies and babies was forgotten when I picked her up and carried her upstairs.

SIXTEEN

AFTER PROMISES OF real pillows, and much to my chagrin, an air mattress, Diane finally agreed to go camping with me the next weekend. Pillows and an air mattress for camping. I could have lost my man card on this trip.

Rather than deal with a crowded weekend campground, I took Friday off of work to head up to the state park on Thursday. Diane adjusted her class schedule and we met up in front of our cabins late afternoon.

"Look, we're twins!" She twirled around, showing off her quilted vest, flannel shirt, jeans, and rain boots. If I didn't know better, I'd have thought she was a real island girl.

"No gray sweater?"

"Nope. Linus without her blanket. Thought you'd be proud."

"So proud. You have all your stuff? Please don't tell me you're bringing a giant suitcase for an overnight trip." When she held up a small backpack, I smiled. "Atta girl. There's hope for you yet."

"Listen, Mr. Woodsman, I've caught my own dinner. No city slicker here."

"That you have," I said with pride. I grabbed her in a one arm hug and squeezed, inhaling her fresh citrus scent. "Ready to fight off some bears and serial killers?"

"Agh, don't start with that nonsense or I won't be getting any sleep."

"You said last weekend you were good with staying up late to take the night watches. Are you reneging on that?"

"That was for zombies. I'd prefer to be killed in my sleep by the likes of whatever is lurking in the woods."

"I'll protect you from the woodland creatures. I promise."

"You better. Let's do this so we can get it over with. I'm already thinking about the hot bath I'm taking on Saturday."

The short drive up the island to the campground didn't prepare her for an old growth forest strewn with moss-covered logs and giant trees. Hidden along a regular two lane island road, the park and campground perched high up on a bluff above a rock scattered beach. Each campsite was relatively private, but I'd chosen the most private one at the far end of the loop for obvious reasons.

"This is gorgeous," she said, spinning around with her head tilted back to see the tall trees. "Has this been here the entire time?"

"What?"

"The park. Why don't I know about this place? It's beautiful."

"Yes, old growth forest. It's existed here forever. Maybe you're a shut-in who hides at home and doesn't explore her surroundings."

"I'm not a shut-in. And if anything, I've been hiding out in your bed, exploring your surroundings." She prowled closer and hugged me before standing up on her toes to kiss me.

I kissed her back. There was a reason I wanted to bring her camping and it had little to do with moss covered trees. Something about being naked in the night air—everything felt different.

"Okay, before we get carried away, we have to set up camp and start dinner," I said.

"Since I have no idea what any of that entails, what should I do?"

"Help, or sit on the bench and be pretty."

"I'll help," she said. "My days of sitting around and looking pretty are over."

I instructed her on tent poles and grommets. A plug adapter allowed me to inflate the air mattress from the truck, much to Diane's delight.

"It's like a bouncy castle in here." She bounced on her knees inside the tent while I finished setting up the rest of our site.

Later we sat in chairs facing the fire, our stomachs full of grilled steak and baked potatoes cooked in the ashes of the coals.

"I can't believe how amazing that food was." Our hands lay intertwined on her knee and she lifted them to kiss the back of mine.

"Everything's better outdoors."

"Everything?" She tilted her head and raised her eyebrows.

"Yep, everything."

"Did you bring me out to the woods to seduce me, John?"

"I won't lie. I did."

"We could've had sex at home."

"True. We have and we will again, but where's your sense of adventure?"

"I don't think I had one before I met you. You bring it out in me."

"Glad to hear it." I smiled at her and leaned forward to kiss her.

A branch snapped in the dark woods behind us.

"What was that?" she asked, turning away from me to peer into the darkness.

"Probably a squirrel. Or a chipmunk."

Her face showed her fright.

"How can you tell?"

"First, it wasn't a loud snap. That means it was a small critter."

"Or a very stealthy serial killer."

I ignored her logic.

"Second, there aren't large predators on the island."

A coyote howled in the distance, echoed by others.

Diane jumped from her chair and into my lap. "What the hell was *that?*"

"Coyotes. From the sound of it, several miles away."

"Coyotes? How could you tell they are miles away?"

"From the sound. Trust me, you're fine. But we can continue this in the tent if it makes you more comfortable—" I didn't even finish my sentence before she leapt from my chair and headed for the tent. "Hey, let's make a bathroom run before turning in for the night. I have the feeling once we get inside, you're not going to want to go back out."

"This isn't the time to remind me about how hot you are. Now is the time to defend me against the blood-thirsty coyotes and whatever is watching us from the darkness."

My brain caught up about five seconds late in telling me it would be a bad idea to laugh. I chuckled, watching her standing by the tent and staring into the darkness around the camp.

"You can see better with a flashlight. There's one right next to the flap inside the tent."

"Are you crazy? I don't want to actually see what's out there."

"We'll need it for the hike to the facilities. I need to grab water to put out the fire, too."

We survived the short path to and from the small building housing restrooms and showers. Diane appeared calmer after we returned to the campsite.

Inside the tent I stripped down to my boxers. The air mattress took up a lot of space in the four person tent, which was sized more for two men. She crawled into the joined sleeping bags and removed her jeans and shirt, tossing them toward her feet.

"Cold?" I asked. She wasn't shy about her body.

"Freezing. Remind me why we are out here?"

I lowered myself over her with the sleeping bag between us to remind her of my promise at the campfire.

"Oh, right. That." She lifted her hips and met my body with hers. "Fresh air." After kissing for a moment, I shivered.

"Why are you on top of the covers?" she asked.

"No idea." I moved to join her, leaving my boxers on top along with my jeans.

A few stars littered the sky through the screen, but the moon sat too low to provide much light. My eyes slowly adjusted and I could see her better; we were both bathed in a cool, blue light from the dark. Cool air pebbled her skin where my mouth or hands didn't. When she moaned, I swallowed the sound with my mouth. Our limbs tangled and entwined in the warmth generated from our bodies. With each thrust we bounced on the air mattress. I flipped us so she straddled me, using the bounce to our advantage. Draped in the blanket, her face illuminated only in shadows, she rode me, hands clenched with mine. I couldn't get enough of her; I never wanted this to stop. Nothing else existed outside the bubble of our blankets and the tent.

Only us. Alone in the night woods.

Gray light diffused through the material of the tent hours later. Diane snuggled into my front and I spooned my body around her. I exhaled and my breath created a faint cloud in the tent, but we were warm. The air mattress and sleeping bag for two combined into the most comfortable sleep I'd ever had in the woods. She was right to insist on pillows. Why sleep on a lumpy pad with a balled up shirt and jeans under your head? There was no way I'd bring an air mattress on one of

Daisy Prescott

my guys' weekends, but I admitted to myself this was better.

Diane softly snored beside me, her head tucked down into the crook of my arm and her hand resting in mine. I remained still because I didn't want to wake her this early. Morning wood pressed against the dimples at the bottom of her back. I knew I should shift, but it felt too good. Staring down at her, I took in the lines of her face and the small mole next to her right eye I'd never noticed before. I memorized the faint laugh lines at the corners of her eyes—eyes that were no longer sad. Ever since our trip to Deception Pass, she seemed happier, filled with light. Laughter and lust danced across her face when we were together. She was more than pretty. She was beautiful. And I was falling for her.

The deeper we hiked into the woods, the darker it became. Tall giants formed a canopy, blocking out the sunlight. Thick, furry moss clung to fallen logs and tree trunks alike, softening the sound. Green dominated everything except the dark brown of the dirt along the trail and the exposed bark of the ancient firs.

"I feel like I've been transported to Middle Earth or some other magical land." Diane threw back her head, attempting to see to the top of a massive cedar.

"Pretty amazing, isn't it? This whole area was almost logged in the 70s."

"Seriously? Who would do that?" She turned her head to stare at me, disgust on her face.

"Not me, if that's what you were thinking. I wasn't even born in the 70s."

"What stopped them?"

"Tree huggers," I said and scowled. I couldn't hold it and laughed. "Honestly, a couple organized the islanders to protect the giants."

"I'm all for tree hugging. In Pilates we do something called "Hug a Tree," and I think of you every time."

"Gee, thanks." I wrapped my hand around her smaller palm. "I'm not for cutting down old trees like these, but sometimes clear-cutting is the best option."

"For the loggers."

"Not only the loggers and timber companies. Clearcut allows for new growth, revitalized ecosystems, and gets rid of all the dead wood which would combust in wild fires."

"But what about the owls and eagles, and little woodland shrews who lose their homes?"

"Woodland shrews?"

"Picture adorable creature with a family of smaller adorable creatures."

"You're adorable." I kissed the tip of her nose.

"Don't distract me with your bearded charms, Day. Not when the shrew family is homeless."

"Okay, back to the shrews. No making out in the woods for you." I kissed her again. This time on her lips. "Sure, there are unscrupulous loggers, but my company doesn't want the guilt of homeless shrews haunting our dreams. Environmentalists will make our lives hell, so it's easier to do the studies. No hippies living in the trees, and no shrews in the streets."

"And clearcut isn't evil? It looks evil."

"It isn't evil if it's reforested or replanted with fast growing crops like hemp or bamboo. Burning everything to the ground and paving it, that's evil. And not what we do."

"I like it when you talk about wood. You sound so knowledgeable." The spark returned to her eye and I wondered if maybe we'd make out in the woods after all. "Did you study this in college?"

"I did."

"Do most loggers?"

I stepped over a log blocking the trail, then turned to help her. "Not the guys running the saws. It's brutal work. When I was in school, I didn't plan on coming back to the island and working in timber. I had bigger plans after Montana."

"Professional soccer player?"

"Maybe. Don't most high school athletes dream of the big time?"

"I did."

"What did you play?" I had never imagined Diane as an athlete.

"Soccer, actually. Dreamed of being Mia Hamm. What girl didn't?"

"I dreamt of Mia Hamm, but in a whole other way."

"Pervert. It's all about sex with men."

"Part of the breeding." I nipped her ear with my teeth, then kept walking. "What happened to Diane Watson, the next Mia Hamm?"

"Boys. One boy in particular. I became distracted and lost my passion. Plus, I wasn't that good, honestly. Not like you were." She paused. "Oh, shit. Sorry. I didn't mean to bring up ... I didn't mean to mention ... that summer." Her eyes expressed regret.

"It's fine."

"It's not fine. I'm so sorry."

"Really. It's fine," I lied.

"Last time you stopped talking for the night."

"Yeah, sorry about that. It's better now. You know the story. It's out there. Sharing it with you made it less painful."

"Good." She nodded and then kissed the back of my hand. "Let's change the subject. I liked hearing about your work."

"Really? It's pretty boring to talk about trees and logging. Not exactly glamorous, especially to a city girl like you."

"City girl? Funny. That girl feels a million years ago. I mean, look at me. I'm wearing flannel and a vest."

"You look hot in flannel. I prefer you in one of my shirts, though. Even better if you aren't wearing anything underneath."

"That can be arranged."

"Can or will?"

"Will. Definitely will." I found her confidence sexy.

"Damn, you're making it difficult for me not to throw you down on the ground and fuck you."

She peeked behind her shoulder, and then peered around me down the trail. "No one's around. What are the rules for staying on the trails?"

"Fuck the rules." I pulled her along behind me when I left the trail and headed toward an enormous cedar that would block us from the trail. She giggled behind me and held onto my hand tighter.

I pressed her back against the rough bark and kissed her hard. My beard scraped across her cheeks. I knew they'd be pink with beard burn later, but I didn't care.

"Are you sure no one can see us?"

"One hundred percent. Hear us? Maybe. Can you keep quiet?"

"Mmmhmm," she said, reaching for the button of my jeans.

I leaned into her and rocked against her hand while planning out the logistics of what we were doing. If I lifted her up, she'd scrape her back against the bark. Making up my mind, I told her my plan.

Before I had the chance to do it, she'd unbuttoned her jeans and shimmied them and her panties down to the tops of her boots. Impressive. She turned around and put her hands on the trunk, and bent at the waist. I stood there, observing her. My hand traced the curve of her hip and the swell of her ass. Her skin appeared pale against the bark and deep greens surrounding us.

"You going to stand there staring at my ass, or are we having sex up against a tree?"

"Patience." I gave her ass a light smack and watched as her skin pinked.

Who was I kidding about patience? This was going to be fast and hard. "Hold on tight."

We passed an older ranger on the trail about a quarter mile from our tree. He tipped his hat to Diane.

"Nice day for a hike," he said.

"Sure is," I answered.

"Make sure you keep to the trails." He winked at me.

"Will do, sir."

"Good. You all have a nice day."

I held it together until we reached the main road and crossed back over to the campground.

"Oh my god. He totally knew what we were doing," Diane shrieked and broke into laughter.

"He did. Might be the moss in your hair."

She swept her hands through her hair. Several pieces of moss and a few small bits of bark tumbled to the ground. "Why didn't you tell me?"

"To be honest, I didn't even notice before."

"I want to die. That sweet, old man knows we defiled his pristine forest."

I threw my arm around her shoulders and pulled her close. "You wouldn't be the first person to hump in those woods. You won't be the last. Plus, you're a sexy wood nymph with the moss and twigs in your hair."

"Keyword nymph, short for nymphomaniac. I'm so embarrassed."

She dragged her fingers through her hair until she found a twig and pulled it out. "I'm going to the restrooms to clean up."

I regretted nothing. Moss, twigs, bark, and the smudge of dirt on her cheek I hadn't pointed out made her more beautiful. She may not have been an island girl, but she challenged the best of them with her spirit. Not many women would put up with fishing in April or be up for a quickie in the woods.

She isn't an island girl, the voice in my head reminded me Diane's lease ran out at the end of May and as far as I knew, she had no plans to stay. My mood headed south and I frowned. Euphoria from sex in the woods evaporated, only to be replaced by dread and the feeling I had when I thought about my mom.

Everyone eventually leaves.

SEVENTEEN

WE CLEANED UP, and after lunch, headed down to the beach. Down the chalky cliff stretched a narrow, rocky shore scattered with a few large driftwood logs, but nothing like the driftwood graveyard near the Keystone Ferry.

"Besides cooking over fire, hiking, and having sex in the woods, what else do you do camping?" Diane asked, poking the ground with a stick she'd found.

"Fish or clam. Nap. Sit around. Maybe play cards. Or drink. The whole point is to take a break from normal life."

She nodded, but didn't say anything else.

"What are you thinking about?

"How simple and easy life is here. Not like the constant social climbing, moneymaking world of New York."

"I could never live in the city."

"Not even Seattle?"

"No way. When I'm over there for business I can't breathe until I'm heading back across the water."

"Have you ever lived in a city? Maybe you need to find the right one."

"Wouldn't want to."

"Ever?"

"Nope. What about you? Think you'll move back?"

"To New York? It doesn't feel like home anymore, but I love living in a city. Seattle might work. Do you think you'd ever live anywhere but here?"

"Don't think so. After I tore up my knee and lost my mom I knew I was meant to be an island boy for life."

"Why do you say that?"

"I dreamed big. Got fancy. Look what happened?" I didn't have to say another word. She knew what I meant.

"That was all bad luck. Nothing to do with you. You know that, right?"

I shrugged.

"John?"

Keeping my gaze out over the water, I refused to meet her eyes, even after she took my hand in hers.

"It's all ancient history. I've made my life, and it's a good one." I dropped her hand and then strode further down the beach, hoping to shut down the conversation.

"This explains a lot. It all makes sense."

"Does it?"

"Sure. You live off the land in this idyllic setting. One of those kinds of people who are entirely self-sufficient in every way. You don't need anyone." Her voice had an edge.

"It's good to be self-sufficient. Life on the island isn't easy for many folks. A lot of people live close to the bone. Hard to make a decent living when there aren't a lot of jobs. You need to take care of yourself."

She sighed behind me. "It's one thing to be self-sufficient and another to be isolated."

"There's a reason island people are island people. Part of us doesn't like how the rest of the world operates. You said it yourself about the social climbing and the focus on money. Here, it's about living a life, day by day, season by season." This conversation reminded me how different Diane and I were. Our pasts were about as opposite as they could be.

"I guess I haven't seen that side of things. The beach is nice, and Langley's so charming and quaint."

"That's what the tourists see. They don't venture into the woods to see people heating their homes with wood stoves and getting help from Good Cheer. Don't let your wealthy girl ideals cloud your perception."

"Ouch. I'm not a wealthy girl. I married a man from wealth, but that isn't me."

"It's not?" I lumped her in with the asshole. This day was heading south and gaining speed. "You miss your life in the city as much as you complain about the bad stuff."

"Sure. I miss my friends and all the amazing things going on all the time."

"Right. No friends or anything going on here." My voice sounded gruff and my skin prickled with anger and resentment.

"Did I hit a nerve or something?" she asked, stuffing her hands into the pockets of her vest.

I exhaled through my nose. She had hit a nerve. What was I thinking getting myself involved with her type of woman? She fit into one of the huge houses on the beach filled with summer people and weekenders.

"People come here for the fantasy of living on a picturesque island, but don't ever bother to observe the reality. You live in a beautiful house that isn't yours. You teach exercise classes to wealthy women who pay you to torture them. You probably never even worry about money or how to pay your bills."

"Wow. I'm not sure where this is coming from, but you're right. I love the island for all I've seen so far, but no, I don't know what growing up here is like. I'm lucky money isn't an issue for me." Her words tumbled out like a river. "I had to bleed and have my heart destroyed in the process, but yeah, I don't worry about paying my bills. I loved living in the city and won't apologize. You clearly have a grudge against city people. I can't change who I am today anymore than I can rewrite my past."

I didn't look at her when she spoke; instead, I faced the water. When she fell into silence, I turned to see her eyes pink and shiny with tears.

"No one asked you to change."

"Why are you shutting me out?" she asked, staring down to where her stick dug into the wet sand at the edge of the water.

I said our code word for the second time, "Pyramid."

I tugged at my beard. My shoulders locked up and I rolled my neck in an attempt to loosen the tension. Talk of the city reminded me again she never said she would stay. She would leave me and there was nothing I could do about it. I knew I was being an asshole, but that didn't stop me.

"A storm's coming. Unless you want to sit inside a wet tent all evening, we might as well pack up and head home," I said more to the gathering clouds behind her head than to her.

"I have no idea what's going on here, but whatever it is, sitting in a tent with you acting like this sounds like a terrible idea. Let's go." Her chin jutted out in resolution and she turned to head back to the stairs leading up to the campsite.

I inhaled a deep breath and exhaled it out of my mouth with a resigned sigh. In a few short hours we'd gone from having sex in the woods to fighting on the beach. Worst end to a camping trip ever.

Except for that time I ran naked through some stinging nettles. The pain I felt watching Diane climb the stairs with her head down hit me higher in my chest and stung much worse than nettles.

The rainstorm never hit us, but I'd created a storm of another kind. During the drive home, Diane stared ahead or out the passenger window, and only answered my questions in monosyllables.

I unloaded her small bag and set it on the driveway at her feet.

"Well—"

"Thank you," she said.

"I'm—"

"No, don't—"

"I—"

"I—" She exhaled. I waited. "I don't know what went wrong back there at the beach, but before then I had an amazing time camping. Thank you."

I didn't deserve her kindness or her thank you. I was being a jerk. "Listen, I'll give you a call this week." My words sounded hollow and lame even to my own ears.

"Yeah, sure. I have a busy schedule, too." She shuffled her feet and didn't meet my eyes. I bent over to pick up her backpack at the same time she did. Our hands bumped each other and I let my fingers brush along hers, trying to communicate the issue was with me. Her eyes lifted to mine, the sadness returned.

I was an asshole.

"Listen, we'll do something next weekend. Up to you. No fishing or camping." I wanted the offer to be genuine.

"I'm going to Seattle next weekend. Some of my clients invited me to go out."

"Oh. Right." I handed her the bag. "Well, we'll see each other. We're neighbors after all."

"Sure. Neighbors." She hoisted the bag onto her shoulder and then kissed my cheek. "Bye, John."

"Bye."

It wasn't good-bye forever, but it felt like it when I watched her trudge away from me.

Instead of trying to analyze what happened, I called Donnely. After he gave me shit for bailing on him the past few weekends, we made plans to grab a beer and play some pool in a couple of hours. Maybe time with Donnely would clear my mind enough so I'd stop being an asshole.

Diane once told me I was a nice guy. She was wrong. I was a wolf in nice guy's clothing. I was an asshole—no better than her ex.

EIGHTEEN

"WHERE'S YOUR GIRLFRIEND tonight?" Donnely asked, racking up the pool balls.

"Girlfriend?" I asked.

"Diane. The woman you've spent all your time with lately."

"She's not my girlfriend. We hang out. Have fun."

Donnely stared at me and shook his head. "Sure. Neighbors with benefits?"

"Yeah, something like that. She's not staying on the island anyway. Maggie and Gil take the cabin back at the end of May."

"So? Doesn't mean she couldn't rent somewhere else. Maggie's isn't the only place on the island."

The idea had never occurred to me.

"You think she'd stick around here?"

"Do you pay attention to anything?" Donnely asked, standing up from taking his shot. "She's happy here. Got herself a job for the first time. Hanging out with the likes of you. Not sure how that added to it, given what a moody bastard you are, but she likes you. Go figure."

"Fuck off. Like you ever stood a chance with her."

"I have a reputation with women for a reason, man. Not my fault she has bad taste."

I threw my coaster at him, but it missed his head and bounced off a table.

"Dude, you could've given me a fucking paper cut. I could've lost an eye."

"Shut up. You wouldn't have lost an eye."

"You don't know that. Seriously. Lighten up."

He was right. I did need to lighten up. I had myself worked up over Diane and for what? It wasn't like I fell in love with her.

I wasn't ready to fall for anyone. Was I?

"You're turn," he said, poking me in the shoulder with his cue. I'd zoned out again.

"Right, yeah." My cue slid off the ball and I scratched.

"You're playing like shit tonight."

"Thanks for the observation." I flipped him the bird.

"Hey now, only commenting on the obvious. Given your shit game and foul mood, I'm guessing things are not perfect with your neighbor. What's really going on there?"

"Can we drop it and finish the game? Since when are you all into talking about relationships and women?"

Donnely held up his hands in defense. "Got it." He filled up my pint and handed it to me. "You gone out fishing lately?"

I grumbled to myself about not being able to escape the subject. "Went out with Diane. She caught a decent size Blackmouth."

"You took her fishing? A woman? In your boat?"

"Not a big deal."

Donnely howled with laughter. "Not a big deal? A woman on the Orca?"

This time when I chucked a coaster at his head it hit the middle of his forehead.

"Ouch!"

"I warned you."

"Damn, you haven't been in this kind of mood for a long time. Not since Kelly." His gaze shifted to the door. "Speak of the she-devil."

No. No way.

I faced the door. Sure enough, there stood Kelly.

"What the fuck is she doing here?" Donnely asked the question for me.

I turned back and shrugged. "No idea. Haven't spoken to her since February." What was she doing here?

"Guess you can ask her. She's walking straight for you."

"Hi, John." Kelly's hand touched my arm.

I stared down at it before greeting her. "What brings you to the island?" I spoke in blunt words without emotion, hoping to express my feelings about her arrival and hand resting on my arm.

Her hand stroked up my arm before curling around my bicep and squeezing. When Diane did that, it felt like a compliment. Kelly's hand felt like ownership she couldn't claim. I stepped back and away from her grasp.

"Came over to see my folks. Figured I'd get out of the house for a drink. Crossed my mind you might be here."

Donnely coughed from his spot at the other end of the pool table.

"Hi, Donnely." Kelly greeted him with a wave.

"Hey, how's it going?" he asked.

Their exchange sounded friendly on the surface, but I knew he wasn't a big fan of hers. Wasn't in high school; wasn't now.

Kelly smiled at me and answered him, "It's going great. Now." Another squeeze of my arm.

"Can I get you a drink?" I stepped back and away from her grip.

"Sure. You know what I like."

"Malibu, cranberry, and orange?" I asked.

"See. I knew you'd remember."

When I returned from the bar, Kelly sat in my chair, attempting to chat up Donnely, who pretended to be watching the news on the TV in the corner.

I didn't know Kelly's motivations, but enough with being polite. "How's Rick?"

She blinked a few times before smiling. "Funny you should ask. He's good. I guess."

I nodded and pursed my lips. She baited me to ask more. But did I even care? Not really. The two months between Valentine's Day and tonight felt longer. Our relationship existed firmly in the past.

My silent response encouraged Kelly to continue.

"In fact, he's coming up here this weekend to look at boats with my dad. He's thinking of upgrading to something bigger for both Lake Washington and trips up to the San Juans."

In a few sentences, she told me everything I needed to know. Nothing had changed. I drained the last of my beer and then made eye contact with Donnely. He rolled his eyes behind Kelly's back. With a tilt of my head I communicated I was leaving. He mouthed "Don't leave me with her," and I smiled.

"Come on, let's finish our last game," he said. "I have an early morning date with a chainsaw."

"Is that your new girl, Tom? Finally worked your way through all the single women on the island." The snarl in her voice caused me to duck.

"Ha ha," Donnely said. "No one invited you to join us."

"True," she said. "But John was nice enough to buy me a drink. At least one of you has some manners."

The word "nice" hit me hard in the chest. Why was it when it came to the wrong woman I was Mr. Nice, but when it mattered, I was no better than the next asshole?

"Kelly, why exactly are you here? Not on the island, but here in this bar," I asked.

"Honestly?"

I nodded.

"I missed you. I missed hanging out here with you and playing pool or listening to music."

I raised my eyebrow at her. "Enough to finalize your divorce?"

Her eyes drifted down my legs to the floor where they stayed.

This was different. Was she feeling guilty? Or perhaps trying to come up with another excuse. I didn't give her the opening. "Didn't think so. I'm not some toy you get to play with when you come home."

The words hung in the air, waiting for her response. Donnely moved over to the bar to settle up with Olaf, giving me some privacy.

"I never said you were a toy, John." She met my eyes briefly before glancing away.

"Didn't have to. Your actions said everything." I grabbed my jacket and shrugged it on. "Have a nice life."

I waved at Donnely when I stomped out the door. "Night, Olaf."

I didn't say good-bye to Kelly, but I could see her sitting at the table, the straw to her drink suspended an inch from her mouth.

No more nice guy for the wrong people. Instead of improving my mood, tonight soured it even further.

At least one thing became clear to me. Took me fourteen years, but I'd exorcised that crush from my system.

Maggie's words from last summer echoed in my head as I took the long way home. She told me it was okay to have expectations, and to want more than flirting and flings. Why the hell did I listen to her? If anything, her advice created more of a mess in my life than being single. Single with clearly defined boundaries and rules. First, Kelly, and now Diane.

I pulled into my driveway. Several lights were on next door. For a moment I was tempted to knock on the door. To say what, I wasn't sure. *What would I say?* I tried to be more open, and it backfired because it was with the wrong woman? Maybe tell her I wasn't the type to fall in love. Or offer to be friends again and still fuck? I shook my head. Even I wasn't that big of an idiot to think she'd be okay with that after earlier today. A voice in my head told me I should apologize for being an asshole. That was a long list and it was late.

While I stood in the driveway having a silent conversation with myself, Diane's house went dark. I guess that was the sign I needed. Tonight wasn't the night to make decisions.

NINETEEN

DIFFERENT BAR, DIFFERENT night. Same feeling of being on the prowl with Donnely. The Tom Cat came out to play tonight. A week after giving me shit about ditching him for Diane, he guilted me into coming out tonight. According to him, I was a mopey bastard. I told him to shove it, but here I was.

Tonight's band sounded inspired by Nirvana and Ozzy Osborne. A strange combination equaled a loud bar and shouting to be heard when ordering a beer. My ears and I wished we were home on the couch watching a movie with Babe.

I stood at the bar, waiting for our beers, when a blonde sidled up next to me, and touched my arm. I glanced down at her.

She said something, but I couldn't hear anything over the music. I leaned down.

Placing her hand on my shoulder, she shouted near my ear, "Can you get the bartender's attention? I've been standing here for five minutes. I don't think he sees me behind all you tall, brawny men."

Did she call me brawny?

Her hand still on my arm told me she probably did.

"Sure," I said and leaned over toward the bartender at the taps to get his attention.

"Thanks. I'm Jenn."

"John."

She smiled, and again her words were lost in the music.

The bartender stood in front of us, placing my beers on the bar. I asked Jenn what she wanted and relayed it over the bar.

"Thanks," she shouted.

I raised my glass in acknowledgement. Her hand brushed my shoulder again before I turned to leave.

Jenn was a toucher.

I slid my gaze from my arm up to her eyes. She was pretty, in a high maintenance way. Lots of eye makeup, glossy lips. My eyes wandered down her body and took in the tight jeans and heels. City girl.

Even in her heels she only reached up to my shoulder. She lifted herself up on her toes. "My girlfriends and I have a table out on the patio. You should join us if you aren't here with anyone."

"I'm with a friend."

"Bring him, too. The more the merrier." She smiled in a way, leaving no room to misunderstand her motives.

I scanned the bar for Donnely but couldn't see him. Jenn's pretty face and forward personality would make for a nice distraction from flashes of light brown eyes going through my head every time I saw a brunette in the bar. I followed her away toward the door to the patio, motivated partially by the promise of less screaming vocals. The band sucked. I spotted Donnely leaning against the far wall chatting up a woman with short blonde hair. He smiled at me when I handed him his new beer and mouthed "thanks" before returning to his conversation. I gestured to the patio door with my beer. He nodded. I'd been dismissed. No use for a wingman anymore.

The patio teemed with people seeking refuge from the band or fresh air. I scanned the space, searching for Jenn. Groups crowded together over tables filled with empty and half-finished drinks. Thankfully the noise out here was lower than inside.

Someone called my name. I turned to find Jenn waving from a table. When I reached her group, I stood next to Jenn's chair and she introduced me around the table. I didn't pay much attention. Unlike Tom, I wasn't on the prowl. Far from it.

"… And this is Diane." Jenn gestured to the woman who sat with her back to me.

Dark hair in shiny waves resting on her shoulders was immediately familiar.

Oh, shit.

I prayed for a coincidence. There were many women named Diane who had dark hair in the world.

"Everyone, this is John." Jenn finished her introductions.

The brunette tilted her head back and up to see me.

Light brown eyes met mine.

All the other women and the guy sitting between Jenn and Diane said hello, but my gaze locked with those familiar eyes. Unlike Jenn, Diane didn't look like she wore tons of makeup, but still managed to be the most beautiful woman at the table. I took in her appearance as if it had been months instead of a single week since I'd last seen her. Her outfit was similar to the other women, but something about her didn't fit with them. Instead of tipsy silliness and an intent to flirt, the familiar sadness lingered in her eyes, emphasized by her frown.

"Hi, John. Of all the bars, in all the towns, you walked into this one tonight. What are the odds?" Her monotone didn't hold the teasing lightness I'd come to expect from her.

I blinked at her words. *Was she angry? Annoyed?* I couldn't read her. She showed her teeth, but I wouldn't call it a smile. I noticed the guy sitting next to her had his arm on the back of her chair.

"You two know each other?" Jenn's voice belayed her disappointment.

"We do," both Diane and I said at the same time, breaking eye contact.

"Where have you been hiding him?" another woman asked. I'd already forgotten her name.

"He's my neighbor." Diane gave the simplest explanation.

"Lucky you to have such a hot neighbor," nameless friend number two said. The other women giggled and smiled at me. My ego absorbed their flattering attention, but my eyes remained on Diane and some random guy's arm way too fucking close to touching her.

"You should join us. Since you two know each other. Pull up a chair." Jenn played hostess, a hostess with a bitchy side. Tom wasn't the only one on the prowl tonight.

It hit me then how this appeared. Diane didn't know I was here acting as Donnely's wingman. Nor did she know I wasn't on the prowl. Not tonight. No interest. What she knew was I followed her friend back from the bar.

Internally I slapped myself. What was I doing here with Donnely? I had no interest in mindless sex or a one night stand. Not anymore.

Fuck.

I found a chair and squeezed in between Diane and another woman named Debbie. Maybe it was Stephanie.

Diane had turned her chair and angled her body toward the guy more than me. Message clearly delivered.

I stretched my arm in front of her to shake nameless guy's hand. "John," I said.

"Mike." He squeezed my hand in a vice grip.

"Where's your friend?" Jenn asked, evidently giving up on me as tonight's conquest.

Mike must not have been here for her. The way he gripped my hand and had his arm touching Diane's chair told me everything I needed to know. Who the hell was he to be touching anything close to Diane? My eyes darted back to him before I answered Jenn, "Inside. I let him know I was headed out here, so maybe he'll join us."

Diane flicked her eyes in my direction at the word friend.

"Tom's a great guy. You'd probably like him. Much better looking than me," I said.

Jenn and a few of the other women perked up.

Diane added, "Tom's nickname is Tom Cat. If no strings-attached, no emotional connection is your thing, he's probably your kind of guy."

The barbs in her words stung. Fear settled into my gut. Did she think that's what we were doing?

I'd never made her any promises. I didn't do that. Ever.

Maybe that was my problem.

I attempted to catch her eye, but she ignored me while she detailed Tom's looks and charms to her girlfriends. Mike's arm remained on her chair while he drank his beer. That needed to stop.

Debbie/Stephanie to my left spoke to me, "Diane's mentioned you down at the studio."

Her words surprised me. "She has?"

"She told us about all the fun adventures you took her on. Whenever one of us thought of a place for her to visit on the island or in the area, she'd already gone there with you."

I nodded.

"I'm Traci, by the way."

Not Debbie or Stephanie.

"John Day. I don't think we've ever met."

"Would we have?"

"I know a lot of people on South Whidbey." I shrugged. My words could come across as arrogant, but I'd lived on the island all but a few years of my life and knew most people or families on the south end.

"I run the studio where Diane works. We live in Langley on Maple Cove."

My mind flipped through names of families I knew in Langley. No Traci.

"You from the island?"

"No, we moved up from California about three years ago."

"Ah." That explained it. Californian transplants. "That explains the Pilates."

She laughed and it was friendly, open. "You're not the first person I've met who's said that. You islanders are a tough bunch to crack."

I smiled. "We keep to ourselves."

"Except with Diane."

My eyes wandered over to Diane, who had turned slightly and seemed to be listening.

"Every rule has an exception."

"Although I'm always surprised by the generosity of islanders. Fresh eggs in our mailbox, a borrowed generator when the power went out for days, rides to the ferry … it's a long list. Islanders live and breathe 'love thy neighbor'. Never experienced anything like it before we moved here."

Diane's lips curled into a small smile.

"Are you eavesdropping, Miss Watson?" I asked.

She ducked her head and sipped on her cocktail. "Maybe," she muttered.

Everything felt awkward with her. Except when she smiled.

Mike excused himself and left the table, providing a little privacy for Diane and me.

"How are you?" she asked.

I stared into her eyes. She gave away nothing. "I'm okay. You?"

Her shoulders sagged slightly. "About the same."

"Who's Mike?" A growl rolled through my chest under my words.

A small smile played in the corner of her mouth. "Some guy Jenn knows."

"He's overly touchy-feely." I frowned and drank more of my beer.

She sighed. "He's a guy. At a bar. On a Saturday." She paused and stared at me. "Probably not a stretch to figure out what's on his mind."

Yep. She assumed I was on the prowl with the Tom Cat. "Maybe his friend dragged him out to be the wingman."

Her nod told me she heard me, but didn't fully believe me.

Most of the things I knew in life couldn't help me when it came to women. Fishing, cars, rules of soccer, and types of trees proved useless. I knew how to flirt, how to please a woman in bed. Emotional stuff? No clue. I never let it get that far. Not even with Kelly. Sure I liked her. Really liked her.

Everything felt different, larger with Diane. I shut down and shut her out on the beach. Now what?

Like the other night when I stood in her driveway, I waited for a sign, something to show me what I should do.

I opened my mouth to say we should talk. Nothing. I balled my fist against my leg and drained the rest of my beer.

She saved us from further awkwardness by changing the topic to include her friends. The latest celebrity gossip and shoes to make your ass rounder weren't topics I had much to contribute on. After a few awkward minutes of staring into my empty glass, I excused myself, offering to get more drinks for everyone.

I retreated back into the bar where thankfully the band had taken a break. With a glance toward the wall where Tom stood with tonight's interest, I shouldered my way through the crowd. The wait at the bar discouraged me. Mike was nowhere to be seen. At least I wouldn't have to talk with the guy. If I hadn't offered to get a few drinks for Diane's friends, I would've bailed altogether. The distraction of a night out faded when I saw Diane.

A hand pressed against my lower back. Warmth spread from the point of contact and for a second I thought it might be Diane. When I turned, different brown eyes met mine.

"Sorry. Excuse me," the not Diane woman said.

"No problem." I hid my disappointment behind a friendly smile.

Slow, tortuous minutes in line gave me time to think, which was the last thing I wanted to do. Tonight wasn't the time to talk with Diane. Not here, not with her girlfriends sitting around like an audience, not when she thought I was here trolling for action like Mike.

My head spun, but not from the alcohol. I'd had two beers all night. Making my decision, I ordered the cocktails and returned to the table. I told Donnely my plans when I passed him

"I'm going to head out. You ladies have a fun evening." I set the drinks on the table and then squeezed Diane's shoulder, trying to communicate I was leaving alone.

A few of the women frowned and tried to convince me to stay. Mike sat in his spot next to Diane, but chatted up Jenn, clearly having shifted his sights. Good. If I accomplished nothing else tonight, at least I'd scared him away. Diane gave me a sad smile and told me it was nice to run in to me. No see you later or around or anything to give me hope I hadn't fucked up everything.

On the ferry back to the island, I stood on deck at the front of the boat to watch the island come into view. Behind me the lights of the rest of the world blinked and burned. Let them. I didn't want them. Solitude suited me better.

I'd fucked things up with Diane. Maybe this was the reason Maggie never gave in to my flirting. Living next door to someone you made a mess of things with would be torturous. I believed I was in love with Maggie at one point last year. Looking back, it was nothing more than a crush. At least compared to how I felt about Diane.

The dark shadow of the island grew larger when the ferry approached the dock. A few bright spots of lights littered the beach and bluffs. Each one was a reminder of the solitary island life of living away from the bright lights and seduction of the city.

"How's Diane?" my aunt asked while spooning green beans on my plate.

I held my hand out to stop her from creating a mountain of vegetables I'd be forced to eat out of politeness.

"I assume she's fine."

"Oh, dear." She frowned.

"What?" I shoved beans off my pork chop.

"I thought you were fond of her."

"I was. I am. We're not spending a lot of time together right now." I shrugged, an attempt to end the conversation.

"Honey, leave the man alone. The more you pester him, the more he'll dig in his heels," my uncle interrupted, holding his plate out for a spoonful of beans. "You should know that by now."

"I know no such thing," she said.

"It hasn't worked for him and Ted, what makes you think your pushing will work with this girl. Leave it be. Give him some room to breathe and figure it out on his own."

Helen set the beans down next to her plate and sat in her chair. "I guess you know what you're doing."

"Guess so."

"It's your life, John."

I waited for her next words.

"I want you to be happy."

"I'm happy. I swear. Got everything I need."

She sighed and gave me a mothering look, which told me she didn't believe me, not by a mile, but would let it drop. For now.

"Great meal," I said, shoveling pork and mashed potatoes into my mouth.

"Don't talk with your mouth full," she chastised. I'd upset her. Great. She was mad at me, too. What was it lately with me and all females?

"Diane's never said she planned to stay on the island. At least not to me. What's the point in starting anything if she's going to leave soon?" I sounded stupid even to my own ears.

"No one can say what's coming up for any of us. Or how long we have." My aunt spoke in clichés when she gave advice. "You find your people in life and you hold on tight. No one is promised a future more than today."

Her words were about Diane, but could have been spoken any time over the last decade about my mom. Or me.

"Holding on won't keep them with you," I said. I held on to my pain over my mother and my anger toward my father for ten years. And had nothing to show for either.

"I have a framed needlepoint around here somewhere your grandmother made. Has a quote about loving and letting go. Want me to find it?"

Needlepoint? What was I supposed to do with a needlepoint? Put it in my powder room?

I don't have a powder room.

"Nah, it's okay. I get it."

"Good," my uncle said. "Now, if you two are done with all your talk about emotions, what's for dessert?"

Pretty sure my uncle just called me a woman.

"I baked a cherry dump cake. Ice cream?"

My uncle patted his large belly. "Of course."

I decided to turn the talk away from me and all the "emotions". "Speaking of sugar, how's the diabetes these days?"

Peter grumbled something about his health being his own damn business.

"Peter, no swearing at the dinner table."

"Damn woman has sonic hearing I swear," he mumbled into his water glass. "Doctor says I need to lose more weight or I'll have to go on some other kind of meds."

"Should you be eating sweets?"

"Probably not. Life's too short to follow all the rules. I stopped all the other fun stuff I used to do. A piece of cake every once and a while won't kill me. You gotta live your life."

"Truer words have never been spoken."

I complimented my aunt on dinner and told my uncle we'd go fishing soon before saying I'd see them next Sunday.

Dinner with them often turned into a free advice session or morality lesson. They weren't old, not by a long stretch, but I guess that's what happened when you settled down. You found other people's problems and lives to advise and mess with.

TWENTY

EXPECTATIONS.

TROUBLE STEMMED from having them. That I knew for certain. When I said the word "girlfriend" aloud to Kelly and she denied me, it stung. I buried it with anger, but the seed of it hurt. No amount of deer fern would remove the sting like it did with nettles.

Damn nettles. I'd run into a thicket of them on the job site today without my gloves. My fingers prickled and the palm of my hand burned even after crushing up fern fronds and rubbing them over my skin. Shows how little focus I had. Lack of focus led to injuries or death in logging, so I spent the rest of the afternoon in the work trailer. Given it hadn't stopped raining for three days, being in the trailer was the better option.

Everything outside was saturated and muddy. Streams flooded, standing water pooled on roads, and giant puddles took over parking lots. Miserable. My own jeans hadn't dried out from the morning and my jacket steamed from where it laid on top of the space heater.

At three, I sent the crew home and cut out early myself.

The rain and mud didn't help my bad mood. On Monday, Helen called to apologize for prying into my life and upsetting me. I told her it was fine. If she didn't pry, no one would. I think that mended things between us. They were the closest family I had and mattered more to me than I let them know.

The source of my mood centered on the mess I'd created with Diane. Things were unresolved with us and I didn't know how much time I had to make them right. She needed to know the issue wasn't with her. I was trying to save her from all of my own shit.

That was a lie. I was so scared about her walking out of my life, I'd kicked her out. Could I admit that out loud?

To add to my self-inflicted misery, I hadn't seen a sign of Diane in over a week. Nothing since I ran into her at the bar over in town. I'd made sure she saw that I left alone, but that might have been too little too late.

Whenever I had checked on her house this week the lights were off downstairs, and it was quiet. I didn't see her Jeep in the driveway yesterday or today when I left for work. It wasn't there when I got home.

Could she have left the island? I knew she came home after Seattle last weekend, but had her plans changed?

A mature person would text or call her, even stop over and knock. That person was not me. Instead, I called Maggie. May was here and she'd be returning to her house for the summer, which meant Diane would be leaving soon. And I didn't know when or where she'd go.

Maggie picked up with a surprised hello.

"Are you okay?" Her voice sounded worried.

"Hi to you, too. Everything's fine," I said, a defensive tone to my voice.

"Are you sure? You never call me. Other than a few texts the last few months, the last time you called, my house was on fire."

"Almost. Smoke, no fire."

"Right. So what's going on?"

"Nothing. Was wondering when you were coming home. And if you've come to your senses about leaving the professor behind in Portland."

"Hush. No, Gil's coming with me. He's looking forward to the summer. In fact, he wants me to ask you if you'll take him fishing."

"Really? I didn't figure him for the type."

"Don't judge a man by his elbow patches. Gil grew up fly fishing in Colorado. Just because he lives in the city, doesn't mean he can't bait a hook."

Her words reminded me of Diane and our fishing excursion. As if reading my mind, she brought her up.

"Diane told me you took her fishing."

"You two talk?" Why hadn't I assumed they did? Maybe Diane had called her and told her about us. About how I'd fucked things up.

"Sure. Email more than anything. I'm excited to meet her soon. Weird we know each other online and she's living in my house, but we've never met."

A perfect opportunity for me to ask about Diane, but when I started to speak, I found my mouth dry and my tongue unable to form the question.

"She's great. Isn't she? I lucked out with her for a tenant."

"Yeah, great."

"You sound distracted."

Here was my opening to talk about Diane and figure out what was going on in my head, but I couldn't find the words.

"Hello? John? Did the call drop?" she asked.

"I'm here."

"Are you moving around? I couldn't hear what you said."

"I'm not. Satellite must have shifted. I didn't say anything."

"You know, Diane told me you two spent a lot of time together the past few months. That's nice of you."

There was that word again. Nice.

"Yeah, we hung out."

"Past tense?" she asked.

I rubbed the back of my knuckles along my jawline, pressing them into the bone and scowled. "Kind of. I'm not sure what's going on there."

"Oh, John."

"Geez, don't give me the "oh, John" in that voice. Your disappointment is palpable."

"What happened?"

"Not sure. We were hanging out and then after we went camping, it all kind of fell apart."

"Wait. Wait a second. You took her camping?"

"Yeah."

"She must like you. Camping *and* fishing. Wow. Are you in love?"

"Why do you ask that?" My words were clipped.

"Come on. A young, single woman who is willing to go camping and sit in your boat for hours surrounded by bait? Only a woman in love would do that."

Again, I lost my words.

"Hello? Can you hear me? Damn island cell service," she muttered into the phone.

"I'm still here."

"Oh, I thought the call dropped. You never answered my question."

"What question?" I played dumb to buy myself some time while the word love bounced around in my brain like a pinball.

"Are you in love with Diane?"

"I don't know."

"Don't know or won't say? And what happened to Kelly? Is she still in the picture? John Day, if you are two-timing these women, you're in big trouble." Her voice rose in exasperation.

"Not seeing Kelly anymore. I thought I told you about that. Pretty sure she's back with the husband."

"Ouch. What a bitch."

"You said it not me."

"I'm glad. The last thing you need is messy emotional baggage."

I shuddered. "Yeah."

"Got it. There's no reason you and Diane can't be together."

Another opening. This time I rallied my courage and took it. "There's a big reason. You're moving back into your cabin. She's leaving."

My phone was silent. I pulled it away from my ear to see if the call had been dropped this time. Maggie's voice squawked from the speaker, but I couldn't hear her.

"What?"

"What what? I asked when the last time you and Diane spoke was."

"Um, it's been over a week. Closer to two really."

"Jesus, John!"

"What? Why are you yelling at me?"

"You haven't spoken with her at all?"

"No, I told you it's been a while."

More unintelligible swearing followed.

"What are you saying? All I hear is cursing."

"Okay, where are you?" she asked.

"I'm standing in my living room."

"I need you to sit down."

My heart stopped and I held my breath. People only told you bad news when they asked you to sit down. Dad told me to sit down when he called me in the middle of the night to tell me about the accident.

Oh, fuck.

Tingling spread up my arm from my finger-tips. Blood rushed in my ears. "Is she okay?" I whispered, backing up until my legs hit the chair. I slumped against the arm and silently chanted, "Please be okay" in my head.

"John? I don't want you to beat yourself up. You didn't know. I figured you knew already. That's why I asked if you were okay. I didn't say anything because I thought, well, I thought you would've been with her at the hospital." Her words were said in what was Maggie's attempt at a soothing tone.

"Tell me," I shouted.

Fuck.

Please be okay, please be okay, please be okay.

"There was an accident."

TWENTY-ONE

Accident.

I NEVER wanted to hear those words again in my life. Ever.

"Is she home?" I stood up too fast and the room swam with stars

Shaking my head to clear my vision, I already had my hand on the door when Maggie spoke, "She's okay. Now. She'll be fine. But she's in Coupeville."

"Coupeville?" Why would she be in Coupeville?

"John, she's still in the hospital."

I started the truck before I even realized I had left the house, the phone and Maggie's voice tucked between my ear and shoulder.

"John? What are you doing? Hello?"

"I'm here. I'm in the truck."

"Stop. You need to calm down before you see her."

Shit. I banged my hand against the steering wheel. The horn sounded.

"Listen, she's okay. I swear. She's being held for observation with a bump on the head, bruised ribs, and a broken wrist from the airbag."

"What the fuck happened?"

"On the way to Langley this morning she hydroplaned after avoiding a deer and lost control. Ended up in a ditch. I'm surprised you didn't hear already. Typically news travels fast up there."

"I've been ignoring everyone and everything all week."

"I'm so sorry. I assumed you knew. I honestly didn't know or I wouldn't have asked all that stuff about love."

The burning sting settled back in my chest.

"It's okay. You didn't know."

"You all right?" she asked.

"Not really. Do you know when visiting hours are at the hospital?"

"I have everything at Whidbey General memorized. You can see her until eight tonight."

The truck's clock showed the time as five-thirty. I exhaled a deep breath and attempted to calm myself.

"You're going up there, aren't you?"

"I am."

"She'll be home tomorrow morning. You could wait. If things weren't good between you, you might want to wait."

"I'm not waiting. This is bullshit. No word to let me know she'd been hurt? What the fuck is that about?"

"Did you tell her about your mom?"

"I did."

"There's your answer. She probably didn't want to worry you. And if you had fought, she wouldn't want to bother you."

"Fuck."

"So you were fighting?"

"Damn it. This is my fault. Stupid self-sufficiency conversation."

"What?" she asked.

"Our fight. It was about her not being an islander and how islanders are self-sufficient. Not even a fight. I was being an asshole."

"Oh—"

I cut her off. "Seriously. Don't sympathize with me right now. I fucked this up and need to take the blame." I banged my fist against the top of the steering wheel.

"Okay."

"I need to fix this."

"You do. Can you?" she asked.

"I have no idea." I didn't have a clue what I would say or do to make it right, but I would. "Listen, thanks for letting me know. I owe you big time."

"No worries. You can pay me back and take Gil fishing."

I grumbled.

"You'll have fun. You two are going to get along great."

"Fine. I'm hanging up. I need to get to the hospital."

"Go get your girl, John."

Luck favored me when I sped up island and didn't encounter a single cop or slow-ass logging truck.

I stood in the lobby gift shop stalling for time and debating on flowers. I didn't know if flowers would be inappropriate or lame, so I texted Maggie, who approved.

All the flowers looked like the biggest cliché ever. Red roses didn't feel right and the rest had seen better days. Balloons felt too festive. Browsing the store like I was casing the joint, I finally found something appropriate.

The older lady at the information desk told me Diane's room number and pointed me down the hall. I thanked her, then took a seat in the lobby, trying to calm my nerves. I hated hospitals and avoided them at all costs.

I couldn't do this. Diane would be home tomorrow. I could see her then. Right. I'd stop over tomorrow and check on her at home.

I stood and the woman at the desk smiled at me.

"It's okay, Son. Hospitals make a lot of people nervous. Even big strapping men like yourself. I don't think your girlfriend has had any visitors all day. I bet she'll be excited to see you."

I started to say she wasn't my girlfriend, but stopped myself. For one thing, it was none of her business what my relationship was with Diane. And secondly, I didn't want to deny anything anymore.

I thanked her and followed her directions down the hall to the patient rooms. Nurses in colorful scrubs passed me, their shoes squeaking on the floor. A few patients in wheelchairs sat outside rooms in the broad hall. I passed the open doors and the sounds of televisions.

I stood outside her room for a minute, gaining my courage. Maybe Diane didn't want to see me. She didn't call me. *Who was her emergency contact?*

Behind me an older man in a blue robe coughed on his way down the hall with his walker. The nurse holding his elbow gave me the once over and asked if she could help me.

"No. I'm here to see Diane Watson."

"Oh, well, you're standing in front of her room. She hasn't had any visitors. You'll be her first."

Fuck. Guilt washed over me. I inhaled a deep breath and slowly let it out.

"Go on in. She should be awake." The nurse encouraged me with a smile.

I could do this.

I lightly knocked on the door and shuffled into the room. The first bed on the left was empty and the curtain was partially drawn around the bed by the window.

"Hello?" I said, peering around the fabric divider.

"Um, hi." Diane sat up further in the hospital bed. She wore a hospital gown and her left arm was in a cast. Maggie had told me she'd hit her head, but I wasn't prepared for the bruises on her face.

I guess I stared at her face too long when she said, "I must look like shit."

"No, no. It's just I didn't know what to expect."

"I look like shit. The shiner is going to take a while to fade."

"Makes you look tough. Like a fighter." It wasn't a lie. She looked fierce. "Or a ninja after a fight."

She laughed, which caused her to suck in her breath in pain. "Ow."

"Sorry." I hated seeing her in pain. "Can I get you anything? Are you on good drugs?"

"The drugs aren't bad. Thank goodness for pharmaceuticals."

"Good."

Silence grew between us.

"I brought you something." I held out the salmon plush toy.

"You brought me a stuffed fish?"

"Salmon, a Chinook. I didn't know what kind of flowers you liked. Or if you like balloons." I shook my head. "I saw the salmon and thought of our fishing adventure. So, yeah, here." I laid the fish next to her on the bed.

Picking it up, she smiled, soft but genuine. "It's about the size of the one I caught."

"It is. It's a fine looking fish."

"I'm guessing Maggie called you." She tucked the fish close to her side.

I scratched my sideburn. "I called her about an hour ago and she told me."

"I couldn't … I didn't want to call you after last week. I, um, didn't want to be a burden." Tears filled her eyes and she wiped them away before turning her head to face the window.

I stood in place for longer than I should have. This beautiful

189

woman cried because of me. Me and my stupidity.

I cleared my throat and gently sat on the edge of her bed.

"Diane." I waited for her to look at me. When she did, I reached to touch her right hand lying on the bed. She didn't pull away, but she didn't lace her fingers with mine either. Still, I kept contact with her. I needed some reassurance she was here and okay.

She sniffled and tried to wipe her nose on the back of her hand in the cast. Leaning toward her, I grabbed the box of tissues off the tray table next to the bed. She held her breath when I moved close to her.

After she blew her nose, she handed the box back to me. I noticed she winced when she lifted her arm.

"Are you in a lot of pain?"

"No, it only hurts when I move, laugh, or breathe." She smiled and I returned it.

"In other words, it hurts." I chuckled.

"Not as much as my ego."

"Why?"

"Crashing the Jeep in the rain."

"The crash could've happened to anyone."

"Ever happen to you?"

"Sure. I fishtailed in my '68 Mustang in high school. Hit the back bumper on a guardrail and did a 360."

"Wow. That's impressive."

"It was. I got in major trouble, but it was pretty cool when it happened."

"Yesterday wasn't cool. The airbag was the worst part and I have it to thank for being in here."

"For being here at all," I whispered.

Her sad eyes met mine and I felt the nettle sting in my chest again.

I tapped the plaster of her neon green cast. "Nice cast. Did you get to pick your color?"

"I did. The Ortho was very sweet and he let me have a color."

"He?" Of course 'he' let her pick a color. He was probably flirting with her.

"Dr. Scott. You know him?"

"Nope. Must be new." My voice rumbled with my jealousy.

"Jealous?"

"No," I said. A little too quickly. "Maybe."

"He's married. Not that it matters."

We fell into silence. I still held her non-broken hand.

"I wish you had called me."

"I wasn't sure… After our good-bye, I wasn't sure where we stood. All your talk of self-sufficiency …"

I had droned on and on about that, but she'd missed the part about islanders taking care of each other.

I frowned at her, then ran my hand over my jaw. "You know I would've dropped everything to come be with you. You have to know that."

She blinked back a few tears and nodded her head.

"Damn it, I hate thinking about you being all alone after the accident and then here. No one should be alone in the hospital. Who's your emergency contact?"

"It's Traci down at the studio."

"That's bullshit. It should be me."

Her head snapped back. "Oh, really? We haven't spoken in over a week."

"So? We're neighbors and have been friends for months."

She frowned, then turned away from me again. "Traci's my boss."

I ran my hand up the back of my head. "Fine."

"Fine," she said.

Her eyes wandered down to my hand holding hers and we both stared at our hands. Everything felt awkward and whatever I said didn't make it better. I wanted to scoop her up in my arms and hug her, kiss her forehead, and let her know she wasn't alone. She had me. If she wanted.

Instead the room rippled with tension.

"When do you get out of here?"

"They're keeping me overnight for observation because I hit my head. And I live alone," she whispered the last sentence.

She was breaking my heart. There was no reason she had to be alone, except for me. I ruined everything.

Again.

"I can give you a ride home."

"Traci already offered."

I glared at her.

"Stop glowering at me."

"Stop being stubborn."

She shifted on the bed and attempted to cross her arms before wincing and dropping the cast to her side where it rested on top of the salmon.

"Truce? I know we need to talk about the camping trip, but my biggest … no, my only, concern right now is getting you home and looked after."

"Since when are you the good Samaritan?"

"You'd be surprised."

"Which is it, John? Nice guy or asshole? You're making my head spin more than this concussion."

Her words held the question I'd be asking myself a lot the past week.

"Probably both. I'm far from perfect."

She frowned. "No one's perfect." Her good hand lifted and gently poked at her face where blue and purple bloomed on the skin. "No one is a complete asshole either."

I raised my eyebrow.

"I'm going to stand by that," she said, and yawned. "Sorry. The meds make me sleepy, but they keep waking me up all the time to check on me so I can't sleep."

We were back on neutral territory and I felt my shoulders relax.

"Reminds me of when I had my surgery after blowing out my knee. It's a unique form of torture being in the hospital."

"I've never stayed overnight before."

"The staff's pretty good here. Are they being nice to you?"

"They are. And the food isn't bad either."

I gave her an incredulous look. "Seriously? You must've hit your head."

"It isn't. I swear." She smiled.

"I'll take your word for it. And on that note, I'm going to head out so you can rest. They'll kick me out of here soon anyway. But I'll be back tomorrow morning."

"John—"

"Don't try to change my mind. I'm coming."

She sighed and rolled her eyes, acting resigned, but a small smile flirted at the corner of her mouth.

I decided to push my luck since she agreed about tomorrow. After standing, I leaned toward her. She didn't flinch or hold her breath when I gently pressed my lips on the top of her head. After I straightened up, I tucked a strand of hair behind her ear and whispered, "I'm sorry. More than you know."

Her eyes closed and her breathing deepened. I waited for her to open her eyes before I left.

Opening her eyes, she met mine. "Goodnight, John. Thank you." She picked up the salmon and held it in her good arm.

I wasn't sure if she was thanking me for the apology, or stopping by, or the fish. Maybe all of the above.

"You're welcome, Diane." She looked so young sitting there with her green cast and tousled hair. Young and alone. I pointed to the fish. "You won't be alone tonight. See you in the morning."

In the lobby, the same woman whom I spoke with earlier sat at the information desk. When I passed her, she gave me a wink followed by a knowing smile.

"Nice long visit. I'm sure your girlfriend feels better having you here."

I didn't correct her. No reason to.

TWENTY-TWO

SLEEP DIDN'T COME easily last night with all the thoughts and dreams spinning around my mind, mixing past and present, accidents in snow and rain. Rain wet pavement switched to white, ditches turned into semi-trucks.

I finally gave up at four a.m. and went downstairs. At seven, I paced a loop around the living room while Babe watched me from his bed in the corner. I called Steve at seven-thirty to get the Jeep towed to him for repairs. By eight, I'd had enough and decided to wait it out at the hospital, visiting hours be damned.

On the way to the hospital I stopped off at the Fellowship of the Bean coffee hut and bought Diane's favorite white mocha along with an extra large black coffee for myself.

A new woman sat at the visitor's desk. An early morning crankiness crackled beneath her sweet smile and brightly knit sweater. No soft smile when she told me I'd have to stay in the waiting room until official visiting hours since I wasn't family.

Diane's coffee cooled while I squirmed in the uncomfortable

chairs facing a lone television playing a Seattle morning show. Talk of flooding, raging rivers, and mudslides were the big stories. I scanned outside and could see rain still poured down from the late spring storm. It looked and felt more like March than May.

May.

I still didn't know if Diane was leaving. Neither Donnely nor Maggie believed she'd be moving away when her lease ended. Somehow the topic had never come up between us. Thinking back, it was strange we hadn't talked much about the future. Lately we hadn't been doing very much talking at all.

Thoughts of naked Diane took over my mind. The way her back arched and the color when her nipples darkened when I licked …

A cough broke me out of my thoughts. I shifted in the chair and tried to relieve the pressure in my groin without using my hand. I glanced up to see a young doctor wearing Birkenstocks with socks standing in front of me.

"Are you here for Diane Watson?"

Despite her snarl, the woman at the front desk must have let someone know I was here to take Diane home.

I nodded and picked up her coffee from the table next to my chair before standing.

"I'm Dr. Scott," he said and stuck out his hand.

I straightened to my full height and shook his hand, my grip extra firm. "John Day."

The doctor smiled at me.

Why was I acting like a caveman to Diane's doctor? The flash of gold on his finger confirmed what she told me.

"Is she ready to leave?"

"Not yet, but she's dressed and you can see her. We're finalizing her paperwork."

"Is she okay? I know what she told me yesterday about being here for observation, but it isn't anything serious, is it?"

"Head injuries are always serious, but she only has a mild concussion. We kept her because she lives alone. She'll be fine. Cast can come off in about six weeks, then she'll need some PT to regain her muscle strength. Nothing too bad. She's lucky. Good thing she was in a Jeep."

She's lucky. It all came down to luck? Whether you die or walk away with a bump on the head? Could it be that simple?

I nodded at him again. "You need anything from me?"

"No, you can go to her room. Take good care of her."

"I will." A promise.

Diane sat on her bed fully dressed. Yesterday's clothes were rumpled and she probably needed a shower, but she looked better out of the ugly hospital gown.

My salmon lay in her lap and she absently played with a fin while she talked on the phone.

I waved to let her know I was here and held up her coffee, before gesturing I'd wait in the hall.

She waved me over and mouthed she was talking with her parents. I handed her the lukewarm cup and she smiled.

After a few minutes of reassuring them she was fine and swearing she had someone to take care of her, she hung up.

"Hi," she said.

"Sorry the coffee's probably cold. I had them put it in two cups to insulate it, but I sat out in the lobby for a while."

She took a sip and moaned in happiness. "White chocolate mocha. My fave. You remembered."

"I did. Is it hot enough? I can find a microwave and try to reheat it or something."

"It's perfect. While the hospital food might be edible, the coffee the nurse brought me earlier tasted like dirt, watered down puddle mud." She frowned and stuck out her tongue.

I smiled at her adorable frown. "That was your mom on the phone?"

"Both of them sharing a receiver. My mother wanted to fly out here and my dad wanted to know where my doctors attended medical school. Typical parental stuff."

"Is your mom coming out? You shouldn't be alone."

"I thought I had a neighbor who was going to make sure I was looked after properly." She smiled at me and sipped her coffee.

"Are you talking about Dave? Cause I wouldn't trust him not to peep through your drawers."

"No, it's you." She gave me a small smile. "If you want the job."

"Consider it a done deal. When are they springing you?" I asked from my chair near her bed.

"Any minute. Dr. Scott said it would be about twenty minutes."

"How are you feeling?"

"I'm good."

My expression told her I didn't believe her.

"I'm okay. Stuff hurts today that didn't hurt yesterday and I'm desperate for a shower. I'll have to bag my arm because the cast can't get wet."

"I can help if you need it." The eagerness in my voice surprised me. And her.

"You don't have to."

"I know I don't. I want to. Plus, I've seen you naked already. It won't be awkward."

She held her side when she laughed. "No, not awkward at all."

"What?"

"Honestly?"

I was completely lost at why it would be awkward. I told her as much.

"It's not you seeing me naked that's awkward. It's all the other stuff that goes along with the naked."

"If you think I'm going to try to have sex with you, I promise I won't."

"Won't because you don't want to or won't because you're concerned about my injuries?"

I opened my mouth to speak, but closed it instead. Then opened it again when I found the words. "Why would you think I wouldn't still want to have sex with you?"

"The whole not talking for almost two weeks thing?"

Right. That.

"One thing you should know about men, is even if we're in a fight or sick or injured, we'll still want to have sex."

Her answer was a roll of her eyes.

"It's true. Want me to prove it?" I stroked my bottom lip with my thumb.

"Oh my god, you're not serious." Her voice raised and she flailed her good arm around. "Hello? Hospital!"

"Think how much fun the adjustable bed could be."

She ignored me. "We're not having sex until we talk."

I frowned and shifted, clasping my hands between my knees. "The 'we have to talk' talk is always ominous."

"Ominous or not, we do need to talk."

I exhaled and squared my shoulders. "Okay. We'll talk. In fact, I have things I want to say, too."

Her eyes widened. "You do?"

"I do. But not here and not until we get you settled."

A nurse guiding a wheelchair into the room interrupted us to say Diane could go home. She handed Diane some forms and told us her prescriptions could be picked up in Freeland.

"Ready to be sprung?" I asked, gesturing to the wheelchair.

"Ready." She sat in the wheelchair, cradling her fish, and then smiled up at me.

I kissed the top of her head before the nurse wheeled her down the hall.

"You shouldn't be alone," I said.

"I'll be fine. I swear." Diane crossed her arms and put on her stubborn face.

"You can swear about being fine all you want. Doctor's orders you shouldn't be alone. I took the day off work, you're stuck with me."

"Hmmph," she said under her breath.

"So what do you want to do first? Shower? Eat? Nap?"

"I need to figure out what to do about the Jeep. I don't even know where it was towed."

I rubbed the back of my neck.

"You know something about where it is?"

"I might." I dragged a knuckle over my mouth.

"Are you going to tell me?"

"Are you going to be mad?"

She huffed. "No promises."

"It's at Steve's garage."

"How'd it get there?" Her eyes were leery.

"Called him this morning. If anyone can fix it, it'll be him."

"You took over?"

"I did," I said without regret. "You misunderstood my words about islanders. We help each other out. Even Traci understands how things work around here."

"I thought you said I was a spoiled, naïve, wealthy city girl." Her words sounded weary and she confirmed the feeling by curling up on the sectional by the windows.

Had I said all those words? I tried to retrace our conversation on the beach. "You're twisting my words. I never called you that."

"Not all at once, but you spoke those words."

I had.

"Would it help if I said I'm sorry?"

"It might. What are you sorry for, John?"

What was I sorry for? "It's a long list. But in this case, I'm sorry for shutting down on you at the beach and ruining our weekend."

She stared at me with her sleepy eyes. "Thank you."

Her eyes closed and her head sank heavy on the pillow in the corner of the big gray couch. I watched her body slump. The tension she held on the ride back to the house left her shoulders.

It was May, but the rain chilled the air, leaving the house feeling damp and cold. While she napped I could build a fire. After a quick mental inventory of what food I had at the house I frowned. Other than some cereal, smoked salmon and a freezer full of fish, I had nothing to feed her.

I covered her with a blanket, and wandered over to the kitchen, doing a quick inventory. Her shelves were about as bare as mine, but she did have boxed macaroni and cheese, which I could manage to cook.

A fire in the wood stove heated the room while pasta boiled on the stove. I snuck next door to let Babe out and he wandered around in the driftwood on the beach. After a quick phone call to my aunt, I headed back next door.

On the stove, the pot of water had boiled over, making a mess. Scalding water splashed on my hand on the way to the sink.

"Shit!" I said loudly, louder than I meant because Diane stirred on the couch and squinted at me.

I gave her a wave from my spot by the sink. "Hey, sorry." Steam rose from the pasta when I transferred the pot back to the stove.

"Isn't this how we met?" She nodded to the wood stove.

"How so?"

"Fire in the wood stove and me finding you randomly standing in the house. Oh, and the cursing."

I smiled. "Yeah, it's kind of like that morning. Without the smoke and the fire alarm."

"Far less dramatic." She stretched and winced.

"You sore?" I glanced at the clock. "You can take some pain meds with lunch."

"Is that what you're making?"

"Yep. The best Kraft has to offer."

"John Day, you'll never stop surprising me."

"You didn't have many options. But I've got that covered."

She gave me a sidelong glance before getting up from the couch and shuffling over to the counter. "It smells delicious."

I shrugged, feeling awkward because I was making her lunch. "It's only boxed macaroni and cheese. You hungry?"

"Sure." She stood on her toes and attempted to reach the bowls in the cabinet, but stopped and took in a sharp breath.

"Here, let me." I took down two bowls and handed them to her.

"Thanks," she said, but her eyes didn't meet mine.

I exhaled long and deep, gathering myself. Getting back to normal with her wasn't going to be easy, but it would be worth it. That much I knew.

We ate in silence and then she said she was going to take a shower.

"I'll wrap your arm so your cast won't get wet."

"You don't have to do that."

"I know, but that's not going to stop me. Until you tell me to leave, I'm staying. Do you want me to go?" Feeling insecure, I lifted my eyebrows and scratched the back of my neck while I waited for her answer.

She sighed and smiled at me. "Okay, you can help. We still need to talk, but today I need a shower. And your help."

I met her smile with my own. "Done. Plastic bag and some tape?"

"Junk drawer."

After cutting the tape, her left arm was waterproofed as best it would get.

"I'm going to head upstairs."

"Holler if you need me." I paused and decided to push my luck. "Or want company."

"Not that again. Keep it in your pants, Day." She laughed and shuffled away, shaking her head.

I chuckled while I tidied up the kitchen. Didn't take much to rinse out a pot and two bowls. The water turned on upstairs.

At the sink, I closed my eyes. Images of Diane and I in the shower at my house floated through my mind. Her dark hair almost black with the water, droplets winding their way over her breasts, down the curve of her waist, further dropping into the dark hair below her navel. I wasn't sure if I'd ever see that vision again in person.

My wet fingers moved across my forehead and scratched along my hairline, and my palms pressed into my eyes. I rubbed my hands in circles over my face a few times and exhaled, trying to stop my mind from sending all the blood to my cock.

And failed.

"John?" Diane's shouted from upstairs. "John?"

I stepped over to the stairs. "Yeah?"

"Can you come help?" She sounded desperate.

I took the stairs two at a time and raced down the hall to the bathroom. "You okay?"

She sat on the closed toilet lid still wearing her shirt and stretchy black pants. "I'm stuck." She held up her plastic bag arm and pouted.

"You want me to undress you?"

"I do." She blushed.

"And this embarrasses you?" I teased. I couldn't help myself. The panic she hurt herself and the run up the stairs had dissolved my hard-on to half mast. If I didn't keep things light, my dirty thoughts would be on full display again.

She nodded and sighed.

"Didn't we go over this in the hospital? Seen you naked already. Know where your moles are. Memorized them. Could draw you a map if you want." I gestured for her to stand up. "Let's get you in the shower before the hot water runs out."

"You memorized my moles?" she asked, standing in front of me.

"I'll draw a map while you're in the shower to prove it." I smiled down at her. "Pants first."

I tucked my thumbs into the waist of her pants. I squatted down and dragged my hands down her legs, removing her pants and underwear both. Her T-shirt came off next. So easily it made me suspicious if she needed my help or not.

"You couldn't take off your T-shirt?" I asked.

She shrugged her shoulders and gazed down at her feet.

I squinted at her face. Hmmm. "Okay, this stretchy bra thing is going to be more difficult." I pushed the fabric up from her waist and she raised her arms over her head. "Ready to be naked?"

"Gah, just do it," she huffed.

I smiled, but she didn't look at me. To get her attention, I traced a circle around a spot on her thigh near her hip. "That's one. You have another one on your ribs under your right boob." I tugged the fabric further up her body and traced my finger over the newly exposed mole. "Right there."

Her breath hitched.

One more pull and the bra was over her head, blinding her, but exposing all of her chest to me.

"This one's my favorite." I pushed the boundaries when I brushed the back of one knuckle over the freckle to the left of her nipple.

She held her breath.

"Breathe, Diane," I whispered, then released her from the confines of the fabric. The bra landed on the rug.

Her cast and good arm covered her chest and she gaped at me. "You're not playing fair."

"Sorry." I grinned at her. "Now into the shower with you." I held out my arm for her to grasp when she climbed into the claw-foot tub. I closed the curtain behind her and waited.

"Um?"

"Yes?"

"Can you … do you mind …"

"What? Ask. I'll do anything."

"It's … I can't." I could hear the tears in her voice.

Opening the shower curtain, I peered at her. She looked as I had imagined downstairs, but vulnerable.

"What do you need?"

"I need you. I can't do anything with this." She waved the bagged arm around. Her lip trembled.

"Okay, don't cry. Please don't cry. I figure we have two options. One, I can get in the shower with you."

Her eyes widened.

"I'll wear my boxers. Promise."

Blinking, she asked, "Second option?"

"We turn this shower into a bath and I wash your hair for you."

"You'd do that?"

"For you? Anything."

"I choose bath."

"Done." I reached for the stopper and switched the water to the faucet. "Do you want to stay in there while it fills?"

"Yes, I'll be cold if I get out now."

I helped her sit down in the tub and grabbed a washcloth before taking a seat on the closed toilet. "Soap please."

She squirted some bath wash on the cloth and I dunked it in the hot water. I moved her hair over her shoulder and swept the warm, soapy washcloth over her back, rubbing in circles as I descended.

She rested her head on her arms, which were curled around her knees and moaned.

The sound headed straight to my cock. I shifted and softly moaned. I didn't think she heard me.

"Did you moan?" She opened her eyes and stared at me.

I nodded. Guilty.

"Are you having perverted thoughts about me while you play nurse?"

"Definitely." No use in denying it.

"Are you hard?"

My hand stilled on her back.

"Maybe."

She turned her head forward and giggled.

"Hey, you moaned too."

"I did not."

"You did. Don't deny it."

"It was more of a sigh."

"Sigh. Moan. Let's agree to disagree." I smiled as I rinsed the cloth and wiped her back. "Lean back."

She rested her head on the edge of the tub and I pulled her hair back. The arm with a cast sat on the edge, while her right arm draped across her breasts.

"How am I going to clean your front if you are covered up?"

"I can do it." She raised her hand to her shoulder and reached for the washcloth.

I moved it out of reach. "No fun in that. Let me make you feel good."

"John—"

"I'm not talking about sex. Let me do this for you."

"I'm not getting rid of you, am I?" Her head lolled to the left and she observed me.

"Nope. Not until you ask me to leave." I smiled.

She sighed. "Okay." Her arm created a small splash when it sank under the water by her side.

I soaped up again and gently swept my cloth covered hand down her torso and over her shoulders. Her eyes stayed closed and a small smile formed on her lips. She looked peaceful and incredibly beautiful.

I successfully washed and conditioned her hair without mauling her despite the pain of my erection pressing into my jeans. However, this wasn't about me. Not even a little bit.

Diane stood on the mat while I dried her off. Occasionally, I added something new to my map of her body. I didn't tell her my new favorite freckle was located between the dimples above her ass. I'd remind her of that one with my tongue. It was good to have goals.

TWENTY-THREE

MY AUNT ARRIVED in the evening with enough food to feed the entire beach. Casseroles were put into the freezer, a crockpot full of chili heated on the counter, and the fridge was stocked with … well, everything. A chocolate sheet cake rested on the island, a small corner of frosting missing and my hand stung from where Helen swatted me with the back of her wooden spoon.

Diane burst into tears when she saw everything Helen brought. She cried harder when my aunt hugged her and told her it would be okay.

"You're never alone when you live here," Helen reminded her.

I stood at the counter and watched them hug and talk over on the couch. The frosting tempted me, but I rubbed my hand and bided my time. All the female emotions made me uncomfortable. I excused myself to run over to my house for a bit.

When I returned with what I needed to spend the night, Helen excused herself with a knowing look at my arms full of clothes. She double-checked Diane had her number and then kissed my cheek on her way out the door.

"What's all that stuff?" Diane asked, blowing her nose again from all the crying.

"Staying the night. In case you need anything."

"You don't—"

I interrupted her, "I know I don't have to, but I'm staying."

"Right. Staying until I ask you to leave."

"Glad you understand finally. I'll sleep in the other guest room. I'd sleep on the sectional down here if it would make you more comfortable."

"Thank you. You didn't have to ask your aunt for all that food."

"I didn't. I called her this morning and told her what happened. That's all her doing."

"Wow. She doesn't even know me."

"She knows you're important to me, which makes you important to her. It's how things work around here."

"Right. The island way of life."

"We take care of our own."

"And I fall into that?"

"You do now."

"I'm overwhelmed. I mean, I moved here not knowing anyone to be independent and make it on my own." She shook her head and tears welled up again in her eyes. "Instead, I'm a charity case."

I walked over and draped my arm around her shoulder. "You are independent and strong, not a charity case."

"I can't even bathe myself."

"You probably could. Not very well, and would probably make a mess, but you could."

"Then why did I need your help in the shower?"

"Obviously you wanted me to see you naked again. I know your wicked ways." I hugged her closer and kissed the top of her head.

"You're making it difficult to stay mad at you."

"Then don't. Or do. But if you kick me out, I'm taking the cake with me. My aunt must like you to make her chocolate sheet cake."

"No way are you taking my cake!" She turned and pushed my chest with her good hand. "And don't think I didn't see you steal frosting."

I absentmindedly rubbed my hand. "If you didn't see it, you at least would have heard the thwack of the spoon on my flesh."

She laughed and took my hand, massaging the back with her thumb. "She's fast with a spoon. I was impressed with her reflexes."

"Don't underestimate the woman. She's put up with me and my cousins for years. Heathens, all of us."

"You're not so bad."

I quirked my eyebrow.

"Don't give me that look." She held my hand still and interlaced our fingers.

I gazed down at our joined hands.

A small gesture, but it was a start.

We ate chocolate cake for dinner sitting on the couch. It felt rebellious and silly Diane said. A perfect reminder her life was her own, to be lived by whatever rules she wanted.

I slept in a twin bed down the hall from her room that night and the next, but she kicked me out on Sunday evening, saying I had to work and she had to figure out how to be a one-armed wonder.

The big talk didn't take place. Part of me hoped it never would, but I knew we'd be better off if it did.

A week after the accident, she invited me over for dinner of taco casserole—one of my favorite dishes, but she didn't know that.

She greeted me at the door, freshly showered and dressed in a blue button down and jeans. The bruise on her face had faded into a pale, greenish yellow.

"Impressive," I said, gesturing to her clothes.

"I know. I'm thinking world domination is next on my to-do list."

"You could probably do it. Will you be an evil overlord or a kind-hearted despot?"

Her brows pulled together while she gave her options serious consideration. "I'm thinking despot, but one who wears a tiara." She cracked herself up over the image. "Come on in."

I laughed at her laughing at her own joke. "Someone's feeling better." I pointed at her face. "That's a lovely shade of green on you."

She gently touched her bruise. "It's almost gone."

When she moved her hand, I traced the line with a light touch. "I've said it before, it makes you look like a kick-ass ninja. I like it."

"Thank you."

"For what? For liking your bruise."

"For always making me feel beautiful. And desired."

"I'm that obvious?"

"It's a good thing." She sashayed into the house ahead of me. "Don't stop."

"I won't," I promised. Somewhere between the shock of the accident and finding out she'd be okay, a shift occurred inside me. Despite the doctor's assurance, this felt like a second chance with her. Life didn't give you many of those and I wasn't going to waste it.

The house smelled of taco casserole. "My mom used to make this all the time when I was a kid."

"I've never had it before."

"I've got to admit when Helen made it for you, I was jealous."

"Maybe she knew I'd share it with you. There's no way I could eat all her food by myself in a month."

I smiled thinking of my aunt's meddling.

We talked about general stuff while we ate. Weather felt safe. The rain had stopped and spring bulbs broke up the continuous green of the island. Mid-May and Memorial Day lurked on the horizon and with it, June. June meant the return of Maggie. Uncertainty pushed me to ask what I'd avoided for the past months.

"Speaking of warmer weather …" I cleared my throat. "Maggie said she'd be returning first of June."

"That's the plan." Her answer sounded deliberately vague.

"Right. And what does that mean for you?"

She gave me a knowing smile.

"What?" I asked. Lost.

"You finally asked me what happens next."

"What do you mean?"

"I've been waiting for you to want to know what happens in June."

I furrowed my brow in confusion.

She leaned across the table and pushed against my eyebrows. "I haven't told you, because you never asked."

"Why keep it a secret?"

"I didn't mean to. In fact, I'd planned to tell you when we were on the beach. But then everything went ass over elbows and I didn't get the chance."

"Ass over elbows?"

"Tits up? To shit?"

"Gotcha." Here it was. 'The Talk.' "Are you leaving?"

"No."

"No?" I asked, surprise written all over my face.

"I love that you're surprised by this."

"I always assumed you'd be leaving when your lease was up."

"Right. Assumed."

I shook my head and my brows pulled together again. My fingers found the scruff of beard at the corner of my jaw and I cocked my head to stare at her. "But you never said you were staying. All that talk of the city and how you missed it."

"I do miss it, but it doesn't mean I want to leave here."

"So all of this …" I gestured between us. "… happened because of my stupid assumptions?"

"Not all of it. I take responsibility for being guarded."

"Why guarded?"

She stared back at me, then reached over and moved my hand off my beard, pulling it to her side of the table. "You scared me. Kind of still do." Her smile soft and shy, she laced her fingers with mine.

"Scared you? Like you believed I'd hurt you? I'd never hurt a woman." My disgust caused me to clench her fingers.

"Not physically, never. I knew you were a big softie. But I was scared you'd hurt me. Break my heart."

"I …" My words fell away. Break her heart? "Did I?"

"No, but you came close in the driveway. I knew you had a big wall around your heart. I could see through the chinks, and thought I'd found a way inside, but that day in the driveway when you said you'd see me around, everything closed up again."

"I'm an asshole."

"Stop saying that. You aren't. You try to be, but you're not."

"I'm a selfish guy who doesn't fall in love." Half was true.

"I don't believe you."

"You should," I lied.

"Have you ever been in love?" she asked.

"Once. Maybe twice. A long time ago."

"Let me guess. Before your mom died?"

I inhaled a deep breath and glanced away before nodding.

"Not everyone leaves, John."

"Yes, they do. At least in my life. They leave or you lose them."

"Your aunt and uncle are still here. Donnely is still here."

I snorted. "Donnely's never leaving this island. Unless he runs out of women."

"Sounds like he ran out of local women a long time ago, but you're not Donnely. Not even close."

"Closer than you know."

"You'd never have a boat named The Master Baiter. There's that. Plus, Donnely wouldn't have shown up at the hospital. Or bought me a stuffed salmon."

"He might've." She stared at me. "Okay, he wouldn't have."

"See? Different type of man altogether."

"What's your point?"

"You're a nice guy. One of the best men I've ever met."

"Well, knowing you married an asshole, it doesn't sound like you met a lot of half-decent guys in your life." I scoffed and let go of her hand.

"Stop. Why can't you accept it?" She stood up and walked around the table to my side.

Grumbling, I pushed my chair back at her instruction. She sat on my lap and draped her cast over my shoulder. My arms wrapped around her waist.

"If you're done grumbling, do you want to know my plans?"

"Sure," I mumbled into her hair. I felt defensive and cranky, but a warmth had begun to spread out from my chest from the same spot the nettle sting hurt a few weeks ago.

"Will you stop growling, please?"

"I'm not growling."

She pivoted back and stared me in the eye.

"Fine. I'll stop growling." I growled and showed my teeth.

This brought out her laughter and a groan. "You can't make me laugh. Bruised rib, remember?"

"Sorry." I loosened my grip around her waist.

"Okay, plans. First, I'm staying on the island."

"When did you decide this?"

A blush bloomed in her cheeks. "Can I plead the fifth?"

"No. When?"

A deep breath and a pause preceded her answer. "March."

I narrowed my eyes at her. "When in March?"

"Late March."

Dates and places filtered through my memory. An image of the two of us sitting on our own tiny island above the water of Deception Pass came into focus.

"Deceptions Past?"

She nodded and the blush deepened.

"Why then?"

Rather than answer, she tucked her head under my chin and curled into me.

"Diane?"

A soft sigh escaped when she exhaled. "I knew then."

My own breath paused and I felt my heart rate increase. I wondered if she could hear it. Or feel it as it attempted to beat its way out of my chest.

"Knew what?"

"I knew. I knew my marriage was truly over after reading Kip's letter. I knew a whole, big beautiful world existed out there, which I didn't know about because I'd always followed others in my life." She paused and took a breath. "And I knew I was falling in love with you."

I exhaled, but didn't speak.

"It's okay if you didn't feel the same. Or don't. That's another thing I figured out."

"What?" I whispered.

"I knew it didn't matter. I would be okay."

"How?" I continued to respond in single syllables while I processed her words. She fell in love with me. In March.

"It was okay because I could fall in love. After Kip and the pain I went through, I had lost any faith I'd ever be able to fall in love again. You showed me I could."

"I did?" Two syllables. I made progress.

"You did. At the time I wasn't sure you knew how to fall or would ever be ready. Or would let yourself. I came to the decision to not live in the land of maybe or should. I'd be in the moment with you. Wherever that led, I'd be open to it. And I decided I'd stay. Maybe not forever, but I knew I wouldn't be going back to New York."

I lifted my hand and stroked her hair where it fell over her shoulder.

"Mmm, that's nice." Her breath sounded out like a purr. Curled up in my lap, she felt solid and warm in my arms. Whatever happened next or outside this bubble, we had this.

"I—"

"Don't feel you need to say anything. Knowing is what matters."

I needed to say something. Something to honor what she said.

Before I could speak, she continued, "Everything that followed after was easy. Falling was impossibly easy, like floating in salt water. I gave into it and fell. I never once believed I would sink."

I felt myself drowning in her words. Each sentence poured over me, stealing my breath while I attempted to keep my head above the flood of emotions. She lay herself bare to me. I discovered myself in an uncharted place.

"I never brought up emotions or expectations with you. I had none. Or so I told myself. Until the beach. My carefully constructed tower of bowling balls toppled over when you shut me out. But it also showed me the truth."

I swallowed and asked, "What truth?"

"Loving and being loved feed each other. You can love without reciprocation, but being in love requires two. And you weren't there with me. Or you were, but I couldn't find you over the huge wall you built around yourself."

My ego told me to defend myself. I didn't have a wall. Being independent wasn't a bad thing. I stayed silent rather than lie to her.

"So I let you go."

"I wondered why you didn't call me."

"No you didn't. You knew."

Caught again, I nodded.

We sat in silence for a few minutes. I stroked her hair and she played with the button on the cuff of my shirt.

"That's the why of my staying. Simple. I have a job, a car, or had a car, and hope life gets better."

"You have me."

Once again she leaned back and stared into my eyes. I got lost in hers and the truth in them.

"You do. I'm not going anywhere."

She repeated the words I'd said to her since the accident. "Not until I ask you to leave?"

"Pretty much. I'm not good at the other stuff, but I'm a man of action."

She smiled at me and leaned forward until less than an inch separated our lips. Her eyes swam in my blurred vision until I closed mine. When our lips touched, I felt everything my mind failed to form into words. No doubt in my mind what I felt for Diane. If I couldn't tell her, I could show her.

I pushed the chair back from the table and stood up, lifting her in my arms, careful not to hurt her arm or rib.

"Oh," she said. "What are you doing?"

"Making love to you."

With that I carried her up the stairs to bed.

TWENTY-FOUR

I CAREFULLY SET Diane down on the big white bed, aware of her bruises and cast. She flopped down on her back and stared up at me. Her arms lay splayed out at her sides and her hair spread out like a dark halo beneath her head. Brown eyes framed in dark lashes stared up at me.

When she opened her mouth to speak, I placed my finger against her lips. "Shhh. Let me make you feel good."

She nodded mutely, but her eyes followed my every move.

After I unbuttoned my cuffs and removed my shirt, I stood there in my jeans and boots. I trailed my gaze over her curves. "You're wearing too many clothes. I think we'll lose the jeans first." The button released with a single finger. The zipper slid down easily, exposing pink lace underneath.

I tapped her hip and she lifted her ass to allow me access to pull down her jeans. After tossing them on the floor, I moved up to her shirt. The blue cotton resembled a man's shirt and I remember how much I liked seeing her in one of mine.

With one finger, I traced down the buttons, pressing into her skin, letting her know exactly where I was.

When she closed her eyes, I told her to open them. "I want you to watch me, see what I do to your body."

Her throat bobbed when she swallowed and nodded her head.

The first button exposed the swell of her breasts. The second showed me her bra matched the pink lace covering her pussy. The third, fourth, and fifth revealed all of her torso to me.

"Gorgeous." I ran my nose down the middle of her chest, between the valley of her breasts, and over the softness of her stomach. Inhaling, I slowly brought my mouth to the top of the lace at her hip and dragged my lips across to the other side. My breath hit her skin, causing her to raise her hips. I hadn't even touched her below the lace. To hold her in place, I rested one of my hands over her navel. My other hand nudged her thighs apart and held them open. From my position between her legs, I peered up at her face; her eyes were still open, but her lids were heavy. Her cheeks flamed pink and her chest rose and fell with her breath. My girl was turned on.

Continuing my slow explorations, I repeated the same pattern on her thighs. Nose, mouth, breath. She smelled of citrus and musk. I needed to taste her, to bury myself inside her and remind myself she was alive, here, and mine.

Her underwear had to come off and now. Once gone, I returned all of my attention to her center. I wanted her to feel everything.

Pleasure, want, need, and love.

A hand curled into my hair and tugged, giving me a sign that what I did pleased her. Inhaled breath held and clenched before a slow, deep exhale guided my tongue. Every moan and squirm, each push and retreat, was noted and obeyed. My sole purpose was to please her. To love her with my body.

My world began and ended with her.

Because the words weren't mine yet to say, I had to show her she meant everything to me.

When she clenched around my fingers, I knew she was close. I observed her face. Her eyes had been closed, but as if sensing my stare, she opened them and stared back at me. Our eyes locked and her orgasm shot through her, rippling through her thighs and pussy until she was shaking with it. She moaned, hands fisted on the quilt and her eyes closed. I slowed my movements, drawing out the high for her until her muscles relaxed into nothingness. With a soft peck to her hip, I rose above her. Resting my weight on my elbows, I kissed her breasts, her chest, her collarbone, her neck, and finally her mouth.

Her mouth opened to me and I lost myself in her—her taste, her breath, her soft, wet kisses. My heart raced and it had nothing to do with exertion, and everything to do with having her back in my arms.

I pulled away until my nose rested against hers. She opened her eyes and tried to focus on mine. "Wow."

I chuckled. It was rare for Diane to be speechless, but I'd reduced her to one syllable.

"Mmm," I said, kissing along her jaw until I reached her ear. I skimmed my teeth along her lobe before nipping it. "I'm not finished with you yet," I whispered into her ear. "Not by a long shot."

"I hoped you'd say that," she whispered back.

I moved to hover above her face again. "You did, did you?"

"Mmmhmm." She rubbed her nose against mine. "You still have your jeans on and I'm still wearing my bra."

"Is that a challenge?"

She nodded and smiled up at me.

Challenge accepted.

And met.

Steam rose up from her body. We stood in Maggie's outdoor shower on the deck with hot water pouring over us. Cool air against my back contrasted with the heat between our bodies when I lifted her hips and thrust into her. Our bodies joined together and my head rested on her shoulder while her good hand tangled into my hair, scratching my scalp. The pressure of her fingers distracted me, helping me last longer for her. After last night, I wasn't sure how I could stand, let alone fuck.

Not fuck. Make love. Making love—heart, body and soul.

I lifted my head and shifted her higher. I wanted her to feel good. It's all I wanted at that moment. If I could consume her, meld our bodies into one, I would have done it.

I chased her orgasm with my own. After, I pulled away from her body, a slight tremor ran down my spine when hot water and cold air hit my cock. With a gentle kiss to her lips, I turned and dunked my head under the water.

Her plastic covered arm wrapped around my waist and she leaned her head against my chest, her other hand pressed against my heart. A happy sigh escaped with her breath.

I enveloped her with my arms and rested my head on hers. Content.

Early morning gray light brightened as we stood entwined and the water cooled. I reached over to the hooks to grab her robe and the towels while she turned off the water. Cold air slammed into us and she shivered.

"I'm freezing." She hopped from foot to foot with her arms wrapped close to her chest.

I smiled at her standing, or hopping there, naked and wet.

I cocooned Diane into the robe and loosely wrapped a towel around her head. She looked ridiculous, like a turbaned marshmallow. She was beautiful.

The other towel I wrapped around my waist before we ran for the door and the warmth inside.

I made a note to myself to install an outdoor shower over at my house before summer. Maybe next weekend. I didn't think Maggie would approve of Diane and I using hers once she returned.

We sprawled naked on my couch later that afternoon. So much for not having the stamina for more. Sunlight created large squares of light on the floor, but we weren't tempted to venture outside. Somehow we went from watching one of Diane's favorite terrible action movies to having sex with her straddling me.

Not that I complained. I hoped the hot sex would chase away the crying karma of the couch. I loved my comfortable couch.

All weekend, I showed her with my body what my mouth couldn't say. Half a dozen times when we were naked I felt the words slip toward my lips, but even I knew better than to say them for the first time when I wasn't wearing pants.

Diane stood and stretched, then dove behind the chair, hitting her cast on the floor with a loud bump when she rolled flat on her stomach.

"What the hell are you doing?" I didn't move from my spot on the couch, but leaned down so I could see her head on the floor near my feet.

"Cover yourself!" she shouted at me, pulling the throw blanket off the chair and tossing it over my lap.

"Why do I need to cover myself? Nobody's here except us and Babe. Trust me, Babe's seen you naked before. And doesn't care."

"People are climbing up the stairs of your deck. People who look like they are going to come knock—"

A knock at the glass door to the deck interrupted her and I turned to see who it was. A couple in jeans and fleeces stood on the deck. The strawberry-blonde hair was familiar and so was her dark haired companion.

"Oh, that's Maggie and Gil," I said, giving Maggie a wave.

"I just want to die," Diane moaned from the floor and attempted to bury her head under the chair.

"You do know your ass and bare legs stick out beyond the chair, right? Pretty sure they can see them through the window."

"You're not helping. Where are my clothes?"

"Too late for clothes. Here, have the blanket." I swept the blanket off my lap and in the same movement covered my crotch with a pillow. "They know we're in here. We might as well say hello."

"Can I die first?" She somehow managed to wrap the blanket around herself before struggling to sit up with one arm holding the blanket to her chest.

"No, you can't die. At least not this minute. Or for a very long time. Now, sit up in the chair and turn, smile, and wave." I stood and held the cushion against my middle, creating a small bit of decency.

I waved the arm not hiding my cock and Maggie waved back before stilling her hand. She covered her eyes before quickly stepping away from the window. When she stepped back, she bumped into Gil and turned her face toward his chest. I laughed and almost dropped the pillow.

"Looks like Maggie's figured out they didn't come at the best time. Although, if they arrived about five minutes ago, they would have seen the whole shebang." If we couldn't laugh at the situation, well, we'd lost our humor.

Diane grumbled about first impressions and being a common hussy while locating her clothes on the floor.

"No one thinks you're a hussy, common or not. They didn't see anything. Plus, this is my house and if I want to make love to the woman I love on the couch in the middle of the day, then I will." I followed this up with a strong nod.

She stood there speechless, holding her arms out with her clothes loosely piled on top.

I gave her a weird look before patting her ass. "Get dressed and we'll go outside and say hi."

She didn't move.

"Hello?" I waved my hand in front of her face. "You were worried about how things looked and yet you're standing here in a blanket with all the world to see."

"You said you loved me."

I blinked at her and ran my speech back through my head. Not a hussy. My house. Making love … to the woman I love. She was right. I had said it.

A slow, sexy smile spread across her face. The blanket slipped a little, exposing her breast to me. Thankfully her back was to the window. Maggie and Gil had moved away from the door and stood facing the water, giving us some privacy.

With the pillow still covering myself, I tugged the blanket up and over Diane's breast. "I guess I did."

"You did. No take backs."

"Are you surprised?"

"No, not at all. I've known for a while."

"You have?" I quirked my eyebrow and tried to appear serious.

"You love me."

"I do." I inhaled a deep breath and slowly exhaled it to calm my heart. "I love you."

Her clothes fell to the floor. A smile split her face and she grinned up at me like a crazy woman with disheveled hair, naked under a blanket with a lime green cast hand covering her heart. She was a glorious mess. My glorious mess.

"I love you, John." On her tiptoes she could barely reach my mouth with her lips, so I bent forward, sweeping her into my arms. The cushion fell to the ground and I pushed myself against her warmth.

She kissed me back and the blanket slipped again. When I felt her breast against the skin of my chest I moaned into her mouth and felt myself harden against her.

My moan broke her out of the kiss. "Um, are they still out on the deck?"

I peeked over her head. "Yep."

"What's wrong with me? I'm thinking about throwing you down on the coffee table right now and my landlord is standing outside."

"I can send her away."

She shook her head. "No, no we're going to get dressed and be presentable. We can do this. They can't stay forever, right?"

"I liked your first idea with the coffee table much better. They'll be living next door to us all summer. We can be proper neighbors then." I kissed her again, but she didn't open her mouth to me. "Okay, okay. I give up. Let's make a run for it down the hall." I turned and ran ass-naked down the hall to the laundry room. Diane shuffled behind me in the blanket.

Once we dressed, I kissed her again and said, "I love you." Because the block between my heart and my mouth was finally gone.

TWENTY-FIVE

IN THE HISTORY of awkward meetings, introducing Diane to Maggie and Gil wouldn't have made the top ten. But it definitely ranked in the top twenty.

Diane's blush covered not only her cheeks. From her hairline down to her cleavage visible beneath her hoodie, her skin turned pink. I pressed the back of my hand to her neck where I felt the heat from the blood racing in her pulse. To calm her, I grabbed her good hand and held it when we wandered outside, squeezing her fingers in reassurance.

Babe bounded past me to greet Maggie's dog Biscuit on the lawn. The two barked and jumped all over each in greeting.

Maggie turned around when she saw Babe and smiled at us. "Sorry to, um, barge up here uninvited. Well, I called both your and Diane's phones yesterday and this morning on the drive up from Portland. And left voicemails." She laughed. "But seeing what can't be unseen just now, I'm guessing you two haven't checked your missed calls."

Diane and I looked at each other. I shrugged. Hadn't occurred to me to look at my phone all weekend. Probably should've done that.

Maggie continued, ignoring my shrug, "Hi, I'm Maggie. And you must be Diane. Please be Diane." She blushed.

Diane released my hand and extended hers to Maggie. "Hi, Diane Watson."

"Oh, please, I've practically seen you naked. No need for formalities. Hugs are in order." Maggie hugged her tight.

"I'm … I can't believe … I have no words," Diane said, grimacing through the hug.

"Don't worry about it. Honestly. I'm glad you're okay and John's taking care of you after the accident." She blushed again. "I didn't mean in a sexual way. Um, Gil? Want to give a girl a hand here?"

I eyed Gil who'd been observing this from his position at the railing.

"Nah, you're doing fine." He walked over and kissed the top of Maggie's head. "Hi, John." He shook my hand, but didn't try to squeeze off my fingers like the first time we met last summer.

"Hi. Gil, this is my girlfriend, Diane. Diane, Gil." My mouth twitched with a smile when I said the word girlfriend. Out of the corner of my eye I could see Diane smile at the word.

Maggie studied us and grinned. "Quinn said you were beautiful, and for once he didn't exaggerate. It's so nice to meet John's girlfriend. Finally."

I ignored her teasing. "What brings you up to the island? Thought you were coming back in a few weeks."

"We are. That's the plan. Unless you need more time, Diane?"

"She can always stay with me." The words rushed out before my brain caught up. All three faces turned and stared at me. "I mean, if you need her to leave before she finds a place. Not forever. Not yet."

Great. Gil stared and Diane gaped at me, her jaw hovering near the ground.

Maggie gave me a wink and smiled. "You're full of surprises," she said. "Who are you and what have you done with John Day?"

I grumbled about nosy neighbors under my breath.

Gil changed the subject for me. "Maggie explained all this in the voicemails, but we decided we'd take Bessie down to Portland now that the weather's nice."

"And I wanted to make sure you're okay after the accident. I wasn't sure if things were settled between you and John or if you had anyone looking after you." Maggie looked at Diane.

Diane smiled at her. "Thanks. John's been great after the accident. I'm in good hands."

I put my arm around her shoulder and pulled her close to my side.

"Well, we don't want to interrupt any more than we have," Gil said. "Have you considered getting curtains?"

I laughed and glanced at Maggie, then back at Gil. "Have you?"

Maggie swatted at my shoulder. "You've never had to see my naked ass running around in the middle of my living room."

Busted. She had turned around again. Let her look, she had her chance. I raised my eyebrow at her and cocked my head.

"Okay, okay. New beach neighbors' rule. No peeping in windows or coming over unannounced."

"Where's the fun in that? I've got nothing to hide," I said with a big smile.

"We're not turning this into some island version of a nudist colony or swingers' beach," Maggie said.

"Who said anything about swinging?" Gil bristled and gawped at Maggie.

I leaned over and whispered into Diane's ear, "See? I told you we had nothing to worry about. She's as crazy as we are. Probably more so."

"I heard that," Maggie said. "I'm not crazy."

"Honey, you were talking about nudists and swingers. In front of your tenant, who happens to be John's girlfriend, whom you've never met before."

Maggie hung her head. "Hi, my name is Maggie and I suffer from word vomit."

Diane smiled. "I think we'll get along perfectly."

"Let's leave on a high note." Gil grabbed Maggie's hand and tugged her toward the stairs.

"Probably a good idea," Maggie said.

Maggie said something about Quinn and chatting on the phone soon about logistics and return dates, but I lost myself in Diane's scent while she stood beside me. It had been a big afternoon besides the surprise visit.

Big words.

Promises of the future.

A calm settled over me. Everything was different now.

I waved at Maggie and Gil when they left, but I'd zoned out on the last of the conversation.

"That went well. Ended better than expected, don't you think?" I turned our bodies and strolled back toward the door.

"Sure. I'm happy it wasn't my naked ass Maggie and Gil saw."

"No one sees your naked ass except me."

"Same goes for you. Maggie today was the last exception. No nudists and no swinging." She frowned before shaking her head.

"Classic Maggie. She's this amazing writer, but when she gets nervous, she can't stop herself."

"She acts fond of you. Should I be worried?"

"Did you see how she looks at Gil? And how he looks at her?" I stroked her hair.

"I did. They love each other."

"Nothing to worry about, then."

"It's the same way you look at me, you know."

I loved the confidence in her voice. "I know."

Maggie called from the ferry to tell us she'd run into Dave on her way down the beach. His brother and family canceled their summer rental, leaving him with an empty place about four houses down the beach from mine—a perfect location for Diane.

Monday after work we walked down the road to see the house. After counting the steps between our houses, Diane made her mind up before we entered she'd take it. For a beach rental it was decently furnished, but she insisted Dave take away the mounted deer head above the brick fireplace. He offered to replace it with a ram's head, missing the point all taxidermy was a no for her.

A summer rental would give her enough time to find a permanent place. With her divorce settlement, she said she could afford to buy a place. We hadn't talked about how much money she was getting from the asshole, but she'd hinted it was a lot. She deserved every penny.

Now she had a place for the summer, Diane told me she'd be going back to New York for a week. At first I hated the idea. I worried the charm of hikes and fishing couldn't hold up to the lifestyle of the city.

The insecurities I wouldn't admit to out loud stirred again. She'd return home and decide she'd rather be there than stuck on an island with me.

"Why do you have to go back? Don't you have friends who can ship your stuff?" My voice whined and I cringed. I sounded like a girl.

We sat on the couch in my house again, fully clothed this time. At least for now. Depended how this conversation went.

"Are you pouting? Big, bad boy John Day?" She poked me in the ribs.

"I'm not pouting." I crossed my arms to protect my chest from her poking fingers.

"You are. It's adorable. And annoying. As only you can be."

"I'm not annoying. I don't want you to leave. I'm greedy."

"Is that all it is?" She ducked her head down to see my eyes.

"What else would it be?" I grumbled at her.

"Maybe something to do with your bad mood all week. You haven't been this shut down since the camping trip."

"I'm not shut down."

"Sure. I promise I'm coming back."

"You can't promise that."

"My return ticket would say different."

"Tickets can be changed."

"Don't."

"Don't what?"

"John." Her voice softened and she tucked herself against my side.

"Fine." I exhaled through my mouth, then reached my arm around her shoulder, pulling her closer. "I don't want you to go back and decide you belong there."

Her hand picked up mine and played with my fingers before she laced our hands together.

"When I arrived here in January, I didn't know I'd stay. I planned to be here for a few months. Everything I own, all my clothes and stuff, is in storage back there. I need to look through it and decide what comes back with me. I won't even see Kip."

I grumbled some more, but inside felt better knowing she wouldn't see the asshole. "At least you'll be spared."

"Lauren's letting me stay with her. I'll be spending my days at the storage facility sorting boxes. Not glamorous or exciting."

"Can't Lauren do it for you?"

"No. This is everything from college and after. An entire life squeezed into boxes and bags. Depressing, isn't it?"

"I could come with you," I said.

"You could, but you'd hate it. You know that."

"I'd do it for you."

"I know you would. Do you want to examine the excesses of my former life? All the silly shoes, last year's must have fashions, and old pictures?"

"Sounds like hell."

"Thought so." She reached up and turned my face to hers. "We're solid, right? You and me?"

I nodded and bent to brush my nose against hers.

"Let me try to understand your man brain. You think I'm going and never coming back?" Her lips touched mine, but when I tried to deepen the kiss, she retreated.

I shrugged at her observation, and willed her not to analyze it.

Studying my eyes, she furrowed her brows. "Oh," she said. "Oh."

I closed my eyes and leaned my head back on the couch. No grown man should be this messed up about something that happened over a decade ago. My breath quickened along with my pulse. I fought the instinct to run, to escape, to make it all fade away.

Her hand stroked across my brow and smoothed out the line between my eyes before moving down my face and over my jaw. A finger outlined my nose and the line of my lips.

I steadied my breathing, then opened my eyes. Diane stared at me. No, more than stared. Her gaze penetrated me as if she could see all the darkness inside.

"I'm not going to leave you. Not unless you tell me to." She repeated the words I said after her accident.

"You can't keep those promises. Things happen. People leave."

"John." Her legs straddled me and she wrapped her body around mine.

Slowly, I returned the embrace, burying my head in her shoulder. Breathing in her scent, I counted to fifty and willed the panic to leave me. She'd fly to New York and be back in a week. A week. Seven days. Six including travel.

Her voice sounded soft and soothing. "If you want, you can come with me. It might be fun. During the day while I work you could explore the city, then at night we'd be together."

It was a nice offer, but the minute the words left her mouth, I knew I wouldn't take her up on it. This wasn't about trusting her. This moment, this point in my life, was about trusting myself. If I went, the demons and ghosts from my mother's death would win. I had to let her go.

TWENTY-SIX

SIX DAYS. ONE hundred sixty-eight hours. Ten thousand and eight minutes. More seconds than I knew.

It felt like forever.

Diane left the next Monday for New York.

The time difference sucked. She tried calling during the day when I was in the woods with no cell service. I'd call her at night and she'd be out with Lauren, or Quinn and Ryan, or other friends, shouting over the noise of a restaurant or bar because she couldn't hear me.

We finally connected on Saturday, five days after she left and one before she'd be back.

Home.

One very long day before she returned home to me.

"Damn it's early," I mumbled into the phone, trying to find the alarm clock. "Why are you calling me at five on a Saturday?"

"Sorry. I missed your voice. Texting isn't the same."

"Are you calling for phone sex?" I rolled over onto my back and my morning wood tented against my boxers.

"I hadn't thought about it."

"You should have. Thought about it." I yawned.

"I'll let you go back to sleep."

"I'm awake. And there's a saying about wasting wood."

"Wasting wood? Is that a timber saying?"

"No, wrong kind of wood." I stroked myself.

"Oh," she said and fell silent.

"Are you blushing?"

I pictured her cheeks heating and reddening.

"Maybe."

"Have you ever had phone sex before?" I asked.

"No. Have you?"

"I have."

"I see. Well, unless you want Lauren to join in cause she's sitting here next to me in the car, we might need a raincheck."

I groaned and rolled to my stomach before immediately rolling back over. Her muffled voice carried out of the speaker.

"John? Hello? Damn island cell service."

"You're still there. Why are you laughing?"

I smiled. "I'm laughing because you sound like an island girl cursing at the bad cell reception."

"I do?" she asked, her smile coming through her voice.

"Yep."

"Well, that's why I'm calling. I've changed my flight. I finished up early and I'll be home tonight. That's the reason I called."

I sat up in bed. "You are?"

"I am."

"You said home, you know."

"I know. It is home. It's been great to see Lauren and everyone, but like you said, I'm an island girl now. I miss the fresh air and the green." She lowered her voice. "I miss the smell of wet pine, earth and sea air."

"You do?"

"I do. I miss you." Her voice was low and sultry, barely above a whisper.

I groaned. "Fuck. You're killing me. I miss you, too. I love you."

"Love you, too."

I would never tire of hearing her say those words. Before we got off the phone I scribbled down the information for her flight with a promise to meet her at the airport tonight.

My girl was coming home.

Babe hung his head out the window the whole way down to Seattle. We arrived at SeaTac and spotted Diane at the curb, surrounded by more bags than she left with.

When she saw the truck and Babe's head sticking out, tongue lolling and tail wagging, a huge grin spread across her face. I stopped and opened the door, not bothering to turn off the engine. In five long strides, she was in my arms. Citrus, dark waves, and soft curves. I gripped her waist tighter and crashed my mouth into hers. We lost ourselves in the kiss, forgetting time and place while we said hello.

A loud cough behind me startled me out of the haze of lust enveloping us. I turned us both around in the direction of the sound, unwilling to part from her body. My eyes met the stare of a cranky looking officer.

"No parking. Loading and unloading only. Sir, your vehicle is unattended."

I pointed at Babe still sitting in the passenger seat with his tongue hanging out. "No, it's not. The dog's still in it."

Diane giggled and hid her face in my chest.

"I'll give you two minutes to load up and be on your way," the officer said without a hint of humor.

I tipped an invisible hat in his direction and grabbed two of Diane's suitcases. She picked up the small duffel she had left with and another bag, and threw them in the back of the cab. Babe licked her face while she attempted to reclaim the passenger seat.

"What's in the suitcases?" I organized the bags behind my seat.

"Summer clothes, pictures, treasures."

"Got any bikinis in there?" I winked at her.

"Will the weather be warm enough for a bikini?"

"Come July and August it will be. At least I can hope."

Before we buckled ourselves with the seat belts, I kissed her again, losing track of time. Plastic tapping on glass and the gruff voice of the cop saying, "Move it along," finally forced us to move.

Diane's laughter filled the truck's cab, causing Babe to bark and bounce around with excitement.

She came back to me. I had my girl, my dog, and life was good. Better than good. Perfect.

Until we hit traffic downtown. Accident over the UW bridge backed everything up, including the express lanes. We crawled along and I grumbled about the city.

Diane pointed at the Space Needle with a tourist's glee. I told her the story of my parents taking me there when I was a kid, even having dinner in the spinning restaurant at the top. Somehow she convinced me to take her there this summer. It didn't take much convincing. Five torturous days apart meant I'd agree to anything to make her smile and hear her laughter.

Despite being stuck in traffic forever, we caught the ferry at Mulkiteo without having to wait. Perfect timing meant we drove down the hill from the toll both and straight on the boat. I'd had enough waiting already, so when Diane asked if I wanted to head upstairs, I answered her by pulling her across the bench seat and into my arms.

Making out on the ferry made me think of high school. As horny as I felt, I could have been back in school. I wondered what she was like as a teenager. I pictured a teenage Diane in white tennis shoes and a too short to be decent skirt. That direction of thinking needed to stop because of our current location.

"Why are you groaning?"

I admitted where my mind had drifted.

"Let me get this straight, you're turned on because you're fantasizing about the teenage me? Kind of perverted, don't you think?"

"No, I'm turned on because the woman I love is home. Finally."

She smiled and kissed me again, dragging her hand through my beard. "I try to picture you in high school, but the beard throws me off."

"Is that girl code for shave it all off?"

"No. I like it." She scrunched up her face and squinted at me. "Although, I'm curious what you'd look like bare."

"Speaking of bare …" I moved my hand between her legs.

"Thought you didn't care?"

"I lied. I've fantasized about dragging my beard over you to watch you squirm."

"Funny, I've had the same fantasy."

"If this damn ferry ever docks, how 'bout we make it come true?"

"Damn ferry." She kissed me. "Damn island." She kissed me again.

Her Jeep sat in the driveway where Steve had dropped it off this morning. Good as new.

"How?" she asked pointing at the front end.

"How what?"

"How is my Jeep fixed?

"Steve said you were lucky you crashed into the ditch instead of hit the deer."

"But with the airbag and everything, I figured the whole front end got crushed."

"Nah, only dented. See why I suggested you get the big SUV?"

"I can't believe it." After getting out of the truck, she walked over to her car and stroked her hand along the side.

"Are you petting your car?"

"I am. And saying thank you to it for taking care of me."

"Did you ever name it?"

"I did."

"Are you going to tell me?"

"It's embarrassing."

"You gave your car an embarrassing name? This I have to hear." I crossed my arms over my chest and smiled. "Go on."

"I call it the lumberjack."

I laughed and raised my eyebrow.

"It's big and strong and handsome."

"It's missing the beard."

"And flannel shirt."

"I don't always wear flannel shirts. Sometimes I wear T-shirts," I huffed.

She moved to my side and tugged on the sleeve of my plaid shirt. "Sometimes you do."

"You named your car after me?"

"I did. I told you it was embarrassing."

"Nah, you love me. It's a compliment. I think."

"I do love you, my big lumberjack."

I rolled my eyes, but if she wanted me to be a lumberjack, I'd show her. She squealed when I picked her up, slung her over my shoulder, and marched toward my house.

Two weeks later Diane moved out of Maggie's house and into Dave's. The official lease paperwork stated as much. In reality, she spent most nights in my bed and most mornings in the shower with me.

Funny how easily she merged into my life.

I surveyed my bedroom and spied half a dozen things belonging to her. A half-full glass of water sat next to a romance novel on the nightstand on her side of the bed. Last night's jeans hung off the back of the chair and a pair of earrings joined her phone on the dresser.

None of her girly stuff had invaded my bathroom yet, but it was only a matter of time. Each object threaded her hook deeper into my flesh and I willingly let myself be pulled up to the light by her.

She stirred beside me and I stroked her hair where it flowed over her pillow. With a turn of her head she faced me and opened her eyes.

"Morning," I said.

She mumbled something into the pillow, but I couldn't hear it.

"What?"

Lifting her head she repeated herself, "I said, morning already?"

"Tired?" I smiled at her.

"You know I'm tired. Someone kept me up late doing unmentionable things."

"Unmentionable? You didn't mind last night when you begged me to—"

Her hand clamped over my mouth. I nipped at her palm with my teeth, not enough pressure to break the skin, but deep enough she pulled her hand away. I took advantage of her distraction to pounce, holding her hands above her head.

"Ouch!"

"Let me kiss it better." I lifted her hand and placed my lips on the mark. Rather than kiss it, I sucked gently, then trailed my mouth to her wrist. She loved it when I dragged my beard against the sensitive skin there.

"Mmmm."

"What about unmentionable things you loved last night, but don't want me to talk about in the bright light of day?"

"Nothing."

I nibbled along the flesh inside her elbow, causing her hips to squirm beneath me. "Some of those things you've done to me in the daylight before. Last week during our hike, you—"

Her lips slammed into mine and she silenced me with her tongue. I loved teasing her. And tasting her.

"You know I get all embarrassed when you do the replay."

"Embarrassed? Or hot and bothered?"

"Less talking, more action." Her hand wiggled out of my grasp and headed south between our bodies.

I lifted my hips to accommodate her. "I think I have my answer."

She may have acted reluctant to hear or speak dirty talk, but I suspected she protested too much. If her grip on my wood proved anything, she loved it.

I looked forward to the weekend mornings when there was nowhere we had to be and nothing we had to do. Other than each other.

Later in the afternoon we drove up to Freeland to the recycling center.

"Remember our conversation the first time we came here?" she asked while we unloaded the bed of the truck.

I smiled and nodded over at the pyramid of bowling balls. "Feels like forever ago."

"It does." She sighed, full of happiness.

While she dumped bottles, I headed over toward the book bus. Her words triggered my memory of that day and I scanned the piles of metal littered amongst grass, puddles, and wildflowers. I spied what I wanted, but didn't pick it up. Instead, I walked inside to talk with the owner to set up a time to come back for it.

Diane gave me an odd look when I returned to the truck, curiosity lingering behind her eyes. I shrugged and said, "Pyramid."

"You're up to something, John Day."

"Maybe I am, and if you know what's good for you, you won't ruin the surprise."

She narrowed her eyes at me, then crossed her arms. "Fine. It's a good thing I've grown to like your surprises."

I hoped she liked this one and she remembered everything about our first trip here.

June brought long days, which didn't end until late until the evening when we approached the summer solstice.

Diane's cast came off, finally. I wouldn't miss getting thwacked in the head, or worse, with it in the middle of the night when she starfished on the bed.

To make her feel better about paying rent, we sometimes spent the time down at her place. Boxes arrived from New York with the belongings she decided to keep. What she didn't unpack we found room for in my garage.

An old, rusted metal birdcage with a missing door took its place of pride on the fireplace mantel in her cabin.

TWENTY-SEVEN

"HAVE YOU EVER not had a beard?" she asked, standing behind me in the bathroom while I brushed my teeth.

I spat toothpaste into the sink. "Sure. I wasn't born with a beard. Nor was I one of those boys who had a mustache in the sixth grade."

She swatted my ass with her towel. It stung. She had a crazy strong arm after physical therapy.

"No, I mean as an adult."

"Sure. I've lost bets and shaved it off. I usually trim it shorter in the summer."

"Any other time?"

Where was she going with this?

"A few times I've shaved it clean for no reason because the mood struck me."

I turned to face her and she ran her nails through my beard. I knew I needed to trim it, but since her return a month ago I'd been distracted most mornings.

"I'm curious what you would look like without it."

"You are?"

"I am. I feel like it's part of you, but at the same time I can't see your face, your whole face, underneath it."

"Are you asking?" Would I shave my beard off for her? Sure.

"Maybe." She stood on her toes and kissed me, running her cheek along my jaw. "It'll grow back."

"It will grow back. Pretty quick, too." I kissed her again. "What are you doing right now?"

"Shaving off your beard?" She smiled. "Can I help?"

"Sure."

I found the clippers under the sink and a new blade for my razor. Handing her the clippers, I showed her how to run them over my jaw.

A clump of dark hair filled the sink and small hairs littered her leg where she sat on the counter facing me with the clippers in her hand.

"You're truly bad at this, you know?" I laughed, examining my face in the mirror when she paused. Areas of clearcut surrounded bigger patches of fully intact beard.

"I've never done it before. Hold still." Her tongue peeked out of the corner of her mouth while she concentrated. As long as she didn't cut me, I'd let her have her fun.

After a few minutes she declared me all done. I opened one eye to peer at my reflection. Not half bad.

Her hand stroked my jaw. "Where'd you get this scar?"

"Soccer. 7th grade. Took a header from Sam Carter straight to the chin. Fifteen stitches."

She held my chin in her hand, turning my face back and forth, studying the newly exposed skin.

"Want me to go for the full monty?" I asked.

Her eyes bugged out and her gaze fell down below my waist.

"No, not down there. No way. I meant shave it smooth."

A look of relief, or maybe disappointment, floated across her eyes before she nodded.

I let her lather my face, but after her less than stellar work with the clippers, I decided we'd both be safer if I used the razor myself.

She sat next to me, gazing at me while I slowly dragged the blade up my neck. When I rinsed off the last of the foam, her hands were immediately on my face.

I leaned close and kissed her, brushing my lips softly across hers.

"It's like kissing you, but a different version of you."

I kissed my way to her ear and then down her neck. "It feels the same to me."

"You're less pokey."

"Give me a few hours and I'll be scratchy again."

"Maybe we should take this for a test run now before you regrow it."

"Test run?" I asked, standing between her legs.

'Uh huh." Her legs wrapped around my waist. "I want to be able to make an informed decision on my preference."

"Well, if that's the case …" I swept her up in my arms and carried her to bed.

Turns out beards were good for many things, but sometimes bare skin made all the difference in the world.

I stood on my deck drinking coffee and enjoying the warmth of the July sun. After a long, rainy winter and spring, blue skies had returned. These were the days that made living here worth all the gray.

Facing the exposed tide flat and retreating water, I spotted a pair of horses and riders far out on the sand, well beyond boats stranded in the low tide. I tugged my newly grown beard and thought about going out this evening to see if the salmon were biting.

I turned to the left and spied Maggie out on her deck with her laptop, probably writing. She waved and raised her coffee cup in greeting. I echoed her gestured and smiled. It felt good to have my neighbor home. I'd even warmed to Gil. At least he no longer stared at me like he wanted to fight.

In the other direction, summer people in shorts and bathing suits dotted the beach and decks. Children ran up and down the sand, dogs played in the water, and the summer wives sunned themselves. A few houses down a woman practiced yoga in the sand. Her shorts were tiny, leaving little to the imagination about her legs and ass. With her ass in the air and her torso bent over at the waist, I couldn't see her face.

I turned back around to see if Maggie caught me staring. From her grin it was clear she busted me. Laughing, she shook her head and mouthed, "Pervert."

The laugh was on her though.

I knew that ass anywhere.

I watched while Diane slowly curled up from her pose and lifted her arms, her dark ponytail swinging down her back when she stood up.

Returning my gaze to Maggie, she called out, "You're still a pervert, John Day!"

I winked at her, then focused on Diane again. She faced me and laughed.

Her mouth moved with words I couldn't hear from the deck. Reduced to pantomimes, I explained I couldn't hear her, then offered her coffee. I never did learn sign language, so I couldn't say for sure what she meant by her hand gestures, but you wouldn't make those gestures in church.

A few minutes later she strolled down the beach and joined me.

"How long did you stand there staring at my ass?"

"Not that long. Maggie busted me, though."

"Did she know it was me?"

"Not at first." I scratched at my new beard. "I, um, had a reputation for admiring women on the beach."

"Had?"

"Before you."

She echoed my words, giving me a sidelong glance. "Before me."

"Yes, there's my life now with you, and then everything else before."

"I'm the dividing line?"

"In more ways than you'll know." I leaned over and pressed my lips to her forehead.

"I like that."

"I like you."

"I thought you loved me." Her voice teased.

"I do, but I like you, too."

"I'm glad. Do you like me enough to get me some coffee?"

"Not that much, no." I was already heading inside to get her a cup when her hand hit my ass.

When I returned, she lay across the deck seat, her knees bent and her arm shielding her face from the sun. My shadow blocked the light, letting her know I was back. She sat up and took the mug from me.

"What do you want to do later?" I ran my hand up her leg and followed its path with my eyes. These shorts were illegal.

"Did you hear me?" she asked.

I had no idea she spoke, lost completely in my thoughts about her legs and hips wrapped around me.

"No."

"What are you thinking about?"

"Sex."

"And?"

"And you shouldn't wear these shorts out of the house."

"Oh, really?"

"No."

"I've worn them around clients when I'm training them."

My growl rumbled low in my chest.

"It's probably wrong, and I shouldn't encourage you, but I love it when you act all caveman with the jealousy and growling."

My eyes flashed to hers, which contained nothing but pure delight.

"Don't make me throw you over my shoulder and have my Neanderthal way with you in my cave. Cause I'd do it."

"Oh, I know you would. You've done it before."

"Damn right." I flexed my pecs and shoulders.

Instead of dropping to her knees in front of me, she laughed so hard she rolled right off the bench and hit the ground with a thud.

"That's great for my ego, you know."

Through her giggles she wiped her eyes. "I think your ego is doing fine. In fact, I think you're even more handsome than when I met you. Although I miss your winter beard."

Her nails scratched the short scruff along my jaw. It wasn't as thick as it had been, but it didn't have the bare look from a few weeks ago. Despite her reassurances, she couldn't convince me to keep it.

Two things I knew for certain. I would never live in the city. And second, I resembled a plucked chicken without my facial hair.

Donnely gave me shit for it and kept telling me I was whipped.

The things I did for love.

"How about a beach fire tonight?" I asked during dinner later that evening at Diane's house.

"We could invite Maggie and Gil. Or maybe Donnely," she suggested.

"Do we need chaperones?"

"I don't know, do we?" She gave me her sultry smile.

"We haven't done it on the beach yet. That's all I'm saying."

"It's not even dark yet."

"But it will be later."

"True."

"So yes?"

"Yes to the fire. Anyone could stroll up and see us having sex."

"No one strolls up the beach at night. It's not like there's a boardwalk out there. We've done it outside before." My mind brought up images of her pale skin in the woods and I smirked.

"All that sand though."

"A blanket will solve that problem. Or even blankets if you're feeling shy."

"Since when am I shy?"

"Given the yoga shorts you've worn, more shy might not be a bad thing."

"You like those shorts."

"I like you naked, too, but no one else should be allowed to see that."

She leaned over and kissed my cheek. "You start the fire and I'll grab the blankets."

"I'll take that as a yes then!" I shouted to her back when she headed down the hall.

She wouldn't have believed me, but sex wasn't on my mind when I suggested the fire. I wasn't in the mood for company other than hers. The past week had been filled with family. Family included my father and Joyce. I needed alone time, which meant alone with Diane.

The fire sputtered and caught when I blew on the kindling. She joined me with her arms full of the blankets. When we shook them out,

I noticed she had something stuck under her arm.

"What's that?" I pointed to the blob of fabric.

She tossed a ball of gray fabric at me—the sweater from the winter.

I held it up and a mischievous grin spread across my face. "Really?"

"You've wanted to burn this thing since January. Here's your chance."

"Are you serious, Linus? I can?"

"Burn away, pyromaniac man. It was my security blanket. Now it reminds me of all the sad things."

I dangled it over the flames, but didn't dip it low enough to catch.

"Is this a symbolic gesture or is it necessary because it's a biohazard?" I lifted it up, pretending to sniff it.

"Burn it or I'll do it for you and steal your joy." She moved to grab it, but I was faster.

"Bye." The sweater fell on top of the logs and slowly caught fire.

We watched it burn, her arm around my waist and mine around her shoulders.

"We're ridiculous. You agree, right?" I stared down at the fire.

"We are. I won't tell anyone if you don't."

"Tell them what? We ritually burn clothing?"

"That and that you're a sentimental softie."

"Am not."

"Right. Like how you're not a nice guy."

"I'm not."

"No one believes that but you."

A few women's faces flashed through my mind—a jury of people of my past who would disagree with her. The last face was Joyce.

"Quit trying to find evidence to support your twisted ideas." She pinched my side. It tickled more than hurt.

"I haven't been all that nice to my dad or Joyce."

"True. But you made more of an effort last week during their visit."

Diane and Helen had ganged up on me to hang out with my dad last Sunday. Soon after we arrived at the house they disappeared with Joyce down the road to pick berries for pie. I knew Diane didn't bake, but she was in cahoots with my aunt and Joyce.

At first we'd sat in silence with Peter, watching the Mariners.

"What do you think their playoff prospects are this year?" my dad asked the room. Sports acted as the gateway to conversation with men of his generation.

"Probably the same as last year. Not great," I answered.

"I'm always optimistic things will pull together for them."

The metaphors of team work, wins, and hope in the face of loss communicated more than game stats. My father spoke in layers of sports jargon rather than express his fears and feelings.

Before the game finished, somehow we managed a conversation that didn't turn into a fight for the first time in years.

Diane and I sat side by side facing the fire. I leaned down and whispered in her ear, "You know, I saw through the whole berry picking for pies scheme. Since when do you bake?"

"I don't bake. I do eat pie and have two hands." She waved her fingers at me.

Her bare ring finger caught my eye. I imagined it with my mother's ring on it.

Wait.

Where did that come from?

No way we were ready for that. She'd only been officially divorced this year. Way too soon for rings and weddings.

Way too soon.

No one was thinking about rings on fingers.

Definitely not me.

I said a rude comment about eating pie, sending Diane into a fit of giggles. All thoughts of rings faded away when I pinned her on the blanket and unbuttoned her shirt.

She shivered when the cool night air hit her skin before I pulled the other blanket over us. I knew no one was on the beach. The lights were dark over at Maggie's and no one else had a direct line of sight to the fire ring nestled near the driftwood and sea grass.

Diane was right about the sand. Despite the blankets, it got everywhere. Everywhere.

Luckily for me, I had a plan to deal with the sand.

Outdoor shower. Installed two days ago and yet to be christened. Set off to the side of the house away from windows and the road, the three sided structure hid our bodies from prying eyes, but I muffled Diane's moans and cries with my mouth. Sound carried down at the beach.

TWENTY-EIGHT

ANOTHER SUMMER NIGHT, another bonfire. A night that ended with a predawn meteor shower and making love under blankets on the cold sand.

Summer began to slip away as the middle of August approached. The island continued its tradition of being overtaken with tourists and summer people. Traffic and crowds drove me to spend more time out on the boat. Whether I caught something or not, the peace and quiet restored me.

The Doghouse burst with non-islanders who clogged the pool table on the weekends. Donnely took full advantage of the season, introducing unsuspecting but willing women to the geoduck hunt. Tom Cat liked to flirt with Diane in front of me, knowing he pushed my buttons. I gave him shit for it, but it didn't bother me. I couldn't imagine going back to life as his wingman.

She teased him with a promise to bring her friend Lauren out for a visit, saying she'd put him in his place. I laughed at the thought of Donnely going up against a big city girl. Never imagined I'd fall for one, so anything was possible.

Observing Diane sitting in a deck chair in her cut off shorts and tank, you'd never know she was a wealthy divorcee. When she told me how much she had in the bank I nearly keeled over. My girl was rich. But instead of spending it on cars and fancy shoes, it all was put into the bank and investments. For our future. Not hers. Ours. She insisted.

A burst of laughter from next door caught my attention. Maggie walked out on her deck with a blond man, followed by another guy with short brown hair carrying a baby.

Diane jumped up from her spot on the deck and screamed, "Quinn! Ryan!"

I forgot she knew him.

"Why is Ryan holding a baby?" I asked, standing and following her down the stairs.

"Oh my god, it's the baby!" Diane took off in a run over to Maggie's deck. I strolled behind her.

Baby? Whose baby? I hadn't seen Maggie for a few months, but at no time did she ever seem pregnant. I would think she'd have mentioned if she was pregnant.

"Diane!" Quinn embraced her and gave her a twirl. "My broken goddess. Look at you! You're as poorly dressed as Maggie." He peered at her face. "And as head over heels in love as she is. Who's the lucky guy?" His head snapped to me standing by the stairs. "No! You snagged the lumberjack? You lucky bitch."

I gave Quinn a smile and wave. "Hi, Quinn."

He gaped at Diane and then whispered something in her ear, causing her to blush. She nodded and he gave her a high five.

"Is this Lizzy?" Diane asked, moving toward Quinn's husband and the baby dressed in pink and black stripes. "Oh, she's beautiful. May I?" She gestured to the baby.

Why did women have to hold strange babies? I didn't get it.

"Isn't she perfect?" Maggie asked me when she appeared at my side.

"Whose is she?"

"Quinn and Ryan's daughter Lizzy. They had a surrogate last summer."

"Huh." I nodded. "Cool."

Next thing I knew, Diane stood in front of me. "Want to hold her?"

"Not so much."

"Oh, come on." She held the baby out to me.

"She's not that scary, John." Gil reassured me.

"Nah, I'm okay." That didn't work either.

Diane ignored my protests and placed the baby in my arms. Lizzy immediately reached for my beard and tugged.

Fuck. Who knew babies were so strong. That hurt. My eyes watered and I tried not to curse out loud. Even I knew to keep it clean in front of kids.

"Lizzy has a thing for the beard, too." Diane smiled at me while she gently pried the tiny fist away from my face.

"Can't blame her," Quinn echoed. "She has the best taste in everything."

Relief filled me when Maggie took Lizzy out of my arms. Over Maggie's shoulder Lizzy smiled at me. I smiled back. I couldn't help myself.

I caught Diane's gaze. She had the expression women get around babies. Other than the strange talk we'd had months ago about babies and zombies, we'd never discussed children again.

Up until this moment, I'd never thought about them. But seeing the love on everyone's faces when they gazed at Lizzy it all clicked into place.

Rings on fingers.

Babies in arms.

I wanted it all.

It wasn't until I fell in love with Diane I believed I could have everything.

I kissed the top of her head when she leaned into me.

Everything.

Maggie insisted we join them for dinner. She didn't have to twist my arm. The woman was an amazing cook.

Diane's excitement over seeing friends again was infectious and I found myself having a great time. Wine flowed and we devoured several pounds of clams and mussels cooked in broth and butter. The baby monitor on the table squawked occasionally to remind us of Lizzy's presence upstairs.

"Wasn't it about this time last year you had a house full?" I asked Maggie.

"Good memory." Her gaze drifted over to Gil. "I guess it's our one year anniversary."

He kissed the back of her hand. "One year, plus twenty something."

Diane asked about the story and Maggie gave her the short version.

"That's so romantic. There must be something in the water here." Her hand reached for mine under the table.

"Must be all the fresh air," I said, squeezing her hand back. Her blush told me she knew exactly what I meant. "Where's the rest of the gang?"

"The rest of them are off on other adventures," Maggie said. "The Ben and Jo's are on the Cape. And Selah's on sabbatical. In Ghana."

"Is that what we're still calling it?" Quinn asked.

"It's the official answer," Maggie answered.

I glanced between them. A bigger story was there. There always was with Maggie's larger than life best friend.

Diane asked the question on my mind. "Is she traveling alone?"

Quinn's smile and wink explained it all. "Selah's never alone for long. She's living her own personal *Out of Africa*." He and Gil chuckled.

Maggie gave them stern looks. "We'll have to wait for her to get back next year to see what happens."

"Or maybe she'll put it into one of her books. First pirates, then lumberjacks, sorry John, now Love: Missionary Style." Quinn cracked himself up.

"None taken," I said.

"Hush," Maggie scolded, but couldn't contain her laughter.

I leaned back into my chair and extended my arm behind Diane. A year ago I'd been the odd man out when Maggie's friends visited. With Diane by my side, all our lives were interwoven. Her friends and my friends had become our friends. It felt good to be part of the group. We were a family not by blood, but by choice.

We made plans to visit the fair the next day. Discussions of which fried foods were our favorites and who would enter the pie eating contest followed.

Pies, goats, 4H kids, and vomit inducing rides all had their charms, but something else at the fair appealed to me more.

I had one last summer surprise for Diane.

Loud beeping noises combined with a thrumming rattle underscored by the low hum of generators. The Island County Fair teemed with people while Diane and I strolled through rows of beeping, flashing, and blaring music of the midway. Behind us followed Maggie and gang.

I teased Diane about the pie eating contest, waggling my eyebrows. Her cheeks pinked, but she ignored me, instead discussing the difference between funnel cakes and fried dough with Maggie.

Our destination wasn't the Tilt-a-Whirl or the Zipper. We were on a mission of a different sort. I asked Gil the time to make sure we weren't late.

The further we walked from the small midway the fair morphed back into its rural roots. Kids in neatly pressed 4H uniforms leaned against fences or led cows around rings. Hay and manure replaced the smell of fried everything. With Lizzy strapped to his chest, Quinn showed her the baby animals while Ryan snapped pictures of everything. I smiled at their enthusiasm.

A pair of tall poles marked our arrival at the log show, a fair tradition. Donnely preened next to his latest eagle sculpture with spread wings. With a wave, he greeted us and went back to chatting up the women admiring his skills with a chainsaw.

Diane stared up at me. Her eyes, wide with excitement, held a single question.

I nodded.

"You said you weren't a real lumberjack."

"I did."

"You lied."

"I stretched the truth. The only lumberjacks who exist these days are in movies, books, and these sorts of competitions. I'm in logging, timber, forestry."

"But you eat pancakes and have Babe and … "

I kissed her hard. "Don't forget the boots and the beard."

She broke out into a grin and grazed her hand down my jaw. "And the beard."

I kissed her again and slowly dragged my cheek along her jaw. She moaned.

"If you moan like that again, I won't be able to concentrate. Not sure I can balance on a log with a hard-on."

"This is every fantasy I've ever had come true."

I ran my thumb over my bottom lip and quirked my eyebrow. "Every fantasy?"

"Let me clarify, every lumberjack fantasy. Is it wrong I hope you fall and get all wet?"

"You want me to fall into the water?"

A devilish gleam lit up her eyes. She bit her lip and nodded her head.

"You're weird."

"But you love me."

"I do love you. And now I have some wood to saw, a pole to climb, and cold water to fall into for your amusement."

She gazed up at me with a swoony face I'd only seen in movies.

I kissed her one last time, and dipped her back and low. I smiled at her surprise while I sauntered backwards toward the competition area where Donnely waited with my gear.

"I love you, lumberjack." Her voice carried over the crowd. Unfortunately, I wasn't the only lumberjack around. Several burly men shouted their love back at her, including Donnely.

Her cheeks reddened and she ducked her head down before she and the others climbed the small set of bleachers.

Between my laughter and my own wood, there was no way I would able to concentrate.

After changing into my cork boots, jeans frayed above the ankle, a gray T-shirt, and red suspenders, I looked the part at least.

I ended up doing a spectacular backward fall off the log into the shallow pool of water. Not on purpose. Of course not.

I shook out my wet hair and took off my shirt to wring it out while

I waited for the log rolling to finish.

As I stood there shirtless, I heard Diane's cheers. They were the loudest by far; I had no idea she could whistle like that. I stood up straighter with my shoulders rolled back, and grinned.

"Whipped." Donnely coughed next to me.

"Shut it." I shoved him in the shoulder.

My comeback in the chainsaw, axe, and speed climb rounds weren't enough to recover from the dive I took in the pool. Didn't matter. When it was all over and done, Diane jumped into my arms, wrapping her legs around my hips like I got crowned champion.

She gave me a scorching kiss fit for a returning hero. In between kisses she said, "That. Was. The. hottest. Thing. Ever. When the sawdust was flying around you? And your biceps bulged when you threw the axe? I thought I might pass out."

I kissed her again.

"And the way your thighs looked so strong and manly climbing up the pole?"

She kissed me and I lost myself in her. Standing there in the middle of the fair, wet jeans clinging to me, Diane wrapped around me, nothing else in the world mattered. I'd be a lumberjack if it made her happy. I'd do anything for this woman.

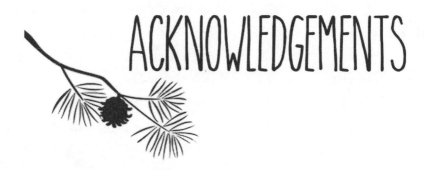

ACKNOWLEDGEMENTS

Thank you to Melissa Ringstead at There for You Editing Services for tackling the edits on this project.

Extra special thanks to my pre-readers Dianne, Heather, Kelly, Marla, and Suzie for reading, hand-holding, guidance, keeping me off the ledge, and swooning over John Day. Your input is invaluable.

Thanks to Sarah Hansen at Okay Creations for another beautiful cover.

Special gratitude for Heather Maven at The Book Trailer for the conversations that inspired me to write John Day's story. If you enjoyed this book, be sure to thank her. Outdoor showers will never be the same.

To the Lost Girls and the Lost Boys, your friendship means the world to me. My sanity would have disappeared long ago without you.

To S L Scott, I'm happy to share a brain with you.

A big thank you to Mr. Purvis, who went above and beyond with information related to all things fishing.

For all the friends and fans I've met along the publishing path, thank you for your encouragement, love, and support.

To my husband, thank you for everything. Including overlooking the Pekingese size dust bunnies when I'm writing or editing. Or any other time.

To my extended family, for their cheerleading and unwavering support, especially my parents for always championing my dreams.

And to all the bloggers, readers, fans, and fellow authors who are the very best part of this publishing adventure, the biggest thanks of all.

ABOUT THE AUTHOR

Before writing full time, Daisy Prescott worked in the world of art, auctions, antiques, and home decor. She earned a degree in Art History from Mills College and endured a brief stint as a film theory graduate student at Tisch School of the Arts at NYU. Baker, art educator, antiques dealer, blue ribbon pie-maker, fangirl, freelance writer, gardener, wife, and pet mom are a few of the titles she's acquired over the years.

Born and raised in San Diego, Daisy currently lives in a real life Stars Hollow in the Boston suburbs with her husband and their dog, Hubbell, and an imaginary house goat. Her debut novel, *Geoducks Are for Lovers*, is a Romantic Comedy and Women's Fiction best seller. She also writes randy pirotica under the pen name Suzette Marquis.

To learn more about this author and her writing visit:

www.daisyprescott.com

Or find her on social media:

Twitter: @daisy_prescott

Facebook: www.facebook.com/DaisyPrescottAuthor

Pinterest: www.pinterest.com/daisyprescott/

GEODUCKS Are for LOVERS

In this Best Selling Romantic Comedy *Reality Bites* becomes *The Big Chill* when a group of Gen-X friends spend a summer weekend together sharing laughter, tears, life's ups and downs, old stories, second chances, and new beginnings in this contemporary romance.

"… I think life is better when you have love. Not a friendly neighbor or old friends kind of love either, but a love that causes your heart to race and your toes to curl."

Maggie Marrion is just getting back on her feet after a horrible year, or two, or three. With their twentieth reunion approaching, she invites four of her closest friends from college for a mini-reunion at her beach cabin on Whidbey Island. What she doesn't expect is her best friends Selah and Quinn to play matchmaker. Will Maggie risk her heart and her quiet life for another chance at romance?

Gil Morrow, former grunge musician turned history professor, joins them as Selah's date for the weekend. With the support of old friends, a few wishing rocks, the world's largest burrowing clam, and a hot lumberjack thrown into the mix, Gil reminds Maggie she isn't too old to fall in love.

PRAISE FOR
GEODUCKS ARE FOR LOVERS

Warm. Heartfelt. Original and engaging. This book was a breath of fresh air. ~**Vilma's Book Blog**

Daisy Prescott is a very gifted writer. ~**The Book Bellas**

Geoducks may be for lovers, but this book is for everyone who believes or wants to believe in second chances and enduring love, hope and life-long friendship. I give *Geoducks Are for Lovers* 5 Stars! ~Dymps, **The SubClubBooks**

If you are looking for a story about adults, without lots of angst, that when you are finished will just leave you feeling good about what you just read, then *Geoducks Are for Lovers* will be for you, silly name and all!! ~Maven, **Love N. Books**

I can't stop thinking about how much I smiled while reading this book! ~**The Novel Tease**

I have to give a rousing 5 stars to Daisy Prescott's *Geoducks Are for Lovers*. She really captures the state of the union for Gen X and also has fantastic characters and gorgeous scenery. Go read! ~Wick, **Amazon Reviewer**

Available on Amazon, Barnes & Noble, and Independent Booksellers